The Last Execution
By
Jerrie Alexander

Cover illustrator and Formatting:
www.BrynnaCurry.com
Edits by: Eve Arroyo
www.evearroyo.com
Proofreading by Red Pen Edits
www.redpenedits.com

Dedication

Kym Roberts

If you Google the word friend, your picture should be there. If it's not, you were cheated.

Chapter One

Doyle Preston cradled the Remington 700 VTR in his hands as if the rifle were a beautiful woman, tenderly and with reverence. Pulling the trigger was like making love: you take your time, use a gentle hand, and then enjoy the sweet reward.

Appreciative of the starless, windless night, he lined up the scope's crosshairs with the target. From his spot, on top of the high-rise, the shot would be easy. He closed his mind to outside influences, silencing the traffic noise surging from one of Atlanta's busiest streets, and ignoring the steady drum of his heart. Every hair on his arms rose in anticipation. Here and now, the destiny of another person's life rested in his power.

Inhale.

Exhale.

Squeeze.

The bullet passed through Officer Brian Slocum's head, exploded his skull like a dropped watermelon, and then embedded itself into the brick wall, exactly as planned. The lifeless body crumpled to the pavement, leaving shards of bone and brain matter splattered on his stunned partner.

Bastard never knew what hit him.

Preston's heart hammered against his ribs as adrenaline surged through his body, but now wasn't the time for euphoria. Methodically, he stowed his rifle, retrieved the shell casing, and inspected the area to ensure he'd left no trace evidence behind. Wearing electrician's overalls and carrying an oversized toolbox, he boarded the service elevator and made his way to his car. After he'd pulled onto the freeway, he allowed himself a moment to be proud of a job well done.

The rifle was his weapon of choice, how he delivered justice. How he helped the abused. How he'd ended the condemned man's brutality.

****

Special Agent J.T. Noble glanced over his shoulder and damned if heaven on two feet wasn't walking straight toward him. He feasted from her shoes all the way up to her luscious lips and—ouch—icy glare.

"Noble." Special Agent in Charge, Casey Granger's all-business tone, broke into J.T.'s thoughts. "Stop scowling. You'll scare the new liaison." He waved his hand in the direction of their visitor. "Bring her here. We need to get started."

"I don't scowl," J.T. grumbled as he moved across the office to intercept her.

With her long stride, she'd already crossed the bulk of the FBI's office space. Head held high, her golden hair had been pulled back into a low ponytail of some sort. Fuzzy curls, which had escaped the bondage, hung at random around her neck and face. The low-heeled shoes and weapon on her hip projected the image of a serious, no-bullshit kind of woman, quite in contrast with her face, which conjured up images of his grandmother's porcelain china.

Her sea-blue gaze scanned from his feet to the top of his head. She got points for not flinching when she reached his face. One of her eyebrows went up at the same time her shoulder shrugged her dismissal. He liked her right-back-at-you attitude. She'd inspected, rejected, and put him in his place all in one easy motion.

"Special Agent J.T. Noble." He extended his hand. "You the liaison?"

"Detective Leigh McBride." She met his palm with a strong grasp and pumped once.

"SAC Casey Granger is expecting you." He pointed toward Casey's office and fell in step behind her.

Normally, he checked his libido at the door when at work, so his reaction to her surprised him. Pissed at himself, he pushed aside his attraction to her.

Entering the room, she introduced herself to Casey before J.T. had a chance to speak.

"Chief Hampton instructed me to provide you and your team the information we've collected on the sniper. As the liaison, I'm to assist in any capacity you deem appropriate."

Her words, formal and disciplined, dropped cold and hard, like ice cubes falling into an empty glass.

"Good. Take a seat." Casey waved to the small conference table in the corner. "Detective McBride comes to us from the police department's criminal investigation division."

She nodded, placed her briefcase on the table and waited, her eyes hooded, not showing emotion. The lady clearly wasn't comfortable with her assignment. He got that the FBI taking over the investigation pissed her off. If he'd been in her shoes, he would've felt the same way.

Silence filled the room while Casey motioned to fellow agents, Olivia Cisneros and Tobias "Romeo" Bailey, to join the meeting. After introductions, Leigh joined the team at the table. J.T. recognized her discomfort at being an outsider. He shied away from getting too familiar with coworkers. It kept him from getting too close and caring when somebody was killed.

Casey shifted in his chair to address Leigh. "Bring us up to speed on the sniper."

"Yes, sir."

"No sirs in here. I run a close-knit, informal unit. It's Casey." He waved his hand toward the group, his signal she should continue.

A pretty face didn't qualify her as an asset to the team, so J.T. leaned back and observed.

Leigh passed a folder to each member of the group. Casey removed a handful of crime scene pictures, stood, and then attached them to a whiteboard. J.T. studied the close-up and wide-angle photos of three men with a large part of their heads missing.

"Hell of a shot. Why the head? A military-trained sniper would've aimed for the heart."

Leigh gave J.T. a frosty look as if he'd interrupted her rhythm, so he shut up.

"March 29, Marcos Ortega, married, father of four, attorney for a local drug czar, was shot and killed in a grocery store parking lot." She stood to indicate the first picture. "Two weeks later, April 12, Qassim Mussa-Shir, the married father of three, taxi driver, was killed coming out of a Stop-N-Shop. Last night, Officer Brian Slocum, married, father of one, Atlanta PD for thirteen years, shot while standing in the parking lot of a Waffle House."

The detective didn't appear nervous, wasn't sweating while under the team's scrutiny. Her behavior would carry some weight with them, but if she'd hoped for an ally when a female agent joined them for the briefing, she'd be disappointed. Olivia wasn't sending any camaraderie-like vibes. Her body language was more closed off than Leigh's. He'd had to earn Olivia's respect through hard work; Leigh would have to do the same.

"Time of day?" J.T. asked, flipping through the papers.

"The murders occurred at ten in the morning, one thirty in the afternoon, and nine-fifteen in the morning, respectively. The first two occurred on a Monday. He changed his pattern with Officer Slocum's death yesterday." Leigh returned to her chair. "So far the bullets have provided no information. Each one had to be dug out of a brick wall. That's a quick overview. The transcripts of the interviews my team conducted and the forensic information are in the folders."

Casey thumbed through the pages in his file. "Good briefing, Leigh." His fingers drummed on the table. "Okay. Let's get started. Olivia, continue to look for a link between the victims. Romeo, you—

"

"I know. I'm going. If anyone needs me, including our newest member, I'll be in cyber-world researching the dead men."

"While you're there, run a timeline on each of them. Compare it with what Atlanta PD assembled. We need to know the victims' movements on the days they died." Casey checked his watch. "We'll meet back here in the morning at oh eight hundred.

"That leaves you two." Casey stood, walked over, and studied the pictures on the board.

"Leigh, you know this case better than anyone, and J.T. is one of the best in the bureau. You'll work this with him."

"Thank you for including me." Her face lit up, and the rigid line of her jaw relaxed.

J.T. understood she wanted to be involved. Atlanta had a nut job on the street killing people, and this was her city, her murders. Now, they were his too.

"You two check in with the lab. See if the techs have run the latest bullet under the microscope. Then offer our condolences to Officer Slocum's wife."

"Good enough." J.T. waited while Leigh gathered her purse and briefcase. A new assignment always cranked up his heartbeat, and this was just the type he liked. When the bastard went to trial, there'd be enough evidence to put a needle in his arm.

J.T. introduced Leigh to Lauren Grant, who everyone knew was the real brains in the organization. "Leigh's going to be with us for a few weeks and needs a workspace."

"Then I guess it's handy that spot next to you is empty." Lauren handed J.T. keys to the desk and then turned to Leigh. "Welcome. He'll show you the way, and I'll get your supplies right away."

"Thank you."

"We're over here." He led her to a cubicle, stepped back to let her check out the arrangement. Low walls separated teams of two and offered little privacy.

Romeo bounded over like a playful puppy, his charm locked on Leigh. J.T. stifled the urge to tell the kid to wipe the slobber off his chin. Maybe twenty-five, Romeo's dark hair, and dark eyes were appealing to women. They flocked to him wherever they went. "Leigh, Olivia, and I are stopping by the Oak Barrel for a drink around six tonight. Come by and knock back a beer with us."

"I'd love to." She looked at her new partner.

"He's too good for us." Romeo pointed at him.

J.T. headed for the elevator. Best to leave before questions were asked. Questions he wasn't going to answer.

****

Leigh checked the time, signed in with the desk clerk at the crime lab, and requested to see Dr. Heintz. She stepped aside for J.T. to do the same.

"This way." She led J.T. through the cold, white-walled lobby and down the hallway.

He drew more than a modicum of attention from the two female clerks they passed. Leigh hoped they stared because he was handsome and not at the jagged scar starting at the outer corner of his right eye, curving downward on his cheek to his chin.

He carried himself proudly, ignoring both women. His crisp white shirt and black slacks molded to his tall, muscular frame, silently shouting dignity and confidence. Regardless of how brave he acted, she knew the stares had to hurt.

Just as they entered the hallway, his stomach growled registering a loud protest. "We should've eaten first."

"We shouldn't be here long, but I wanted you to meet somebody." She led him into a small break room and over to an empty table. "I'm afraid there are no snack machines in here. Sit. I'm pouring."

"No worries. I know of a much nicer coffee shop." When she returned, he accepted the paper cup with a nod. The left side of his mouth lifted. "Don't worry about me."

Leigh sucked in a breath. Oh, boy. He gave her a half-smile, which so far today was a first, and a dimple winked in his left cheek. That simple movement transformed his granite face to heart-stopping handsome. "How long have you been with the bureau?"

"I've been in Atlanta a few months. With the bureau for nearly five years."

"I figured you more for a career man."

"Marines first then Quantico." His thumb stroked up and down the scar. In a flash, he dropped his hand and glanced away.

Leigh's gut clenched. Was it a constant reminder of war or a knife fight with some criminal? She wouldn't ask.

"When do I meet this person?"

"Right now. He's walking through the door." She stood and breathed out a sigh of relief. "Smartest guy in this department." Leigh waved Willem to their table. "Doctor Heintz oversees the lab and is a ballistics expert. Willem, this is Special Agent J.T. Noble. He's working the sniper case."

"J.T." He stood and shook the smaller man's hand.

"Willem." Wearing jeans and a white lab coat, he straightened his wire-rimmed glasses and locked his gaze on Leigh. "How'd the feds get involved?"

A nerve in Willem's jaw twitched. Leigh sensed he hadn't heard about the taskforce and didn't like the idea his ballistics lab might be bypassed.

"I should've called ahead." She jumped in to explain. "The chief asked the FBI to take the lead on the sniper killings."

"You're going to want the evidence transferred, Agent Noble?"

"Too soon to say. You've compared the bullets?" J.T. asked.

"Yes. The bullet that killed Officer Slocum is as damaged as the other two. The impact in the brick building made identification on a particular rifle impossible. You want to see for yourself?"

"Not if it's that damaged. I may want Quantico to take a look, get their take on it," J.T. said.

"Let me know, and I'll handle the transfer myself," Willem said on a sigh. "We're proud of our equipment, however, yours may be newer."

"Contact me with any new information." J.T. fished a card from his wallet, handing it to Willem.

They said their good-byes, and she led her temporary partner to the exit. He fell in step with her as they made their way to his car. He didn't talk much. Silent and handsome made a powerful combination.

He slid behind the wheel of the standard-issue, dark sedan. "Let's get a burger before we talk to Officer Slocum's wife."

"Works for me." Leigh had schooled herself not to react to men, professionally or personally. They were simply off-limits. Every free minute she had was one hundred percent Ethan's. He was her only priority. Yet, something about J.T. intrigued her.

****

The Slocum's house in Smyrna made Leigh long to own a place with more outside space. Her home had a stamp-sized backyard with a swing set. Ethan would go wild, playing and running at full speed on such a large patch of lawn. Scattered toys and tricycles reminded her how desperately he wanted a big-boy bike.

She and J.T. stepped out onto the well-groomed lawn.

"You go ahead. I'll catch up." Leigh paused at the curb and turned her back to afford herself privacy. She tapped in her mom's number and asked about keeping Ethan so she could go with the gang to the bar.

When she turned, J.T. stood three feet away, leaning against the hood. How much had he heard?

"You ready?" His right hand swept in an arch toward the sidewalk.

"I don't discuss my personal life at work." She pulled a calming breath into her lungs.

"Exactly how was I too 'personal'?" He scowled at her as if she'd grown a second head before he marched up the sidewalk without waiting for an answer.

Well, hell, he'd spoken his longest sentence of the day, and all she'd done was piss him off. Over the years, through transfers, promotions, and attrition, the number of cops in her division privy to the details around the birth of her son had dwindled, making it easier to keep her private life…well, private.

A cold hand gripped her heart and squeezed. She shivered while standing under the warm sunshine. The nightmare wasn't a bad dream anymore, he'd come home from prison. Her nightmare walked the streets of Atlanta.

****

Leigh McBride squared her shoulders, put a smile on her face, and stepped inside her parent's real estate agency. A small yellow ball greeted her. She faded right as it whizzed past, missing her head by inches.

"Hey, watch it," she admonished the blond-haired, six-year-old bundle of energy.

"Mom," he squealed. Dropping his toy, he ran to her.

Leigh caught Ethan in midair, shifting him away from the badge and gun onto her left hip. She nuzzled his warm neck until he shrieked with delight.

"You don't look sick to me. Maybe you should've gone to school this morning."

"I like staying with Papa." Ethan wiggled from her arms, grabbed the plastic golf club, and waved it through the air.

"I'd say he's well." Her dad's blue eyes sparkled. His hair, the same shade as hers and Ethan's was in its constant state of disarray.

She glanced around the room. "Where's Mom?"

"Grocery store. I thought you were going to be late."

"Look." Ethan swatted the practice ball and it skittered across the floor.

Leigh ruffled his curly mop and sighed as he raced off in search of the ball. "I'll be a little late. I just needed a kiss from my guys."

"How'd the day with the feds go?" Her dad moved her out of Ethan's earshot.

"Better than I expected."

"You're still part of the hunt?"

"Yes. And assigned to work with one of their top agents."

"Carrington's release is keeping you up nights. No use denying it. I see the dark circles under your eyes." The lines around her dad's mouth deepened. "I don't understand. Carrington received twenty-five years and served seven. It's not right." His fingers lifted her chin. "You're not sleeping well."

"Yeah. I felt a lot safer with him behind bars." She glanced at her innocent son. Love, fear, and uncertainty flooded her heart. She'd tell Ethan the truth about his birth father someday. Please, God, not until he was a lot older.

"Have you heard from that SOB?"

"Nothing except the few hang-ups on my cell and home phones." Leigh's stomach rolled. "Has to be him."

"How did he get your numbers?"

"If you've got enough money, there are ways."

"You had the calls traced?"

"I tried. He's using a burner phone." She glanced toward the door. "Maybe I'll blow off tonight. Stay home with Ethan."

"Go. You don't get out enough." Her father patted her back as if she were the child in the room. "Your new friends are waiting."

His jaw was set, bringing a smile to her face. As usual, he was right. She stepped into his arms. The familiar scent of Old Spice cologne gave her spirit a boost.

"I won't be too late."

"No worries. Pick up Ethan at the house anytime."

"Thanks." She knelt on one knee. "Come kiss me. Mom's going to hang out with the men in black."

Chapter Two

Doyle sat at his kitchen table staring at the personal advertisement section in the *Atlanta Constitution*. He'd paid through the month for the ad. Not expensive, still, the one line "Preston from New York needs help" had drained his cash. He'd been instructed to flee to Atlanta and wait for someone to contact him. Therefore, he waited, drifting like a ship without a rudder.

He missed his wife's steady logic and warm body next to his. She was one of the reasons he'd become a member of the Final Justice Unit in New York. She'd asked him to get justice for their daughter. A justice he'd personally administered.

Where was his support? He'd given up everything to join the underground movement. When the FBI had discovered their home base, he'd been forced to run. Now he lived in poverty, mopping floors in a hospital. Doyle refused to give in to the panic gnawing at him. He'd live up to his commitment. He prayed not to be the only one who'd escaped.

****

Leigh joined the taskforce at Casey's conference room table with a lot more confidence today. Olivia, with her short, wavy, brown hair and dark chocolate eyes, was the last member to arrive. Casey with his sun-streaked hair, warm blue eyes, and serious square jaw, got down to business.

Olivia reported she hadn't found anything new in any of the victims' backgrounds. Hearing a federal agent reaffirm the research Leigh had provided was rewarding.

Romeo's timeline for Officer Slocum and his wife's activities before his death gave them no additional insight. Slocum had reported for duty on time, and the call log reflected nothing out of the ordinary up until he and his partner had stopped for breakfast.

"This sounds more like a random killing. How did the sniper know Slocum and his partner would go to that restaurant?" J.T. moved closer when Casey asked the two of them to update the group, and Leigh found herself wedged between the table leg and J.T.'s rock-hard thigh. The warmth from his body made concentrating difficult.

"Unless they were being followed," Romeo answered.

"It's possible," J.T. agreed.

"Hard to believe Mrs. Slocum said her husband had no enemies." Casey shook his head. "There's not a cop on the force who hasn't pissed more than a few people off."

"She lied," J.T. stated in his usual clipped speech. "She wouldn't look at us."

"J.T.'s right. There was a lot she didn't say," Leigh agreed. "Her husband's dead, yet she was completely unaffected."

J.T. leaned forward. "Leigh noticed the bruises on the widow's face before I did."

"The discoloration on her cheek was obvious, along with a leftover black eye. We're betting she'd been abused." Sympathy for the widow blurred her thoughts, forcing Leigh to struggle to keep her tone professional. Bruises faded, but memories of a beating never went away. The feeling of helplessness and desperation lingered long after.

Olivia spoke up. "What else, Leigh?"

She detected a hint of respect in Olivia's tone. Maybe having a beer with her and Romeo last night had been worth the time away from Ethan.

"Mrs. Slocum's body language was closed off. She kept shifting her gaze toward the door. Perched on the edge of her chair, she gave me the impression she wanted to bolt. Her eyes weren't swollen from crying. That was no teary-eyed widow talking to us about her husband."

Casey stood and paced for a minute. "Romeo, look into the Slocum's finances and see if she made a lot of trips to the doctor." Casey gathered the morning's notes and glanced at J.T. "You and Leigh see what the neighbor's say about Mr. and Mrs. Slocum. Tread lightly."

"We'll be discreet." Leigh closed her file, stood, and walked back to her desk. She'd only just nestled into her new chair when her cell buzzed. The ID screen read "unknown caller." Was this another hang-up? Reluctantly, she answered.

"McBride."

No one spoke.

"McBride," she repeated. Fire raced across her skin. "Aren't you a little old to be playing games?"

"Games? What makes you think I'm playing?" A hard edge vibrated through the voice. Cutting and cruel. "Okay. Let's play," Jason said.

"Don't threaten me. Don't call me. Don't come near me. You'll pay the price if you do." She hit the end button, tossed the phone in her top drawer, and then slammed it shut. Leaning her forehead into her hand, she closed her eyes and tried to control her runaway anger. Hate rolled through her. Sweat broke out and trickled down her chest. She sucked in a quick breath.

Her skin tingled as if she stood in an electrical storm. J.T. was behind her. She dared not face him. He'd spot her urge to kill expression for sure.

"Any way I can help?" His tone of voice, deep yet soft, oddly comforted her.

"It's nothing. Thanks for offering." She lifted her head, meeting his gaze. The heat from telling such a blatant lie crept up her cheeks. She prayed he'd drop the subject.

"Let's make that run back to the Slocum's." If her abuse theory proved out, she'd earn a little more of the team's respect and trust. "Bet there's a neighbor who'll gossip about them."

"Okay." He stared into her eyes, his jaw stiff as carved granite. "Afterward, we can stop by the sixth precinct. Talk to Slocum's coworkers."

"You won't be welcomed with open arms," she warned.

A lopsided grin lifted one corner of his mouth. "Not a new experience for me."

Leigh slung her handbag over her shoulder. "Really? I'll bet your mama welcomes you with open arms."

"Don't. You'd lose," he mumbled.

****

Originally, the idea of working with Leigh hadn't bothered him, but the lady had secrets. And secrets could get you killed.

She sat forward, opened her mouth then closed it.

"What?"

"Just a thought."

"Let's have it."

"The sniper has killed on Monday or Tuesday. It might be a pattern."

"It's something to track because he will strike again."

"Yeah. I don't buy Romeo's copycat, gun-for-hire theory. Mrs. Slocum didn't pay to have him killed."

"Romeo talks out his ass sometimes." J.T. drove into the Slocum's housing subdivision and parked on a side street. "Let's talk to the neighbors first."

She easily kept up with his long stride. She'd worn black slacks with her blue blouse tucked in at her narrow waist. Her loose jacket did nothing for her figure. He'd bet she purposely dressed in a nondescript fashion. Probably to keep men like him from speculating about what lay under her clothes.

"We'll play it by ear. If a woman answers, you take point. You did okay yesterday."

Leigh shot him a cool look over her shoulder. "I wasn't aware I was being judged. Good to know I passed," she snapped.

He stepped directly in front of her.

"Easy, hotshot." She was still pissed about the phone call she'd received earlier, so J.T. tried to understand. "My every word's not an accusation."

The firm set to her jaw said she'd never admit she'd snapped at him. The smile playing at the corners of her mouth gave her away. "I'll try to remember."

****

Nurse Ellen Rosen pulled the curtain back and motioned him to come to her. Doyle, alias Don, limped to her, dragging his cleaning cart with him. His favorite ER nurse lifted her lips into a slight smile.

"We had an accident. Will you lend me a hand?" The nurse leaned closer and spoke in a soft voice. "Her husband came in to check on her. Right after he whispered something to her, she threw up. I sent him to the waiting room. If you'll get the floor, I'll take care of her."

"No problem." He grabbed the mop from the cart, hurrying to clean up the mess.

"I'm sorry." The woman's words were barely audible.

"There's nothing to apologize for. We don't mind. Do we, Don?"

"No, ma'am. Don't mind at all."

The patient's voice had a broken tone, one he'd come to recognize. He turned in her direction while he rinsed his mop. Her swollen, blackened eyes and busted lip kept two interns busy assessing the damage.

Don dropped his head. Would the beatings never end? Would the abusers never learn? The world continued to produce an endless supply of spineless bastards who preyed on women, maiming them for life. Bile rolled up in the back of his throat, hot and bitter.

"You all right? You look like you saw a ghost." Nurse Rosen's concerned face eased the fire raging in his veins. "I said your name three times."

"Sorry, I didn't hear you. I'm fine." He wasn't and he'd seen a ghost. Cheryl, at nineteen years old, stood before him. For a fleeting second, his daughter's bruised, cold, and dead body had flashed through his memory. He had to pay closer attention. *Remember, your name is Don Porter.* He pulled the curtain closed and pushed his cart down to the janitor's area.

He usually dusted the waiting room later in the day. Luckily, he controlled his schedule. Carrying his furniture-cleaning tote, he limped through the door to the visitor's area, where he moved around the room wiping tabletops. The abuser was easy to spot. He sat playing a game on his cell phone, his red knuckles not slowing his thumbs. The bastard looked up and straight through Doyle without giving him a second glance. After all, he was a lowly orderly. A nobody.

****

Leigh dipped her spoon into her dessert. "Riding with you for long would be hard on my waistline." The down-home café that J.T. had stopped at for lunch struck her as odd. Small and cozy, the old house converted to a diner was charming. She'd pegged him for a Big Mac kind of guy.

"Never happen. We'd hit the gym. Regularly." He scooped up a spoonful of dessert. "I've been to a lot of different cities and countries. Atlanta and my grandmother's house are the only two places in the world I've found truly good peach cobbler."

She leaned back in the booth and stared in amusement. "I'll be damned. You do speak in sentences of more than four words." Leigh's spirit lifted when he chuckled. The warm, throaty sound made her smile.

"Of course I do. Why'd you think otherwise?" His right cheek twisted and curled at the tip of the scar when he laughed.

"Yesterday you spoke in only four-word sentences."

"People talk too much." He dropped his gaze to the bowl in front of him and ate without looking up again.

"You want to go back to Carol Slocum and question her again? Her neighbor overheard more than one fight between the couple."

"No, ma'am."

Great, now he was down to speaking in even shorter sentences. Her cell vibrated on her hip. The screen read "unknown caller." She pressed the decline button and turned back to find green eyes focused on her, seeing everything, missing nothing. Expecting what? A tingle spread across her chest. Her breasts tightened, and the muscles in her lower stomach clenched.

"Was that somebody you need to speak with?

"It wasn't important," she managed to choke out. She reached for the check, anything to slow the flush washing up her cheeks.

"I've got it." He tossed a twenty on the table, walked to the front, and held the door open for her.

"Thank you."

The scent of wild honeysuckle greeted her on the way to the car. Summer was coming, and school would be out soon. She and Ethan loved the outdoors, spending hours in the park. "April makes me want to find a hammock, stretch out with a good book, and. . . a cold beer." Damn, she'd almost said with Ethan at her side.

His shoulders stiffened. "You need alcohol to loosen up?"

The breath of fresh air she'd taken soured at his odd question. J.T. slid behind the wheel and drummed his fingers on the steering wheel.

"Call your friend at the lab. Ask him to send me side-by-side comparisons of all three shell casings. All three spent bullets ending in brick is a bit convenient. It's no accident. The son of a bitch knows exactly what he's doing."

"If you're right, and he's not military trained, maybe he's SWAT." She hated what she was thinking. Worse yet, she hated the possibility she could be right.

"Jesus Christ." He shifted his gaze upward. "Gear up for a shit storm if he's one of us."

Chapter Three

Jason held the amber liquid up to the light before taking a sip. He smiled appreciatively. His father's taste ran to the expensive, and the single-barrel Jack Daniels helped make the pompous bastard tolerable.

Carlton Carrington's presence filled the room with the scent of greed and prosperity. Jason barely contained his disdain.

"Son, if you're sure you're ready to come back to work, your office is waiting."

"Thanks, Father. Your belief in my innocence meant everything to me.

"I never doubted you. We'll just put this nasty business behind us."

Jason leaned back on his new, tan leather couch in the apartment his mother had rented for him in an outrageously expensive neighborhood of Atlanta.

This "nasty business" wouldn't be over until Leigh McBride paid for every night he'd spent in Metro State Prison. His money had bought solid contacts on the outside. Through them, he'd closely monitored Leigh for six long, fucking years. Because of her boy's age, the little bastard had to be his.

First, he'd convince his parents their baby boy was a dedicated son who wanted nothing more than to be a good dad. He'd have an ironclad alibi for each time misfortune visited Leigh over the next few weeks. With careful planning and patience, no one would doubt her suicide. When the time was right, that brat of hers would die in front of her. Then she'd hang. The vision of her kicking feet, her tongue swelling, and the life oozing from her cold eyes had kept him going for six years.

"I'd like to discuss something with you before we join Mother for dinner." Every nerve ending sizzled. "Something of great interest to you both."

"What's that, son?"

Blood raced through his veins. Rocking the old man's world was going to be fun. Jason had mentally rehearsed the words, measured each one for impact. He savored the moment the way he had the fine whiskey, rolled the words around on his tongue, and tasted victory.

"An heir to the Carrington fortune."

****

Olivia ruffled Romeo's hair and dropped onto the chair next to Leigh. "Hello, gang."

"Morning." Leigh hoped the warm greeting meant she'd been accepted as part of the team. "How did you get the nickname Romeo when your name's Tobias?"

"God, don't ask," J.T. grumbled.

Romeo waved J.T. off. "Because ladies love me. A fact certain people can't accept. Plus, I can romance information from the network when no one else in this office can."

"He's a geek. And needs a personal keeper." J.T. pushed his empty coffee cup across the table then slid his tongue over his lip.

Leigh's gaze locked on J.T.'s mouth. A ball of heat started in her stomach and shot south. The reaction surprised her, and, in a way, came as a relief. She hadn't experienced that particular stirring in years. Maybe, there was hope for her after all.

"I get a lot of phone calls from women," Romeo continued. "And J.T. gets? None."

Olivia, who kept glancing toward the doorway, interrupted. "Here comes our leader."

"Sorry, folks." Casey hustled in, dropping his briefcase on his desk before joining them at the conference table. "I had an early morning call from an old partner. What did I miss?"

"Not a damn thing." J.T. crossed his arms over his expansive chest. "We didn't get a chance to stop by the precinct yesterday. If we decide it's necessary, we'll do it today."

"I, on the other hand, had a productive day." Romeo preened, running his hand through thick, wavy, dark hair. "Mrs. Slocum falls a lot. She's had more than one brush with the stairs at her house. Broke her jaw once."

"Bastard," J.T. muttered.

"If you're referring to Brian Slocum, I concur." Romeo read from his iPad. "Mrs. Slocum writes a check for these 'accidents' instead of filing an insurance claim."

Leigh handed J.T. the pictures he'd asked for of the three rounds recovered. His hand folded around hers when he reached for his copy. "Not much help here. The bullets were fired from a rifle. That's all we know."

Olivia pushed a diagram to the center of the table. "I agree. Based on the estimated trajectory and damage to the victim's head, the sniper's rifle has long-range capacity."

"My guess is he's using a Remington 700," J.T. said.

Casey leaned across the table to study the diagram. "It's been the weapon of choice for years by hunters and SWAT, even some military, but our gut isn't telling us military."

"Why not military?" Leigh asked.

"Because a trained sniper from any branch of the military aims for the heart." J.T. taps himself on the chest. "It never fails. One-shot. One kill. Head shots are for television and the movies. Too small of a target. If you don't drill them dead center, the bullet can ricochet off the skull and hit somebody else."

Leigh sat in awe. Not only did J.T. talk, but he also spoke in full-blown sentences and with conviction. Mrs. Slocum's bruises and broken jaw nagged at Leigh. "We should check out the other victim's wives. Abuse may be the link we're looking for."

J.T.'s gaze caught hers and held. A flicker of approval flashed in his eyes as he winked with a slight nod. "Let's start with the first widow. Maybe all of them had trouble with stairs."

****

"I'm sorry. Mrs. Ortega not home." Leigh noticed the diminutive housekeeper shift from one foot to the other and the tightly gripped dust rag and can of furniture polish.

"It's important we speak to her," J.T. said in a take-no-prisoners tone.

Leigh stepped in front of him. His size, scowl, and identification probably scared the poor woman to death. "Were you working here when Mr. Ortega died?"

"Sí. Long time."

"Before his death, did Mr. Ortega hit his wife?"

"I don't want trouble." She fidgeted, looking at everything except the two of them.

"We're not from immigration, don't know and don't care about your papers," Leigh assured. "We need the truth about Mr. Ortega."

The woman studied Leigh for a few seconds. "Mr. Ortega lose his temper a lot. Was me called 9-1-1 last time. He fire me. Missus bring me back after he is dead."

"What hospital did they take her to?"

The frightened woman shook her head and tears welled in her eyes.

Leigh looked up at her new partner. "Any questions you'd like to ask?"

"Nope. We got what we came for."

She thanked the terrified woman and followed J.T. down the steps to the car. He paused at the curb.

"So, hotshot, if I compliment you on being right and how well you handled her, you gonna bite my head off?"

"Not if you don't bite mine off for being stone-cold-surprised when you talk to me in complete sentences." Leigh heard him scoff at her comeback. "And stop calling me hotshot."

"Like your fiery temper doesn't shoot sparks?" He arched an eyebrow before he ducked into the car.

"I'm the calmest person you'll ever meet." Truth was, her nerves jumped faster than a hamster running on a wheel. "Next stop the Mussa-Shir home. See if his wife was abused." Leigh entered the address in the GPS, buckling up when he eased the sedan onto the freeway.

"We need a cup of coffee." He drove in front of a Starbucks and growled at the long line at the window. "Sit tight." He parked, and in a couple of ground-covering strides was out of sight.

Nightmares had plagued her last night, no doubt triggered by Jason's phone call and comments. Why had he contacted her? Was Ethan in danger? His words left no doubt he intended to torment her. How far would he go?

Ten minutes later, J.T. shouldered the door open and crossed the parking lot to her side of the car, a coffee in each hand. A gust of wind picked up a lock of black hair and blew it away from his face. His shirt and slacks plastered against his body, and Leigh's heart did a cartwheel and landed with a rapid thump. Her hand shook slightly when he passed her the coffee.

"Th-thanks." She stumbled over the word. He leaned down to the window.

"Didn't know how you took it, so I brought cream and sugar." Eyes narrowed, he searched her face.

Had he noticed her reaction? He never uttered a word as he slid behind the wheel and maneuvered through traffic toward the Mussa-Shir home in North Decatur.

****

The widow had provided nothing J.T. hadn't already figured out.

23 |

She'd been putting up with abuse for years. He just didn't get understand how a man could beat a woman or why she'd tolerate it.

Shake it off, he thought, as he drove around to the backyard of his grandmother's white framed house and parked. With black and white striped awnings, it might've been a cottage in the woods instead of a ranch style on the outskirts of Newnan, Georgia. Her yard was an explosion of azaleas, magnolia trees, and gardenias. Nana was exactly where he'd expected, on her knees, hands in the dirt, planting more flowers. The smile on her face made the drive from Atlanta worthwhile.

"Hello, gorgeous." He slid his arms around her slender frame and helped her stand while soaking in the goodness she radiated. She'd been the one constant in his life when he was a kid and the only reason he'd returned to Atlanta.

"What a nice surprise." She dusted the dirt off her hands before reaching up to cup his face. "Come down here and let me look at you."

"If you wore your glasses, you'd see lots of things." He carefully lifted them from the lanyard around her neck and slid them onto her pale face. He leaned over as she'd instructed.

"It's still daylight, and I don't need them to plant my flowers." Head tilted back, she pursed her lips and studied him, then gently patted his right cheek.

His heart tugged. She treated the scar as part of him. Hell, at least she admitted he had one. "The fresh air must be helping. Your color's good."

Her silver eyebrows dipped, and she chewed her bottom lip. "Was I supposed to fix your dinner tonight?"

"No, ma'am," he lied. "I came to check on my favorite female." J.T. wouldn't tell her she'd forgotten. "Have you eaten?"

"Hadn't thought about it."

"Great. Let's dig through the fridge. I'll bet we find something I can cook on the grill."

"Good, I'll wash up while you look." She slipped her fragile hand through the crook of his arm and led him inside.

"When did Elva go home?" J.T. walked through the house with a critical eye. Satisfied everything was clean and in order, he joined his grandmother at the kitchen sink.

"You can stop checking up on her work." She finished drying her hands with a paper towel. "I can't set a dish down and turn my back without her washing the darn thing. I blink my eyes, poof, my tea glass is gone."

Over the next few hours, they cooked and ate supper, and he laughed at her complaints of how Elva bossed her around. At seventy-six, Nana thought she should be mothering her sixty-seven-year-old housekeeper.

"Have you heard from your mother?"

"No, ma'am." And, so ended a pleasant evening. "I'm guessing since you mentioned it, you did." He fought to keep from snapping. "You didn't give her money again?"

She let out an audible sigh, the one she always used when he tried her patience. "No, Teddy. I haven't heard from her." Cool fingers wrapped around his wrist. "But she's my daughter. If she needed financial help, I wouldn't refuse her."

He fought back the urge to remind her not to call him Teddy. To do so was an exercise in futility of the grandest proportion. "Nana, she's fine. We'd know if something had happened."

His mother had taken advantage of Nana's open heart and perpetual forgiveness many times. After she'd dumped J.T. on Nana, she'd pop in every few years to dry out her liver. Stay just long enough to remind him he had a mother. Then she'd con his grandmother out of money and disappear, leaving Nana and J.T. to recover and rebuild.

Her grip tightened. "Promise me, you'll try to find her."

"Nana, she may not be in Atlanta."

"This is her home, she's in the city. I know it. And if anyone can locate her, you can." She held his gaze until he nodded his agreement.

He hadn't told Nana he'd been searching since the episode with her heart. Trolling beer joints in seedy neighborhoods, sitting across the bar from hundreds of bottles of liquor wasn't J.T.'s ideal way to stay dry himself, but Nana's health took precedence over his failings as a man. Finding his mother would be a challenge, staying sober would test his conviction.

Chapter Four

Jason tightened his hold on his mother's fingers. Her belief in him was critical. She gave him a reassuring glance and patted his knee with her free hand. The high-priced lawyer droned on, explaining the Georgia judicial system. The pompous ass spoke slowly, insisting their request would fail.

His mother flicked her hand through the air to indicate she'd heard enough. She didn't like being told no, and, apparently, Morgan Anderson was about to learn the hard way.

"Morgan, we didn't come for a lecture or to solicit your opinion. If our request wasn't difficult, we wouldn't need you."

He suppressed a shudder and hoped the attorney was right. The possibility of the little snot-slinger getting close to him turned Jason's stomach. This was simply a critical exercise in establishing himself as reformed and rehabilitated.

Morgan's gaze shifted from Jason's mother to his father. "Not difficult, Carlton. Impossible. Your son is a convicted and registered sex offender."

Morgan swiped sweat from his forehead with the back of his hand. His discomfort was obvious after learning they expected him to help prove Leigh McBride's son was a Carrington. Jason bit back a smile. "You must understand the court will refuse to hear this request," Morgan said. "Elizabeth, I checked the records as you requested. The father's name is not on the birth certificate. I'm afraid you've taken up an impossible cause."

"Nothing's impossible. Lies fabricated by a hysterical woman put my son in prison. Do not expect me to accept he fathered a child he will never hold in his arms. Whom I will never hold."

He resisted the urge to break contact when his mother's diamond rings cut into his palm. Instead, he tightened his squeeze, silently encouraging her. The more the stupid cow believed in him the better.

Morgan pulled his hand over his face and shook his head. "No judge in Atlanta will grant his request for a paternity test."

Jason fought to keep his tone pleasant. "I'll show the court I've turned my life around. I'll do whatever it takes. I'm positive he's my son."

"For your own sake, stay away from the boy and his mother."

Carlton Carrington stood. "If this boy is my grandson, I want irrefutable proof."

Daddy dearest had lost his patience and what Mama wanted Mama got. Morgan was close to losing a lucrative account.

"My son has no desire to come in contact with Leigh McBride," his dad continued. "Arrangements can be made for supervised visits. He wants to live up to his responsibility. As grandparents, we intend to ask for visitation privileges."

"With your wealth, the media will be all over the story and you've already gone through one scandal."

Jason's father sat with a grunt. Morgan had scored a direct hit. Jason's underarms soaked through his shirt as support from his parents threatened to slip through his grasp.

Jason spoke up. "In today's environment, everybody sues everybody over anything. You can at least talk to Leigh McBride, can't you? Threaten her with legal action. She's a law enforcement officer with a son and career to worry about. Maybe she won't want her name plastered all over the front page either."

His father's hand landed hard on Jason's knee. "Excellent idea, my boy. I'm proud to say you've matured a lot over the last six years."

Jason glanced up at his beaming father. "You have no idea how much I've changed. No idea."

****

Doyle parked across from the high school. Carrying his equipment in an oversized toolbox, he felt comfortable no one noticed a technician. While he made his way to his chosen vantage point, he considered the dangers of executing Steven Sanders. Granted, the television interview with the FBI boss and learning they'd taken over the case was flattering. It also added a new dimension of care he had to exercise.

Gaining information on Sanders and his battered wife hadn't been easy. The Junior Varsity baseball coach and the often-missing Faith, who taught seventh-grade science, kept to themselves. The excuses for her many absences and injuries would've made an interesting read. This most recent beating would keep her out a minimum of two weeks.

The site selection for Sanders's execution had presented a dilemma, too. Thankfully, the coach made a habit of staying until everybody left, allowing for minimal risk.

Doyle entered through the back door and climbed the stairs to the roof of the auditorium where he unpacked his rifle and got comfortable. In addition to a clear view of the parking lot outside Sanders's office, the entrance to the freeway was a mere two blocks south. He inhaled deeply. Today's execution would be easy and safe.

Doyle wiggled his fingers, which had grown numb from holding the rifle steady. Maybe, he was getting too damned old. Then he remembered the bruised and beaten woman he'd seen in the ER and imagined the fear and pain Faith Sanders had endured. Hell, he'd prefer the law protected battered women, but it didn't.

The door opened and his target walked out, alone. Nice of Sanders to park next to the building. Doyle mentally slipped into the zone, lined the crosshairs up with Sander's forehead, and gently squeezed the trigger. The 700 produced an incredible report, echoing across the almost empty lot. Doyle stowed his rifle and casually left the premises.

****

J.T. arrived on the scene just as the sun dropped behind the giant scoreboard, shooting the last of today's dying rays through the open places on the sign. The team had jumped every time the phone rang all day, but the call hadn't come until late afternoon. He rocked back on his heels and scanned the area. Committing all that lay in front of him to memory.

Leigh's voice drifted up from behind him. His blood flow kicked up a notch, and he cursed himself for the surge of pleasure. He'd called her over an hour ago with an offer to swing by and pick her up. Her refusal had been fast and firm.

"Took you long enough." He'd heard music in the background when he'd called. Maybe she'd gone out after work for drinks. *Who cares where she hangs out?*

"Sorry." She offered no further explanation. Instead, she turned and walked away.

J.T. joined the small group of firefighters and EMTs, introducing himself all the way around. Atlanta patrolman, Ricky Phillips, nodded at J.T. and waved him over.

"Phillips." J.T. shook the cop's hand. "The sniper is keeping everybody jumping."

"This bastard's got everybody in the city on edge." Phillips rolled his shoulders. "A fuckin' car backfires, and we get called out. We had two wasted runs today before this one. Body's over here."

J.T. followed Phillips across the parking lot where an area was taped off with a cluster of crime scene officers working. Phillips ducked under the protective divider and lead J.T. to the body.

"Shit," J.T. muttered, looking down at the bloody mess that used to be the guy's head. "This guy is determined to take the victims' heads off."

"J.T.," Phillips lowered his voice. "In case you didn't know it, Jenna Hawkins is all over the place. She's trying to get the vic's name. Watch out for her. She ain't nothin' but a pretty piranha."

"She's with FOX?"

"Yeah."

"Appreciate the tip."

"You want to speak to the custodian who called 9-1-1?"

"Yeah, where'd you stash him?"

"In the field house." The cop indicated a clapboard structure next to the baseball field. "There's an officer stationed outside. I figured you'd want the guy kept on ice."

"Good idea. I need your help. Let's keep the lady reporter clear of this building. Will you take care of that for me?"

"You got it."

J.T. doubled back past the body and walked over to the field house. A female cop stepped between him and the door. "Can I help you?"

He pulled his ID from his hip pocket, extending the leather holder out for her inspection. "I need to question the custodian."

"Detective McBride's with him now." The cop raised her chin a notch as she stepped aside.

"Good." J.T. decided Leigh had a few friends on the force.

He entered the building and followed the sound of voices down the hall. When he opened the door, Leigh turned in his direction and paused. She lobbed him a smile, motioned for him to join them, and introduced him to Henry Elder.

"Mr. Elder was telling me where he was when he heard the gunshot."

"Don't stop. I'll jump in if I think of something." J.T. pulled a chair over and sat while the older man walked Leigh through his experience.

Leigh made paying attention difficult. Now he understood why she wore her hair in an old-lady, schoolteacher knot at work. Left loose, a riot of blonde waves, swirls, and curls hung midway down her back. A headband of some sort kept her face clear. His fingers itched to tunnel deep, to test the softness. Her jeans and Braves jersey removed the stiff cop image she portrayed during the daytime.

J.T. pushed his idiot brain into gear. "Mr. Elder, what would you estimate your travel time from inside the gym to the body was?" J.T. stood, moving next to Leigh.

"Maybe, five minutes. I know what a gunshot sounds like, heard my share in the military."

Elder tapped the tattoo on his forearm. It was identical to one partially exposed by the sleeve on J.T.'s T-shirt. He tipped his head in recognition and let the man continue.

"Takes me longer than most, but I hurried." The older Marine knocked his knuckles against his knee. "I got too close to a Bouncing Betty in Nam." He snorted a wheeze of air through his teeth, looking at J.T.'s face. "You get that in Iraq?"

"Afghanistan," J.T. said, keeping his voice low. Leigh had zero interest in his scar, and he didn't want to discuss any part of the war around her.

She pulled a business card from her hip pocket and handed it to the older man before shaking his hand. "If you think of something else, give me a call."

"I appreciate your help." J.T. stood and extended his hand, welcoming the strong clasp he received. "Here and over there."

"Semper Fi." Henry nodded his recognition before limping out of the room.

"Marine." She stated the word with a proud lilt in her voice and approval on her face.

"Once a Marine—"

"Always a Marine," she finished for him.

"Who?"

"My dad."

Finishing each other's sentences couldn't possibly be a good thing. He'd earned his reputation for being a tough investigator and catching killers. Leigh was distracting, making concentrating a challenge. One he couldn't allow.

* * * *

People had gathered on the sidewalk under the streetlamp hoping for a closer look. Curiosity from the locals came with the territory. J.T. made a final round, ensuring all the information was gathered and sent to the lab.

Casey had held a press conference earlier in the day, so J.T. had expected heavier media coverage, but this was ridiculous. Four news vans and at least ten reporters were on the scene. He paused long enough to refer all questions to the SAC.

"Now to break the news to the widow," J.T. said.

Leigh joined him, holding up her wrist up to check her watch. Light bounced off her blonde hair and pale skin, giving her an angelic glow.

"Somebody waiting for you?" He wanted those words back.

"Yes." Her eyes widened.

His bold question hadn't pissed her off. Instead, a spark of panic flashed behind her blue eyes. *Why?*

"Then, by all means, go." The coarseness of his voice rocked her back on her heels. "I'll talk to the widow without you."

"No, you won't. This is my case, too. Remember?"

"Of course." Shit, he'd dig his foot out of his mouth later. "Where are you parked?"

"Across Belton. What about you?"

"Behind the field house."

"I'll follow you." She bit her bottom lip, glancing at her watch again.

His gaze dropped to her lush mouth. Stop or kiss her. Do something. "Fine. Go get your car."

She hadn't taken three strides before her cell was in her hand.

Calling a significant other? Check in with someone? Why did he give a crap?

He had two mysteries to solve. It would probably be easier to catch the sniper than to unravel the secrets of his temporary partner.

Chapter Five

Unable to sleep after breaking the bad news to the widow Sanders, J.T. had expanded his search and looked for his mother. Going from bar to bar in the old neighborhood, flashing a twenty-year-old picture wasted his time. Down deep, if he were into soul searching, he'd admit his hunt had been half-assed. He flip-flopped between actually trying to locate his mother and merely going through the motions.

He shoved the door open and stepped out into the night air. The odor of stale beer, sweat, and cigarettes spilled onto the sidewalk with him. An unexpected blow came from behind, and he stumbled forward a couple of steps. He regained his footing, whirled, grabbed the shoulders of the asshole who'd run into him, and shoved him away. The nutcase rushed him again. He swung. An error in judgment.

"What the hell?" J.T. blocked the guy's right only to take a blow to the midsection. He had no idea why the man had hit him, but enough was enough. J.T. delivered a hard punch to the attacker's jaw. The guy landed flat of his back. "Don't fucking get up."

A uniformed cop ran up and slid to a stop.

"FBI." He jerked his ID from his hip pocket and identified himself when he saw the Taser. "Does this piece of crap belong to you?" J.T. rubbed his right hand, pissed about his bruised knuckles.

"Yeah. We caught him making a sale a couple of blocks back." The cop pulled in a deep breath. "The sorry bastard ran."

A second uniform parked a patrol car at the curb and got out. "Next time, I'll chase, you drive," he said to his panting partner. A smile of recognition lit up his face. "J.T. Noble? You son of a bitch. Where the hell have you been?"

J.T.'s feet were lifted off the ground when arms the size of a gorilla's wrapped around him. Davey Campbell finally set J.T. down and pounded on his back. A welcome and friendly face in a city of strangers.

"Everywhere and nowhere, Davey. How about you?"

"Great. You look fit. I heard the feds recruited you right after you left the Marines. Then you fell off the radar."

"After Quantico, I spent a few years in the Chicago office before being assigned here."

"What are you doing on this side of town? You working a case?"

J.T. looked to the stars as he blew out a breath, not wanting to discuss his mission. His high school friends knew all about his mother's drinking problem. She'd shown up at Nana's one day and stuck around for the better part of a year. Then dear old Mom had cleaned out Nana's purse and run off with a new love. His experiences as a kid had made a cynic out of him; there'd be no marriage and no children for him.

"No. This is personal." He handed the old snapshot to David. "I'm hunting Roxanne Noble or whatever her last name is now."

David studied the picture for a minute before passing it back. Pity clouded his face and he shook his head. J.T. remembered when that look used to hurt. Now sympathy bounced off his thick hide.

"I've been working this side of midtown for the past year and haven't seen her around. Have you filed a missing person report?"

"Hell no," J.T. said on a huff of air. "There's a difference between missing and not wanting to be found. She doesn't want any part of being located."

"I'll keep an eye out for her."

J.T. handed David his card. "Thanks. I'll take all the help I can get. My grandmother's been asking for her."

"No problem. We've got to get our passenger checked in." David turned and waved his hand to let his partner know he was ready to roll. "Stay in touch," he said over his shoulder.

"You, too," J.T. called out. He jaywalked through traffic to his car and hit the highway fast. Soon the bars, filled with whiskey, vodka, and ice-cold beer were in his rearview mirror. Playing Russian roulette was a fool's game, and every time he got close to alcohol was another spin of the chamber. How many rolls did he have left before his number came up?

****

"There's a gentleman downstairs asking for you." Leigh turned away from her discussion with J.T. and discovered the administrative assistant was speaking to her.

"Who is he?"

"Didn't give his name, but he specifically asked for you."

Leigh's heart hit the superhighway. Only a handful of people knew about her new assignment. Atlanta PD would've been allowed to come up. "Must be Dad. Something's wrong."

She jumped to her feet and started for the elevator. Her stomach dropped when J.T. matched her stride for stride. He reached around her and hit the down arrow. She whirled to face him.

"Don't argue." His eyebrows dipped. "If there's trouble, I'll be there."

The doors slid open, and he stepped inside. The determined set of his jaw and his insistence he'd be there for her confused her. "I appreciate the offer. Your presence isn't necessary."

"Sure it is."

A silent eternity passed while they descended. Horrible scenarios rushed through her mind. The fire in her stomach increased with each passing floor. At last, the bell dinged, and the door slid open. Leigh rushed out to face the problem, praying Ethan wasn't hurt.

Her gaze swept across the lobby full of strangers' faces. Confused, she turned toward the guard. A chill raced across her arms.

"Detective McBride, your guest wasn't cleared for an appointment." He handed her a business card. "However, Agent Noble can escort him, or you can use one of the meeting rooms down here."

"I understand." Leigh read the information on the embossed card. Why would an attorney who specialized in family law want to speak with her? Her brain scrambled. "The lobby's fine."

"I'll wait for you." J.T. leaned against the desk.

Leigh crossed the lobby to where a man, dressed in a tailored, dark gray suit, stood. He straightened his jacket and approached her. Salt and pepper hair, leather briefcase in hand, she didn't need his card to make him as an attorney. An expensive one. What did he want with her?

"Morgan Anderson."

She accepted his outstretched hand. "Mr. Anderson, I'm Leigh McBride. How can I help you?" His limp grasp and sweaty palm warned her. His mission made him uncomfortable.

"May we speak privately?"

"What about?"

His dark brown eyes went flat and emotionless. "Your son. A subject I'm sure you'd prefer to discuss in private."

Heat flamed in her lungs. "Something's happened to Ethan?"

"Please. I believe you're going to want this conversation kept private."

"Has my son been injured?" She forced her knees to stay rigid.

"I'm sure he's fine."

"Tell me what you want." Comfortable Ethan was okay, Leigh's patience with the attorney's evasive answers had ended.

"I'm here on behalf of Jason Carrington. He is Ethan's father, correct?"

Leigh backed up a step. She needed space.

"No, he is not." The whispered words seethed from deep in her soul. "I don't know what game you're running, and I don't care. You and Jason Carrington stay away from me and my son."

"Mr. Carrington hired me—"

"Wait here," she interrupted. What she had to say should be said privately. She pulled from her deepest reserve and returned to the front desk. With shoulders back and a forced smile, she requested a private space. Leigh avoided J.T.'s gaze, afraid his ever-watchful eyes would pick up on her fear.

"Room D is empty." The guard indicated the south hall.

Leigh thanked the guard and motioned Morgan Anderson to follow her. By the time she closed the door, adrenaline she'd held in check exploded through her body. "Talk fast." She checked the time when she turned to face him. "You've got five minutes." She glanced down. "Four and a half minutes."

"Mr. Carrington's a changed man. If he's fathered a son, he wants the opportunity to do the right thing."

A nightmare she'd lived with for almost seven years became reality with the speed of a hummingbird's wings. His words slammed into her and the earth shifted under her feet. Maternal fury replaced temporary shock, and Leigh moved closer. Inches away from Anderson's face, she enunciated her words carefully and clearly. "Read the conditions of Carrington's parole. If he comes near me, I'll send him back to prison. Don't doubt my sincerity on this matter."

"Carlton and Elizabeth Carrington believe in their son and are willing to spare no expense supporting him in his cause." Anderson continued as if she hadn't spoken.

"Jason Carrington is a skilled liar without a conscience. He convinced his parents of his innocence seven years ago. If you think their money scares me, you're dead wrong."

"You can end his speculation by agreeing to a paternity test."

A wave of nausea hit Leigh. Her mind rebelled against his ludicrous and threatening statement. "Advise your client he's wasting his time." Leigh flexed her fingers, anything to slow her racing heart. "Your five minutes are up."

Morgan Anderson didn't flinch. "The Carrington family can

survive another scandal. Can you?" His friendly voice had turned low and menacing.

"Damn right, I can." Leigh jerked the door open and walked out.

True to his word, J.T. had waited for her. Feet apart, arms folded across his broad chest, he looked more like a bodyguard than an FBI agent. She prayed the anger didn't show on her face.

"Something wrong?" J.T.'s gaze tracked the attorney until he'd exited the front door.

"No. Thank God," she lied with as much conviction as she could muster.

When the elevator doors closed, she leaned back against the mirrored wall and held on to the brass handrail for support. Questions flooded her mind. How'd the sorry bastard find out about Ethan? How did he know where to find her today?

She walked straight to Casey's office. She paused, waiting until he finished a phone call.

Casey motioned her in with a smile. "You and J.T. headed out?"

"Not yet." She stepped to the edge of his desk. "You have a minute?"

"Sure." He pointed at a chair, indicating she should sit. "What's on your mind?"

"How much do you know about me?"

"The chief and I spoke at length before your assignment. I didn't hear anything to make me doubt your ability to stop a murderer or to contribute to the team." He moved around his desk and sat in the chair next to her. "Why do you ask?"

She blinked hard when tears pushed their way to the surface. She wouldn't cry in front of him. She'd get through this by keeping her head and wits under control.

"I may have a legal issue on the horizon." She choked on the knot in her throat, waited for a beat, and then continued. "I give you my word before I embarrass you or the team, I'll request to be removed as the liaison."

"Keep me informed and let me know if I can help." Casey's face was a study in non-emotion.

"This whole thing should be short-lived. Thanks for understanding." She left his office more uncertain than when she'd gone in. The possibility the chief had shared more than her work background nagged at her.

****

J.T.'s lip-reading ability had provided him with the name of the man who'd visited and upset Leigh. Morgan Anderson's website had been pulled up on the computer screen before Leigh walked into Casey's office. Anderson practiced family law. Hello? The word family swam in front of his eyes. The attorney's address on Clairmont Road placed him in one of Atlanta's highest rent districts and explained the high-dollar clothes. Whatever news he'd delivered had shaken Leigh to the core. After her meeting, the color had disappeared from her face, and her entire body had trembled. She hadn't collapsed. She'd supported herself. Her actions led him to believe she was accustomed to not having a shoulder to lean on.

The lady had problems. J.T. had doubts about her. Drunks, liars, and bad mothers firmly planted any woman in his no-fly zone. *All the more reason to keep your dick from making decisions while at work.*

Her stride was deliberate when she crossed the office, sat, and pulled her chair up to her computer. She worked in silence for a few minutes, taking notes while concentrating on the screen. Abruptly, she pushed back and turned to him. Maybe now he'd learn what the hell was going on with her.

"If you'll give me fifteen minutes we can head to the lab." She carried her cell and the notepad with her into the hall.

Then again, maybe not.

****

Doyle had spent the better part of the morning in front of the TV. The feds hadn't caught him in New York, and they wouldn't here in Atlanta. Let them hunt. He'd left nothing at any of the executions. Why didn't the female newscaster drive home the real message? Dead men don't beat their wives.

He dressed and headed out for a run. He hated days off, they left him idle and at loose ends. The park was a couple of blocks away, and within minutes he'd set a steady pace around the jogging track in the park. Tension eased with each slap of his tennis shoes. Sweat beaded on his forehead and vaporized when the southern breeze hit him in the face.

Thirty minutes later and winded, he dropped to the ground to catch his breath. When he looked up, Nurse Ellen Rosen stood over him.

"Are you okay?" She knelt beside him and grasped his arms. Her cheeks were red from running against the wind.

"Yeah. I ran out of steam." She was the last person he'd expected to see.

"You must've been in the zone. I called your name again and again." She leaned over, placing her hands on her knees. "I couldn't run you down."

Her gaze scanned his body. Damn, she'd caught him running as opposed to the usual limp she saw at the hospital. Thank God, he'd stuck on the fake mustache before he left the apartment. "I'm sorry, Ms. Rosen. I didn't hear you."

"Obviously." She laughed and patted herself on the chest. "I'm out of breath. May I join you for a minute?"

"Sure." He moved over to give her a spot in the shade.

"It's Ellen. Ms. Rosen makes me feel old." She stretched her legs out in front of her and leaned forward to touch her toes.

"Okay. Ellen." She was quite attractive. Funny, he hadn't noticed before. "You're anything but old."

"I'll be fifty-five soon." Her cheeks flushed at his comment. "I'm glad your leg is better."

She'd supplied him with an easy explanation about his labored walk at work. "Yeah. Better each day." He'd wanted to shed the limp and the fake hair on his upper lip. Ellen had given him the perfect opportunity.

He'd given up his wife and way of life to become part of the Final Justice Unit. The handlers frowned on their members having personal relationships. Now, he was alone and without the organization's financial support. No one had answered his advertisement or come forward to offer guidance.

Instead of leaving, he kicked his legs out in front of him and joined her in a stretch.

Chapter Six

To call Leigh's behavior restrained during the update meeting and on the ride to the lab would've been the understatement of the century. J.T. didn't question her. He drove around to the back lot and parked, still respecting her silence.

When he turned the ignition off, she caught his hand in hers and rubbed her thumb across his slightly swollen knuckles. Flames licked up his arm.

"Did you apply a cold compress to this?" She tightened her grip when he tried to pull away.

"No. The pusher needed the ice."

"Pusher? You made a drug arrest last night?" She perked up with the question.

"No. I helped the locals stop a runner." J.T. seriously needed his hand back, and she needed to stop rubbing it. Warm and soft, her touch sent those flames from his arm straight to his dick. *Shit*. He didn't need to see the hint of vulnerability behind her blue eyes today. *Or ever*. He was a pushover for women with problems. Add the fact she had trouble brewing, you might as well tattoo the word "sucker" across his—

She pressed a finger on a particularly sore knuckle. "Ow."

"Where'd you go?"

"Sorry." His brain scrambled. "We better get inside." Thank God she released his hand.

The autopsy wasn't scheduled until tomorrow, but J.T. wanted to check on the condition of the bullet right away. They signed in, picked up their visitor's tags, and started back to the lab. Their interview with Faith Sanders last night still bothered him. "Why do you think Mrs. Sanders lied to us about the abuse?"

"She's ashamed. Doesn't want anyone to know her husband was capable of doing such despicable things."

"The guy's dead. He can't hurt her anymore." J.T. didn't get the reasoning. "Why not tell the truth?"

"The bastard beat the hell out of her. That shit's demoralizing enough without other people knowing." Leigh's eyes instantly fired laser blue flames. "Would you tell if you were her?"

"Hell, I might kill him." J.T. stepped back at her intense anger.

"Exactly." She spit the words at him. "When you trust someone and they hurt you, mentally or physically, the shame and embarrassment can be overwhelming. It's a huge obstacle to overcome. The bastard probably convinced her the beatings were all her fault. These women are made to feel they're lacking or unworthy. Mental torture can be as damaging as physical."

J.T. wasn't sure exactly who they were talking about anymore. Her tirade ended when she whirled and stormed into the women's restroom, leaving him with his jaw hanging and a bunch of freaking questions running through his mind. Like, where the hell had the anger come from?

He'd swear that somewhere, somehow, abuse had touched her. She'd added a whole new layer of mystery to her persona. He couldn't question her ability to separate her personal and professional feelings because, lately, he'd done a piss poor job of keeping his own shit straight.

Willem shook J.T.'s hand and then Leigh's. In his opinion, Willem held on to her longer than necessary.

"Good to see you again. The bullet's under the microscope. We're ready when you are."

Willem hit the button to open the swinging doors. A couple of white-coated techs raised their eyes from what they were working on, and one joined them at the front table.

"Pull up the bullet for us," Willem instructed the young man.

An image appeared on one of the computers. As expected, the damage made the damn thing unrecognizable except for the type of weapon used.

"What can you tell us?" J.T. asked.

"We can't identify the weapon," Willem answered.

"If I find the rifle?" J.T.'s experience warned him against getting his hopes up.

"Wouldn't hold up in court."

J.T. ran his hand through his hair. "I knew that, but was hoping you'd prove me wrong. Go ahead and send all four bullets to Virginia."

"I expected as much." Willem passed a clipboard over with the work order filled out for J.T. to sign.

"Thanks for your help." J.T. pushed open the door and headed to the parking lot.

As Leigh entered the passenger side of his car she said, "I have an appointment this afternoon. Will you drop me at my car?"

****

Leigh picked up one of Ethan's shirts, straightened out the wrinkles, and added it to the stack her mother had started. She stopped folding clothes and leaned back, her gaze on the pile of clean laundry. She'd shared her conversation with Jason's attorney with her mother and father. They'd already been through so much with her and dumping more crap on them seemed unfair.

"I hired a lawyer today. Someone to fight for me."

"Why didn't you let one of us go with you?" Her father kept his voice low.

"You guys already do too much for me." She patted the laundry. "Like this."

"Nothing we're not happy to do." He dismissed her statement with a shake of his head. "Your attorney . . . what's her name?"

"Karen Parker."

"This Ms. Parker, she specializes in children's rights?" He glanced toward the den where Ethan lay sprawled on the rug. His favorite cartoon had captured his attention.

"Children and parental rights. I'm confident the Carrington name and fortune won't intimidate her." Leigh's parents were deeply involved in hers and Ethan's lives. She held nothing back. "Legally, Jason has no claim on Ethan. Tomorrow, Ms. Parker will speak to Morgan Anderson and reiterate my position." Leigh rubbed her temple where a headache rode right under the surface. "I don't get it. What does Jason really want?"

"The SOB better not come on my property, not after all he's done." Pink flushed high on her dad's cheeks, and his hands flexed into fists.

Leigh blinked back the emotion swelling behind her eyes. Her father's anger reminded her of the last time she'd heard this much rage in his voice. He'd stood over her in the hospital, murmured soothing words while tears had cascaded down his face. That her stupidity had caused so much pain and anguish ripped her heart open.

"I should've killed him," he whispered to no one.

Leigh went to him, clasping his hands in hers. "Dad, don't even think such thoughts. We'll get through this." She laid her head on his chest. The strength she drew from him had kept her going more than once. "We'll all keep an eye out for Jason. If he tries to come near . . . well . . . I'm sort of hoping he'll violate his probation. Then I'll send him back to prison."

"Exactly what can he do?"

Leigh's mother had remained quiet until now. The heart and soul of the family, she tended to sit back and analyze while Leigh and her dad were quick to act.

"I honestly don't know. I told him to go to hell."

"Can they force you to agree to a paternity test?" her mother asked.

"Not according to Karen Parker. If they find a judge who'll order one, we'll fight it. If Anderson contacts me again, I'm to refer him to her."

"We don't scare easily." Her dad sounded much calmer than before.

"Anderson threatened scandal. I said bring it on."

Her mother reached across to the laundry basket, picked up one of Ethan's shirts, and held it to her chest.

"You're warning us that Jason isn't going to back off, right?" Her mother frowned deeply.

"I'm sorry, Mom. That family is friends with Atlanta's most important people. One could be a judge who'll allow a lawsuit. It's a possibility we have to face." Leigh's spirits sunk even lower. "And who knows what else he'll try."

****

Jason parked his Lexus GX on the side street of Woodland Park. Anywhere else, he'd turn off the engine and roll down the windows while he waited. Not here. He left the motor and the air-conditioner running. Neither he nor his car belonged in this disgusting part of town. He'd spent a long time living with drug dealers, thieves, and cold-blooded killers. You couldn't trust them. Vermin. Every one of them made him sick to his stomach.

The Carrington money and Jason's penchant for using his fists had kept him from bending over for every swinging dick in prison. They'd mistakenly thought because of his looks he'd be an easy fuck, but he'd fought his way out from under his share of sweaty, stinking bastards. When he'd met Vick Coventry, life had changed for the better. The desperate-for-cash con had taken Jason under his wing and become Jason's protector-enforcer.

Paroled at about the same time, Vick remained on Jason's payroll, supplying information on Leigh and her bastard kid. Jason knew everything about her and her parents. She had no secrets from him.

He'd started planning how he'd kill her the day the handcuffs had snapped around his wrists. The bitch thought she could walk away from him, tell him not to call or come around anymore? Nobody fuckin' told him what to do. Especially not a woman.

"Shit." Startled by the passenger door opening, Jason reached for his gun. "You trying to get shot?" His hand relaxed when Vick settled in the seat.

"I taught you not to get caught off guard." Vick leaned his head back and breathed in deeply through his nose. "New car smell. Better than a clean woman."

"Turns you on, does it?" Jason hated that eventually, he'd kill the closest thing to a friend he'd ever had.

"What's up with the SUV? You'd pick up more pussy in a sports car." Vick grinned. "Unless you're into soccer moms."

"I'm buying a booster seat next and having it installed. This car shouts 'I'll be a good father' to anyone interested." Jason marveled at having to explain the simplest things to Vick. He was streetwise, and, at forty-five years old, he could snap your neck with ease. Nobody on the yard out bench-pressed him, but he was dumber than the weights he lifted.

Vick smiled at Jason like a proud papa. "I get it. Good thinking."

"You find out why she's riding with the feds?" Jason's patience waned. Small talk with Vick was a waste of time.

"Yeah. She's on loan. They're hunting that sniper. Been on all the news stations."

"Good. Between the government and us, we'll keep her off balance. You buy a bike?"

"Yeah. I drove to Alpharetta and paid cash at a Walmart. It's ready to be left on grandma and grandpa's doorstep."

"And my stand-in?" Jason removed an envelope of cash and a small sack from the console. He handed both to Vick, worried he didn't understand the plan. "Are you sure you can pull off both projects on the same day?"

"I got you covered. The bike will be delivered early, and your look-alike's lined up for late that night."

Jason sighed at Vick's sheer stupidity. "I don't give a fuck whether he looks like me or not. Just be sure he's close to my height and weight. And you put this cologne on him before he visits Leigh."

"It's all set. He'll leave her shaking in her shit."

Vick's sinister laugh worried Jason. He wanted Leigh terrorized and beat up. No more. Vick had to follow the plan. Jason pulled his pistol from beside his leg and laid it across the console.

"He's not to fuck her or hurt the kid." Jason's voice rose and reverberated through the inside of the SUV. "You understand?"

"He doesn't want her. She ain't his type." Vick's dark eyes glazed over. "When you take her out, I wish you'd give me the boy." He sighed and pushed his hand through his shaggy, brown hair.

"I'm giving you money. Leigh and the boy are mine."

"I know. I was just wishing out loud."

"You remember what to do with this guy after he visits Leigh."

"Yeah." Vick's yellowed teeth shone in the semidarkness. "Him, I can have. Right?"

"Him, you can do anything you want with. As long as you kill him when we're done. Now, get out. I've got places to go."

Without a word, Vick exited the car. Jason didn't want to know what the sick bastard had planned for the poor schmuck. He'd learned in lockup not to question or denigrate another man's perversions.

****

Leigh's nose detected something sweet when Olivia hurried through the door.

"Will this make up for my tardiness?" She placed a donut box in the middle of the table with a guilty smile.

Leigh took the first one. "Works for me."

"Food absolves all sins." Romeo grabbed a donut. "Right?"

He pushed the box to Casey, who snagged a bear claw. "Romeo's got a point. I forgive your tardiness this once."

"What'd I miss?" Olivia slid into a chair directly across from him.

Casey swallowed a sip of coffee and tapped the file in front of him. "I pulled information on the Final Justice Organization, a case I worked in New York last year."

"I remember. You threw a wide net. Caught a few big fish," J.T. said. He studied the contents of the box before taking a glazed donut for himself.

Casey nodded and continued, "When NYPD SWAT raided the underground headquarters a large portion of the records had been destroyed. What they managed to retrieve resulted in several high-ranking officials across the country being arrested. However, we have no idea how many people walked away. The group had factions in lots of major cities. Assassins, each one with a talent for killing and an axe to grind with the judicial system, had been recruited and trained."

The room had gone still. Leigh's gaze drifted to J.T.'s expressionless face. The hard-line of his jaw and scowl over his dark green eyes made her wonder what thoughts ran through his mind.

"What about the rogue cop?" J.T.'s face was still as a granite statue, the intensity of his gaze said he'd immersed himself in Casey's words.

"As I said, he went to the other side after the killer who beat his daughter to death went unpunished." Casey pushed the thick file in J.T.'s direction. "Doyle Preston faked his death. He's alive. I've cleared the transfer of additional evidence from New York that shows this."

"It's a place to start." J.T. turned to Romeo first. "Contact your counterpart in the New York office. There are probably numerous boxes of evidence. Make sure we get everything. Olivia, dig into the Preston family. Look at their finances. See what they have, where it comes from, and where it goes. Leigh and I will look into Preston."

J.T. spoke with conviction and in full-blown sentences. To her delight and relief, he'd included her. She was working on the case of a lifetime, a chance to make a real difference. She followed J.T. out to their work area, unable to wipe the smile from her face.

"You all right?" J.T. asked. "You win the lottery?"

"I feel like Alice in Wonderland. I keep waiting for someone to wake me up." She laughed at the confused look on his face. "Let me explain it better. Being here, with this team, it's a dream come true."

"Good thing you explained, because I don't know anybody named Alice." He gave her a half-smile. Her heart fluttered. Geesh, he was beautiful. He leaned over her as she backed up and sat.

"However, I know a lot about the big bad wolf."

Holy shit. He was flirting. Did he use that soft and sexy voice on all women? She'd bet when he turned on the charm, the ladies lined up to be serviced. Well, she wasn't a car in need of a lube.

"Pass me the folder on Preston. Please." She intentionally spoke in the same tone she used when Ethan behaved badly and achieved the desired results. J.T.'s face had the same deflated expression as her son's after getting himself in trouble. "We should start with his wife."

J.T. rolled his chair around beside hers and laid the open file on her desk. He mumbled a string of words to himself. Something about the knot at the back of her head being too tight. Leigh wasn't about to ask him to repeat himself. She had her hands full controlling her heart rate when he casually dropped an arm across the back of her chair.

The phrase "big bad wolf" swirled through her mind. She swallowed, ignored his woodsy scent and body heat, and drilled down into Mrs. Preston's life.

Chapter Seven

Leigh walked ahead with Olivia on the trip back to work. Romeo and J.T. tagged along behind. Two weeks into the temporary assignment, and if they weren't in the field looking for a break in the case, lunch at Antonio's Sandwich Shop was routine because the bistro was next to their parking garage.

A light breeze ruffled the loose hair around Leigh's face. Sunshine warmed her. She hadn't received one anonymous call today. Her attorney had contacted Morgan Anderson and delivered the message that Leigh would face Jason in court if necessary. The line she'd drawn in the sand must've worked.

"You seeing anyone?" Olivia asked when they stopped at the corner.

"No." The question had caught Leigh by surprise. She shifted the conversation to Olivia. "Are you?"

"Not lately. I suck at relationships." Olivia sounded a little defeated and a whole lot jaded.

"I understand."

Romeo stepped between them, draping an arm over each of their shoulders. "I'd rather walk with you two. What's the topic? Sex? Men? Me? I have no secrets. Ask me anything."

"Anything?" Leigh glanced over her shoulder. J.T. walked behind, apparently ignoring all three of them.

"Go for it." Romeo flashed his brilliant smile at a young woman as she approached. She rewarded him by rolling her eyes.

"Is your hair dyed?" Leigh spoke in a low conspiratorial voice.

Romeo's feet stopped moving. "What?" His eyes flashed wide, and his hands went to his luxurious head of hair.

"J.T.'s hair is black, and I wondered if—" She fought to hold back a smile. "Maybe you wanted yours the same color."

The laughter from behind answered her real question. J.T. projected a stoic, disinterested persona, but he heard and saw everything around him.

Leigh assured Romeo she was joking. She suffered a small blip in her heartbeat when her phone vibrated, and she saw the caller ID. Her mother seldom called during working hours.

"Mom?"

"There's been an accident."

"Ethan's hurt?" A razor sliced into her heart, peeling it open. Her stomach roiled against the sandwich she'd eaten minutes ago.

"He's fine. No one's seriously injured." Her mother's voice shook.

"Where are you?" Leigh felt a hand on her back. J.T. had moved into the spot next to her.

"At home. Can you come—"

"I'm on my way. What happened?"

"That bicycle . . . never mind. I'll tell you when you get here."

"Bicycle?" Leigh said to the dead cell phone.

Romeo and Olivia walked shoulder to shoulder in silence, directly in front of Leigh. They turned and led the way as if they were escorting a dignitary. Their unspoken support helped Leigh hold herself together.

J.T.'s strong hands guided her into the parking garage, and Olivia opened the passenger side of a black Corvette.

"What's this?" Leigh stiffened and took a step backward.

"You're not driving." J.T.'s tone left no room for argument as he headed around to the other side.

"Go." Olivia nudged her into the car as the engine surged to life. "Don't worry about Casey or the job. We'll explain."

"Talk to me," J.T. commanded. "Where to?"

A new wave of panic surged. She was about to break a long-standing rule just because she was rattled and shouldn't be behind the wheel. Romeo and Olivia had overheard Leigh's phone conversation. J.T. would be privy to a part of her life she shared with few people. No one she worked with had met her son.

"Leigh. Let me help." His voice, soft and warm, reassured her. "Where to?"

"Peachtree City."

"No problem," he said. The sports car's roar echoed through the building. Its tires screeched around corners. The Corvette burst onto Century Parkway like a hungry panther on the heels of its prey.

Leigh's blood raced through her body, breaking all speed records. An accident? Where no one was injured? She pulled her cell from her pocket and stared at the blank screen. The fact her mom was busy with the emergency stopped Leigh from calling, so the cold piece of technology lay useless in her hand. Her fingers drummed over the numbers. Leigh patted down the loose hair curling around her face. A strong hand gripped her knee.

"Leigh."

"Ethan doesn't own a bike," she said, struggling to hold her panic under the surface. "I'm sure that's what my mother said."

"Leigh." J.T. shook her knee. "I'm leaving the highway and entering the city. I need directions."

"Sorry. Stay on the main drag for the next five miles, take a right on Turner." She'd lost herself during the thirty-mile drive. Other than her parents and Ethan's sitter, Leigh didn't rely on anyone for anything. Now she'd put herself in J.T.'s hands. She pressed her thumbs to her temples as thunder rolled through her head.

"I appreciate you driving. My mind hasn't been on the road," Leigh admitted.

"No problem."

"And my imagination is running wild."

"You're holding it together." He glanced at her with something resembling pride in his eyes. His hand remained on her knee, strong and comforting.

"My mother made no sense at all."

"Ethan's your son?"

The swish of blood rushing flooded her ears. J.T. was about to meet the entire McBride family.

"Yes." Leigh shuddered, a chill racing across her skin. "My parents keep Ethan while I'm at work."

Leigh directed J.T. through the older, established neighborhood. She was grateful he hadn't asked any more questions. No doubt, he'd have plenty after today.

"Turn right at the stop sign. It's the last house on the left." Leigh opened the door to the car before he turned off the ignition. She hit the ground running. She didn't pause at the entry. "Mom?"

"In our bedroom," her mother called out in return.

Leigh ran down the hall and didn't stop until she reached the side of the bed. Her father had raw abrasions on his arms, his knees, and an angry gouge in his forehead. She looked around franticly. Ethan was nowhere to be seen.

"He's fine." Her dad gave her a reassuring smile. "He's playing his Indy 500 game on the den television."

"He didn't hear you come in, not with those headphones on." Ever the calm one, her mom had cut the legs of her husband's jeans open. A bottle of peroxide, cotton balls, and bandages sat on the nightstand.

"He's not hurt?" For the first time since her mother's phone call, Leigh breathed without the sharp pain in her chest.

"Not a scratch." Her dad smiled up at her.

"You don't look so good." Tears held inside trickled unchecked down her cheeks.

"I'm fine." He moved over, making room for her to sit.

"What happened?"

"Ethan landed on the grass carpet our neighbor two houses down calls his front yard. Cushioned his fall. I, unfortunately, skidded a few feet on the pavement."

"Poor Dad." Leigh gripped his hand, breathing a sigh of relief. "I still don't understand."

"Ethan was doing great. I was running along beside him holding on to the back of the seat when old lady Ferguson backed out of her driveway without looking. We're damn lucky she ran over the bike instead of us. Ow." He yanked the wad of cotton away from his wife, pushed himself up on the bed, and doctored his scrape. "If June Ferguson had looked behind her, I wouldn't have had to try and pull Ethan to a stop. And we wouldn't have fallen."

"Mrs. Ferguson was scared to death. She rushed inside and called for an ambulance."

"I told her I wasn't hurt badly."

Her mom patted him on the back. "But we couldn't be sure about that until the EMT took a look at you."

Leigh rose from the bed. Anger that followed her relief arrived, and the storm in her head worsened. "Why didn't you talk to me before you bought him a bike?"

"I didn't buy the damn thing. We assumed you had and forgot to tell us."

"I didn't. It must've been delivered to the wrong house." Leigh gently pushed her dad back down on the pillows and inspected the bloody spot on his forehead. Her mother handed her a cotton ball soaked with peroxide, and Leigh dabbed at the dried blood.

"No permanent damage was done to anything except the bike."

Leigh shook her head when he tried to rise.

"You rest. I'll check on Ethan—" Leigh groaned.

"What is it?" her mother asked.

"My ride. I left him outside in his car." Leigh and her mother walked down the hall to the front door. J.T. wasn't in his Corvette. Her lungs constricted, and she turned back to her mother. "He's here somewhere."

"He? You brought a man home with you?" A smile spread across her face.

"One of the agents drove me." Leigh walked to the back of the house to the den. She stopped in her tracks in the doorway. Her mother, trailing too closely behind, bumped into her back.

"Oh. My. God," Leigh muttered.

"What is it?" Her mother pushed her way around in front.

Sitting on the floor, propped against the couch, J.T. and Ethan sat side by side. Each held a toy steering wheel. A racetrack filled the big screen TV. Both man and boy appeared to be oblivious to their surroundings. Suddenly, the number eleven car hit the wall and burst into flames. J.T. collapsed back on the couch. Ethan threw his hands in the air, celebrating victory. His laughter filled the room.

"You got that right," her mother whispered.

"Got what right?" Leigh's heart did something weird, a cartwheel or maybe skipped a beat at the scene in front of her. Nothing brightened her day like her son's laughter.

"Oh. My. God." Her mom repeated, fanning herself with her hand.

J.T. turned his head in her direction. The smile he'd shared with Ethan faded. J.T. removed the headphones and unfolded his muscular body from the floor. The starched white shirt was realigned, his hair pushed back into place, and he crossed the room to meet her mother.

"J.T. Noble, Mrs. McBride. Ethan says your husband's okay. I'm glad." He barely released her hand in time to maintain his balance when Ethan landed against his leg.

"It's Sara. Thank you for driving my daughter here."

"Not a problem."

Leigh ruffled Ethan's hair, grateful her mother hadn't blinked at J.T.'s scar. God knows what Ethan had said. "You've been entertaining Mr. Noble?"

"And I won," Ethan exclaimed, looking up at his new friend. "Wanna go again?"

"Not a good idea. Right?" J.T.'s hunter green gaze turned toward

Leigh.

"Can we, Mom? Puleeze."

"Don't I at least get a kiss?" Leigh's mind spun at J.T. and Ethan's instant bonding.

"Sure." Ethan tiptoed and puckered for a quick buzz. Then he was back with both arms wrapped around J.T.'s leg.

J.T. squatted down at eye level with Ethan. "You beat me fair and square. My pride can't take another hit today. Maybe another time." He stood and turned to Leigh. "I'd suggest you call it a day, but your car is in Atlanta."

"I'd better stay. Make sure Dad's not hiding a knot on his head." Her attempt at humor fell flat as neither her mother nor J.T. laughed. "Mom can drive me later. Thanks again for bringing me."

J.T. nodded once and shifted from one foot to the other. He showed clear signs of being uncomfortable. "See you tomorrow. Nice to have met you, ma'am."

He shook her mom's hand, didn't comment on the idol worship expression on her face, and then knelt back down with Ethan.

"Come on, little man. No pouting. Okay?"

"Okay," Ethan pushed out the words over pursed lips.

Leigh walked J.T. to the front door. Time to move him along before her dad hobbled out into the hall and invited him to stay for dinner.

"I'm glad everybody's okay."

"Thanks for everything."

"No problem." He thumbed under her eyes, drying leftover tears. "Ethan's a good kid." He turned and walked to his car.

Standing on the porch with the trees and honeysuckle scenting the spring afternoon, Leigh breathed deeply. The crisis was over. All the possibilities, the things that could've happened slammed into her. She trembled. Her legs liquefied. She eased herself down on the porch swing while J.T. drove away. She touched her cheek, remembering the tenderness of his large hands.

Questions were sure to come after Olivia and Romeo asked him about this afternoon. Leigh had nothing to be ashamed of, but more often than not, people treated her differently after they heard her story. Telling them she was a single mother would have to suffice. She didn't want pity or scorn from J.T. or his coworkers. Hell, exactly what did she want from him?

Her heart shriveled in her chest. What kind of failure was she? If she didn't have the nerve to face people, how would she answer Ethan's questions? Someday her evasive answers wouldn't satisfy him. What words should she use? Her heart ached, would he hate her when he learned he was a child of rape? She'd never once considered abortion. She'd loved her son from the moment she'd learned she was pregnant. After all, none of what happened had been his fault.

Her mother stepped out on the porch. Her expression more relaxed now that the crisis had passed. "I'm sorry I gave you a scare. Your father's injuries weren't as bad as I first thought, but when I heard the tires screech and your dad shout Ethan's name, I ran out and it looked really bad. I panicked."

"You did the right thing." Leigh scooted over on the swing to make room.

"What happened to J.T.'s face?"

"I don't ask personal questions, and he hasn't volunteered the information. I'm guessing he was injured while in the Marines." Her stomach tightened. "I hope Ethan didn't say anything rude. I'll talk to him tonight."

"I'm sure if he did, J.T. understood." Her mother sighed. "Scar or not, he's gorgeous."

Leigh chuckled. "Does Dad know you lust after younger men?"

"As if he doesn't light up when Angelina Jolie comes on the screen."

"Information I don't need to know." Leigh rocked for a second, enjoying her mother's company. "Where's Ethan?"

"Admiring your dad's bandages."

"Where is this mysterious bike?"

"In the garage."

"It just showed up?" She steadied the swing, chills crawling across her skin.

"We picked Ethan up at noon. Today was early out. Remember? The darn thing was parked in the driveway when we got home."

"I want to take a look before you take us to my car."

Her mom stood, tugging Leigh off the swing. "Why don't you two stay the night? You both have clean clothes here. Call DeeDee. Tell her we're taking Ethan to school tomorrow. I'll drop you at work."

"Hmm." Leigh nodded. DeeDee would probably appreciate a day off. She'd watched Nathan from the first day Leigh had returned to work and was like family.

She had no doubt who was responsible for the bike. Had Jason's intended to hurt Ethan? Or was it another way to terrorize her? Either way, he knew way too much about her and her family. Her lungs constricted. Getting a breath became difficult.

****

J.T. ignored the entrance ramp to the freeway and drove straight across the overpass into Newnan. Separated by Interstate 85, Peachtree City and Newnan had grown to the point the natives weren't sure where one started and the other ended. No way he'd get this close to his grandmother's house without stopping. Luckily, Nana never expected him to call ahead. The trip west wove through the older part of town. A few antebellum homes remained single-family residences. Most had been converted into bed and breakfasts. She used to pick him up after school and drive through this area on the way home. She'd tell Newnan's history of how the area had been largely untouched by the Civil War due to Newnan's status as a hospital city. Back then, he'd gripe about hearing the same stories over and over. Now, he missed that connection with his grandmother.

Leigh having a son had knocked J.T. on his ass. Bitter memories from his childhood had him comparing himself with the boy. She'd gone to the bar with Romeo and Olivia. Probably left the kid with the grandmother. How often did that happen?

Pushing his thoughts about Leigh from his mind, J.T. drove around to the back of the house. He'd expected to find his grandmother outside in her garden or at least in her chair close by. Elva stepped out onto the porch and waited for him to park. Icy fingers clutched his spine when the housekeeper's normally jovial face remained solemn. He crossed the yard in long strides.

"Nana?" J.T. held his breath and braced for the bad news.

"She's resting. The hardheaded old woman was determined to finish weeding before she quit for the day." Elva's hand fidgeted with her apron, smoothing out nonexistent wrinkles. "She overheated as bad as my granddaddy's old Ford used to do. I made her lay down for a while."

The tension between his shoulder blades eased. "If she's asleep—" He backed toward his car.

"Come in. You leave without seeing her, and she'll blame me."

J.T. kept his footsteps light while he passed through the kitchen and down the hall to his grandmother's bedroom.

"Sneaking around wasn't your long suit when you were a teenager. Your skills haven't improved."

The teasing in Nana's voice melted his frozen spine. He leaned against the doorframe. "The Marines thought my stealth to be quite good."

She looked small and frail in the antique bed with the old-fashioned quilt across her legs. Her skin had a sallow tinge today, accentuated by silver hair smoothed back from her face. Her green eyes sparkled with mischief, allowing the knot in his stomach to unwind.

"Your targets didn't have my superior hearing." She chuckled at her joke, pushed herself upright, and patting the bed next to her. "Elva called you, didn't she?"

"Hello, gorgeous." J.T. leaned down for a kiss. "No, ma'am, she

62 |

didn't."

"Then why are you here?" Doubt clouded her eyes.

"A woman from work had a family crisis. I dropped her off at her parent's house in Peachtree City. You know if I'm this close to home, I'm gonna come check on you." He lowered himself to the edge of the bed. "Enough about me. Promise me you'll listen to Elva. No more getting too tired or too hot."

"Is she pretty?"

"Elva? I guess. She pales in comparison to you." Nana swatted him on the arm. Another clear sign she felt better.

"Not her. The lady you left work for. Nothing pulls you away from a case."

"Yes, she's pretty. Don't get your hopes up. We work together, that's all."

"You're thirty-three. It's time you gave me a great-grandchild."

"You got married late in life. Don't rush me," he protested with a smile. Marriage wasn't happening and being a parent wasn't going to happen either. Discussing it with her would only get him a lecture.

"I regret not meeting your grandfather long before I did. Maybe if I had . . ." Her words trailed off as her gaze drifted across the room.

J.T. stood, crossed to the row of pictures displayed on her bookcase, and studied the black and white snapshots of Nana and his grandfather. He'd drunk himself to death before J.T. was old enough to remember him. The smiling faces and fake happiness were for the camera. The family shared a dark secret, a disease the old man had passed on to his daughter.

And J.T. carried their genes. He'd stopped drinking after a weekend binge while on a weekend pass in Afghanistan. Hell, he'd opened his eyes Monday morning with no memory of Saturday or Sunday. Scared the fuck out of him. He'd had experience with the destruction alcohol could cause, so he'd sworn off drinking. Not that he didn't want a drink, the temptation was always there; just wasn't an option.

"You had a hard life bringing up a child alone. The woman I drove to Peachtree City is doing the same thing. Luckily, her mother and father help with the kid."

"Speaking of mothers. You have any luck locating yours?"

"None." He moved to the back window and pulled the curtains open. Nana's garden was thriving. He could almost smell the gardenias. "You remember Davey Campbell? He's a cop now. I ran into him. He's gonna keep an eye out for her."

"I remember him. Keeping him fed was a chore."

J.T. leaned over and kissed his grandmother on the forehead. "Like I told you, if a person doesn't want to be found—"

"You'll find her sooner with Davey's help. Now go be a hero. And ask your lady friend to dinner Saturday night."

"We don't have that kind of relationship. Besides, I'm spending my weekend crawling through local beer joints."

Alone. Sober.

Chapter Eight

Jason didn't like this part of town. He didn't like the odor of grease lingering in the air around the booth in which he sat. Most of all, he didn't like it when someone failed him. Jason stabbed his spoon in the cup, stirring the swirling black liquid.

"Your instructions were clear. The delivery of the bicycle and the break-in were both to happen yesterday."

"It's not my fault the bitch never showed. I had your stand-in there, primed and ready." Vick didn't flinch or back down. His tattooed knuckles fisted then straightened.

"She probably spent the night with the fed." Jason didn't care whether she was fucking the federal agent or not, it was just a complication.

"You want to reschedule?" Vick picked at a piece of food lodged between his teeth with a dirty fingernail.

"After I set up a new alibi. I spent all day in meetings and then a miserable evening with my parents. I sat through a fundraiser for the fuckin' library. Like I give a shit if they need money to buy new books." He pulled out his phone and scrolled through his schedule.

"Is that a no?" Vick laid his open hand on the table, palm up.

Did the prick think he'd get paid? "Tomorrow I'm attending a play at the Civic Center with my parents. Make it happen between nine at night and one in the morning. No later. My mother's always at home and in bed by then."

"You got it."

"Look into having Leigh's house bugged. And make sure your man wears the cologne I gave you. Call me with an update and be sure you use the burner."

****

J.T. leaned back in his desk chair and listened to Leigh's voice as she read the case file on Angie Preston.

"After the beating death of her seventeen-year-old daughter, Angie had slipped into a severe depression. A year later, her husband supposedly died in a fiery car explosion. Shortly after the body was autopsied and the corpse turned out not to be his, Mrs. Preston shot herself in the right temple. According to a friend's statement, it was all too much for her to handle." Leigh closed the file with a snap.

"Do you always read out loud?"

Pink flags of color hit her cheeks, spread upward, disappearing into her hairline. Her hands went to her head, and she patted at the curly wisps of hair around her face. "I'll let you read the rest for yourself."

Her gaze lowered to the page in her hand. She either couldn't take a joke or was having a bad day.

He decided against asking Leigh about her father. Being in the house with a full complement of family, including a kid, well, had been more than unnerving. Ethan was the first child J.T. had ever been around—unless he counted the line at the grocery store. The kid had befriended him instantly and without question, which meant he was too trusting and too friendly. The child's open-mindedness freaked him out. And, Jesus, he never shut up.

Why had Leigh kept the fact she had a son a secret? And where was the boy's father? He almost knocked his chair over when a hand clamped down on his shoulder

"Hello?" Olivia stood, bent over him, her mouth next to his ear. "Anybody home?"

"Sorry. I was deep in thought." J.T. stood and pulled a chair from an unused desk over so she could sit next to him.

Olivia whispered, "I saw what 'thought' you were 'deep' into. Do you like Leigh? Go for it. Nobody here cares."

"Moving on. What've you learned?"

"Leigh." Olivia motioned Leigh to come closer. "Want to hear my news?"

Leigh stood and joined the conversation. "I do if you've learned Preston's wife covertly sent him money, and you found a paper trail."

"I wish. However, she did leave a sizable trust fund. The money is for her husband, should he ever come forward."

"I'm not surprised," Leigh said. "Her suicide note stated she didn't know Preston had faked his death. If I had to guess why he wanted her to believe he was dead, I'd say to protect her."

"Love from the grave." J.T. took a dim view of taking the coward's way out. "I don't get why she killed herself?"

"Who knows?" Leigh said. "Sounds like she died still in love with her husband."

Was that melancholy in her voice? If so, it was quite different from her work persona. J.T. got more curious about her by the day. She pulled him to her like a magnet. If he didn't shake the attraction building in his gut, they'd never get this case solved.

"Maybe, we can use the trust to our advantage." J.T. remembered the newswoman from the last crime scene. The pretty piranha, the firefighter had nicknamed her. "We get the media to run a special interest piece on why Angie Preston left money to a dead man."

"But he's not dead." Olivia raised an eyebrow in question.

"The article can't come out and say we know he's alive. We tweak the story. Don't tie it to our sniper. Her leaving a trust fund to a dead man makes the situation bizarre enough. We need to find somebody who'll run it," J.T. responded. "Handled right, Doyle Preston won't know the information came from us. If he needs money, maybe he'll try to get his hands on it."

"Certainly couldn't hurt." Olivia stood. "Okay then, back to work for me."

"Thanks. Keep digging. I'll call Clarisse Chancellor." J.T. pulled up the local FOX station on his computer and found the work number for the newswoman he'd avoided at the crime scene.

"Is Ms. Chancellor a friend of yours?" Leigh's tone had a frosty tinge to it.

"Jealous?" His blood spiked hot. The sound of her accent laced with envy had a profound effect on him.

"Not hardly. You two would make a cute couple."

"I do prefer blondes." He leaned toward her, inhaled deeply to pull her scent closer. Even in that God-awful tight knot, her hair smelled of citrus. Lemon or grapefruit? Man, he loved grapefruit.

"Do tell."

"They're easier to find in the dark."

"You do think a lot of yourself. Don't you?"

"I care more about what you think of me." Damn. He considered biting the tip of his tongue off when her pupils widened. Why did he care? "Surely, you know someone at the newspaper."

"I don't 'know' any reporter who could compete with Ms. Chancellor."

Her instant temper flare puzzled him. Which statement pissed her off, the reporter or his way-out-of-line comment about what she thought of him? She probably didn't think of him at all. Ever. Period. He'd hit her hot button when he mentioned the reporter and had no idea why.

"There's that temper again, hotshot. I have zero contacts here in Atlanta. You must've made at least one friend in the newspaper office."

She shifted her gaze away from him. "I might know someone who'll help."

"Good. As long as we can trust him." Relieved, he closed down the picture of the FOX reporter.

She pulled out her cell. "I'll try to catch him before he goes to lunch."

****

Leigh sat on a bench in Piedmont Park and finished entering her notes while J.T. walked Alan Forge to his car. Her skin chilled. Alan had been the lead reporter for the *Atlanta Journal Constitution* during Jason's trial. Should she worry he'd divulge her personal information? No. She shook off the goosebumps on her arms. He hadn't known about the pregnancy.

J.T.'s gaze lifted briefly and locked on hers. When had he stopped scowling? Had it been her imagination? He sure wasn't frowning now. Her lower stomach heated, muscles contracted, and warmth spread south. *Stop.* He'd made his feelings about marriage and children loud and clear. She wasn't shopping for a husband anyway.

Her mother had been right. The scar didn't diminish his looks. Leigh doubted any movie star could fill out a starched, white shirt and black slacks as well as he did. The day had grown warm, and, without a breeze, the park turned steamy. While J.T. had talked, he'd rolled his sleeves up far enough to reveal muscular forearms. She'd feel safe and protected if he wrapped them around her. Did a bed of black hair nestle in the middle of his broad chest? She'd have to remove the shirt and T-shirt to find out. Ah, she sighed, maybe in another life. She returned her laptop to its case after Alan drove off and J.T. returned.

"Nice guy," he commented. "Meeting here was a good idea."

He surprised her by extending his hand to assist her in standing. As he folded his fingers around hers, heat shot up her arm. Fearful J.T. was experiencing the same sensation, she pulled away, hooking the laptop case strap over her shoulder.

"And he keeps his word."

She hadn't thanked J.T. for not discussing the trip to Peachtree City with anyone at work. Before she got in the car, she stopped and took the opportunity. "You didn't discuss my family or the bicycle incident with Olivia or Romeo, and I appreciate your discretion."

"How do you know I didn't?" One corner of his mouth rose into that lopsided grin.

"They asked me who Ethan was. So, you must not have told them."

"Not my place to tell. Besides, then you might've told them your kid beat me on a video game." J.T. slid in behind the wheel and waited for her to buckle up.

"Your secret's safe with me." She kept seeing flashes of the nice guy he worked hard to keep hidden. Funny, she liked both sides.

"How's your dad?"

"He's fine. The bike died."

"I got damn good at fixing my broken toys. Want me to take a look?" He started the car, letting it idle.

"Thanks, it looked past resuscitation to me. We don't know who it belonged to." The blood drained from her head. The urge to say yes had almost overwhelmed her. Taking him up on the offer meant inviting him to her house. Other than her dad and the babysitter's husband, she'd never allowed a man inside her home. Maybe she was paranoid but trusting came hard for her.

"Your folks didn't buy the bike?"

"No. Somebody had it delivered already assembled. Dad assumed it came from me."

"Bicycles don't normally show up assembled, ready to ride, without shipping documents and no signature required." J.T. shut off the engine and turned to look at her. His scowl had returned.

"I know. And I know who sent the damn thing. Just can't prove it. Nobody on the block saw anything, and that bike's sold by every major retailer in the area." She rolled her hands into tight balls. "I should box the pieces up and send them back to him."

"Him?" J.T. rested his hand on her knee. The same warm comfort she'd felt before settled in her heart. "Ethan's father?"

Seconds ticked by. Leigh's shoulders ached from carrying the weight alone. Dare she open up and share the secret she'd guarded for almost seven years? What if she told him the whole story? Would he condemn her for bringing a rapist's child into the world? Would he understand how hard she'd leaned on her rape crisis group to help her out of the dark hole she'd been in after the attack? Would he agree with her final decision that nurture overrode nature when it came to children? Too risky.

"Listen. You've been a basket-case since the attorney's visit. I may not be able to help, but I can be a friend."

She searched his face. The compassion in his green eyes wrapped around her. She nodded. That slight movement wouldn't mean anything to him. To her, the nod, the admission, was huge.

"You can trust me."

His words slid across her, soft and soothing. Shards of loneliness filled her lungs. She pressed her fist between her breasts and leaned into the pain. J.T. released her seat belt, let it slide off, and then covered her hand with his. His touch, tender and gentle, brought tears to the surface. She blinked them back. For a fleeting second, she considered resting her head on his broad chest and listening to his strong, steady heartbeat. She wouldn't. He'd offered friendship, and Leigh wouldn't ask for more.

"Jason Carrington's not listed as the father on Ethan's birth certificate. That attorney was hired to pressure me into agreeing to a paternity test. I refused. My instinct says he had the bike delivered to prove a point. He wants me to know I can't hide Ethan from him."

"The bastard waits until the kid's half-grown and then wants to be part of his life? I'd tell him to kiss my ass."

His reaction helped her maintain her composure. J.T. moved back to his side of the car and sat quietly. She instantly missed having him near. Missed having him close enough to breathe in his scent. Missed having his strong hand on her body.

"Ethan's six. Not quite half-grown." She breathed deeply to push all the words out as a joke. "Jason Carrington's been in prison. He was released on parole a couple of weeks ago."

J.T.'s stoic face never changed. No flinches. No raised eyebrows.

No shocked expression. Maybe he was non-judgmental. She prayed he wouldn't question her further.

"All the more reason not to let the bastard make demands."

"I agree. I don't care what Jason wants. He's not getting near my son." God, she wanted to take J.T. up on his offer of friendship. Her stomach tightened.

Take a risk.

"I know jack about children, but Ethan seemed okay."

"You were his favorite topic last night. Ethan showed more interest in you than in Dad's bandages; I think it hurt his feelings"

"The kid annihilated me. Winning gave him something to brag about." J.T. started the car but turned to face her. "Maybe I can help put Carrington back behind bars."

"No. Please." Her thoughts ran wild. "This is for me to handle."

The nerve in his jaw twitched. "If that's the way you want it."

Leigh waited for the panic to subside before she worked up the nerve to speak. "Ethan has other toys in need of mending." Her cheeks burned. Her words sounded lame and stupid. Opening up was like walking down a dark alley blindfolded with no gun. Thirty-two years old and she didn't know how to invite a man to her house.

He shot her a glance and another peek at his dimple. "I'll bet. Do you live with your parents?"

"No. Ethan and I live in the city. I'll give you my address." How many rules had she broken today? Her spirit soared. Go for it. Break another. "If you come Saturday, I'll cook dinner."

"Ethan doesn't keep a second Indy 500 game at your place, does he?"

"No. Your pride's safe at my house."

For now, on a warm spring day, Jason and his demands faded to the background.

****

Doyle never paid much attention to the front section. Politics and sports didn't hold his interest, but his wife's name caught his notice seconds before he tossed the newspaper into the garbage bin. Son of a bitch, she'd been dead for over a year. Dead from all the pain life had dumped on her. He ran to the sink and hung on while his breakfast spewed from his belly.

God rest her soul, she'd left everything in a trust fund for him. It should've made him feel better to have money stashed in case he ever needed a defense attorney. It didn't.

He splashed water on his face and stumbled to the couch in his living room, wondering why the story surfaced in Atlanta. He lay down under the rotating ceiling fan. The steady squeak of the motor his only company.

****

The soft hand on Doyle's shoulder belonged to the one person who'd befriended him since he'd hired on at the hospital. "Ellen. How are you?"

"I'm good. I wonder if you are. Your eyes were red and swollen at the beginning of the shift. I decided I'd better check on you." She joined him at the table, glancing at his half-eaten sandwich on the tray. "Don." She covered his hand with hers. "Are you ill?"

"Allergies," he lied. "I started taking my medicine this morning. Thanks for asking."

She nodded. "May I eat with you?"

"I'd like that." He sat up straighter. "I'd like that a lot." His mood immediately lightened. Who wouldn't welcome having such a nice person as Ellen around?

"Be right back." Ellen breezed through the cafeteria line. When she returned, she sat and placed a sliver of pecan pie in front of him. "I had them cut it in half. Like I told you the other day, I'm watching my figure."

"Nothing's wrong with your figure."

"Thanks." She studied his face. "I like you without the mustache."

"Thanks." Once before, he'd thought Ellen had flirted with him. He wasn't taking any chances this time. "You working this weekend?"

"I'm not. Would you think me too forward if I invited you to dinner?"

"No. I like a take-charge woman."

The small laugh lines around her mouth deepened. Damn, she was a nice-looking woman. He swept the niggling guilt aside. His wife was gone, and Ellen was here.

"Nope. Not forward at all," he said with certainty. "I was about to ask you out."

She beamed at him. "Awesome. Don't leave tonight without my address. I'm off Sunday and Monday." Ellen waited until he'd started on his piece of pie before she picked up her fork.

"Me too. I'll bet we can think of something to do for both days." The jolt of sugar on his tongue from the pie couldn't have been sweeter. With her kindness, she'd wiped out the horrible taste in his mouth.

She'd made his decision not to stop for a newspaper on his way home tonight easy. He'd continue building a new life, selecting his executions, and carrying them out.

They returned to the ER, stepping to the side for an orderly who wheeled a sobbing woman down the aisle on a gurney.

"Oh, no," Ellen whispered.

"Son of a bitch," one of the doctors muttered under his breath, turning to Ellen. "I've seen her around the hospital. Her husband's an intern on four; he's standing over there."

Ellen glanced toward the hallway where a man stood looking on. "That's Dr. Holibeck. He's got a reputation among the nurses as a hothead."

"Send him to the lobby. Get him out of here," a doctor ordered.

No one noticed the porter cleaning, so Doyle carried out his duties in the ER quietly. He emptied a small trash receptacle into a larger bag and moved within listening distance. The doctors recited a list of injuries. They ordered x-rays over concerns about broken ribs and internal bleeding. God, was there no end to the brutality men caused? The woman on the bed had suffered horribly.

Doyle casually moved his cleaning material to the waiting room. He liked to look into the eyes of the guilty before their death. Dr. Nathan Holibeck was like the others.

Dead.

Chapter Nine

Parked in front of Leigh's white farm house, complete with a wraparound porch, J.T. grasped his car's door handle for the third time. Was he afraid of one woman and a child? Hell, yes. *Grow a pair, get out, and go in.* He had, after all, mouthed off and bragged he was a fixer of toys. He'd learned how because nobody else had been around to repair anything for him.

J.T. administered one last mental head slap, got out, and was halfway to the porch when the front door swung open.

"Ethan!" Leigh's voice came loud and firm.

Shit. The kid sprang off the porch and came barreling down the walk like the house was on fire.

"Ethan," she called out. Louder, angrier this time.

Too late. The six-year-old missile launched himself into the air, giving J.T. two choices. Catch the kid or let him fall to the ground like a deflated football. J.T. grabbed him and held Ethan out in front, as he would a wet, smelly dog.

Leigh jogged down the sidewalk, sparks flashing from her eyes. She pulled her son out of J.T.'s grasp and plopped the kid down at her feet. She knelt and got right in his face. J.T. made a mental note to not piss her off.

"What have I told you about running out the door?"

Ethan's head bowed. "Don't even think about it." He stared at the tops of his bare feet.

"You didn't listen." She tugged the knot at the back of her head tighter before she looked up. "Sorry about the attack."

"Kid's a natural-born high jumper." J.T. stuffed his hands in his pockets. She'd wadded her hair in the old-lady-school-teacher-bun-thing she wore at work. Probably just as well. If she'd left all that blonde silk loose and sexy, he might've thought it was a date or something, which it wasn't. His presence was entirely the fault of his big mouth.

"Please." She waved a hand toward the wide-open front door. "We were about to come and get you."

"You knew I was here?"

"A black Corvette rumbling around in our neighborhood doesn't go unnoticed."

Dressed in blue jean shorts and a thin-strapped top the same blue as her eyes, Leigh looked more like a model than a mom. J.T. was glad he'd worn a T-shirt and Wranglers.

His chest double-clutched and pulled a weird stutter step when a small hand gripped two of his fingers and two small feet shuffled hurriedly to keep up with him. Tonight was a mistake. Holding hands with the kid was a mistake. Hell, all of it was a huge mistake. His brain churned in circles. J.T. knew nothing about families. He sure didn't know how to act. He and Ethan had played one video game, and Ethan had done all the talking.

Once inside, J.T. relaxed some. Mainly because Leigh's living room had a lived-in, comfortable feel. Toys, books, and boxes of puzzles lined the shelves on one wall. A small TV with what looked like a decent sound system, tons of CD's, a couch, and a well-worn rocking chair finished off the area.

"Can I show Mr. Noble my room?" Ethan had already started pulling J.T. down a hall.

"May I," she corrected Ethan's grammar. "Just a quick look. I'm taking the roast out of the oven."

"Name's J.T." He waited when Ethan turned to his mother and

received her nod. This was way too domestic for J.T.'s comfort zone. How the hell had he gotten himself into this mess? Leigh had her nest built and one little chick to care for. With his family history, no way was he up for long-term stuff like family or kids.

"Want to play a game?" Ethan asked, dragging J.T. to his bedroom where the largest piece of furniture was a twin bed. A Falcon's poster was thumbtacked to the wall. Matching football gear was scattered everywhere. And lots more books. The McBride's were big on reading.

"No games," Leigh called out from the other room. "Come eat."

"She reads your mind?" The kid's bewildered nod said he believed she did. J.T.'s joke had gone right over Ethan's head.

"We better go," Ethan whispered.

J.T. ignored the urge to take a peek at Leigh's bedroom. He'd get his hands slapped big time if caught. Still, her private space played havoc with his imagination. Was it feminine? Decorated in pink with pillows everywhere, or organized with everything in its place? A lot about her intrigued him, and his interest confused him. She was not his type of woman.

He and Ethan followed the aroma of hot biscuits to the kitchen. A table with four chairs sat in the corner, covered with dishes. She'd fixed roast with potatoes, which he and Ethan sat down and ate like they hadn't been fed for days. Ethan dominated the conversation except when his mother got on his case for talking with his mouth full. The evening made J.T. appreciate Nana and how she'd juggled a house, him, and a career. Good memories.

Leigh retrieved the tea pitcher from the counter and refilled his glass. "You keep grinning at me as if you know something I don't," she said. "What's up?"

"Well, you couldn't have known we were about to play a game without reading our minds. It's a talent you should use at work."

"I do have a third eye. Too bad it only works at home." One eyebrow shot up at J.T.'s doubtful look. "Tell him, Ethan."

"She's got one back here." The boy turned in his chair and pointed to the back of his head. "Under her hair."

J.T. choked back a laugh at Ethan's wide-eyed innocence. "That's a mom thing. My grandmother had one. It goes away when they get older."

"A long, long time from now." Leigh stacked dishes. "You two go work on our newest puzzle while I clean the kitchen."

"No way. I eat. I help clean." J.T. turned to see Ethan disappearing into the living room. J.T.'s hands covered Leigh's when he took the plates from her. Her mouth opened a fraction, and her tongue moistened her bottom lip. A simple movement and the sexiest thing he'd ever witnessed. Damn, he wanted to kiss her. He moved closer. Stopped when she pulled the dishes away from him.

"Go. I'm just sticking these in the dishwasher." Her voice cracked, and she swallowed hard.

Between the puzzle and putting the wheels back on a toy dump truck, J.T. shocked himself by having a good time. Ethan's protests fell on deaf ears when bath and bedtime came. J.T. had settled on the couch and turned on the sports channel when Ethan, dressed in pajamas, appeared at his knee. Leigh stood in the doorway, waiting. J.T. bolted to his feet. This was way too comfy.

"Good night." Ethan's lips pushed out in a pout, not wanting the night to end.

He had his mother's blue eyes. They pulled you in. Touched you. J.T. shook off the feeling of tenderness. It wasn't a coat he wore well.

"It's time for me to go," J.T. told him. "Why don't you and Mom walk me to the door?"

He felt Leigh's eyes on him. What was she watching for? When he met her gaze, she smiled and nodded. The small boy staring up at him, clinging to his hand, scared J.T. worse than his last tour of duty. And that one had damn near killed him.

On the porch, Leigh scooped up Ethan, parking him on her hip. "Thanks for coming. We rarely have company, and we enjoyed tonight. Didn't we?" she asked Ethan.

"Yes, ma'am."

"Thanks for supper."

"You're welcome."

She stood on the sidewalk, beautiful in the amber glow of the porch light. God, he wanted to say something else. Something profound. Something to show he understood the honor and trust she'd bestowed on him by allowing him into her home. Something to let her know he'd never betray her confidence. Instead, the intimacy of mother and child smiling at him, scrambled his brain, clogged his throat, and sent him hustling to his car.

****

Leigh's eyes flew open when something heavy landed on top of her. A gloved hand clamped over her mouth. Ethan! Mother and cop instinct took over and she struggled, fought to free her hands. The bedcovers helped the bastard hold her prisoner. Please. God. She'd give this jerk whatever he wanted. Just keep Ethan safe. Panic rode high in her chest when the stranger straddled her body, pressing her farther into the mattress.

White lights exploded in front of her eyes and fire burned straight through her brain as he delivered two fast blows to her cheek. Stars flashed, forcing her to scream into the gloved hand. A third punch landed below her breastbone, causing a gush of air to expel from her lungs.

"Be quiet," the voice whispered. Fingers gripped her throat and tightened. "Understand?"

Leigh stopped struggling and managed to nod her head up and down. Be submissive. Wait for an opportunity to strike. Survival was all about staying calm. The gloved hand moved, and she asked, "What do you want?"

She had to protect Ethan. She gathered her wits and forced her body to relax. She committed every move he made to memory, gathering clues using the dim light from her alarm clock. He wore all dark clothing. His head and face were covered with a ski mask.

Silently, he tugged her sleep shirt up. Cold reality hit hard. Memories of the past rape blasted through her mind. The intruder covered her breast with his hand and squeezed. He rolled her nipple between his fingers then pinched. Twisted, harder, and harder. She clamped her lips tight to muffle the sound when she cried out. He leaned close and rubbed his covered face against hers. The familiar scent of his cologne sent her stomach into overload. The voice was muffled, but the smell identified her attacker.

"Jason. You're going back to prison."

His fist crashed into her jaw. Her world spun out of control. His fingers came back to her neck, tightened. Tighter. Tighter. Ethan. She fought against losing consciousness. Darkness pulled her under.

The weight lifted. She gasped for air. Coughed. Gulped oxygen into her burning lungs. She was alive and breathing. He'd released her. Why? She rolled off the bed, tangling the covers around her legs. Was he still in the house? She crawled to the nightstand, opened the drawer, and found the key to her lockbox. Sweat broke and ran down her face as she scooted to the closet. Opening the door posed a risk but she had to reach her gun. The house was quiet except for her pounding heart while she fumbled with the small key. A whoosh of air left her lungs when the lock opened.

The forty caliber Glock in her hand offered a measure of reassurance. She flattened her back against the wall and listened. Leigh ran down the hall to Ethan's room. She turned the knob, pushed the door open with her foot, and then clamped her left hand over her mouth to muffle a sob. Ethan, sound asleep and undisturbed, had one leg sticking out from under his sheet, his Atlanta Falcons helmet stuck on his foot. Leigh checked inside his closet and under the bed before making sure the window was still locked. The tightness in her chest eased. One more look at her son, and then she backed out, pulling his door closed.

As soon as the 9-1-1 operator answered, Leigh identified herself and provided the appropriate information. She insisted the patrol car come in cold with no siren or lights to disturb Ethan.

A quick check of her house revealed the breach. The kitchen door stood open. She knew she'd checked the doors carefully before going to bed. The locks were old, but the deadbolts should've held. Damn it, she should've gone ahead and had alarms installed.

Jason's cologne burned her nostrils. Stuck to her skin. Maybe forensics could find something so Leigh slipped off her sleep shirt and stuffed it in a paper bag. Sweat covered her body, yet she shivered while pulling on jeans and a blouse. The reality of what might have happened reduced her knees to rubber, and she sank to the floor. Inside her head, jackhammers worked overtime. Her entire body trembled. Her face and right breast throbbed.

She grabbed her cell, begging her fingers to stop shaking. She dialed a number, taking one more peek at her sleeping son.

J.T. answered on the second ring. "What's up?"

His sleepy voice ripped the last vestige of self-control away from Leigh. "Somebody broke in," she blurted the words out on a sob. "Can you come?"

"On my way. You call it in?"

His voice, heavy with concern, opened her up. Try as she might, the emotions bubbled over. "Yes."

"Are you hurt?"

The tears started and wouldn't stop.

"Hang on. I'll be there soon."

****

J.T. slid to a stop behind two patrol units and ran to Leigh's front door. He flashed his ID to gain entrance then froze when he stepped inside. Leigh's face was bruised but it was her eyes, full of pain and fear, that cut right through him. Sitting on the couch with her feet tucked under her, she looked like a wounded child. He eased down beside her, not demanding answers, letting her retell the events at her pace.

She bounced up to go open Ethan's bedroom door every few minutes. Amazingly, the kid slept while the cops tromped around inside and out, asking questions. The boy missing the excitement and not witnessing his mother's attack was a good thing.

When she'd called, J.T. had heard her tears. The sound had almost ripped his heart out. The way she'd pulled herself together amazed him. She'd dressed and rounded up her hair into something close to that infernal knot. She was pissed because her identification of the intruder by his smell wasn't enough to arrest her ex-boyfriend.

The paramedics checked Leigh over and agreed that if somebody drove her to the ER, she could skip the ambulance ride. She called her babysitter, apologized profusely, and asked if she would stay with Ethan for a couple of hours.

J.T. walked the paramedics out, insisting Leigh would keep her word.

"Should you call your folks?" he asked when he returned from outside.

"No need." The last thing she wanted was to scare them. Reluctantly, she let him drag her to the Piedmont Emergency room.

****

J.T. parked in Leigh's driveway and watched the sleeping beauty in his car. Between the adrenaline wearing off and the probing of the ER doctors, Leigh had to be exhausted. She'd dozed off within a few minutes of leaving the hospital.

"I'm awake," she said, her tone soft and groggy.

"Let's get you inside."

Leigh sent the sitter home, promising to call if she was needed. Nerves and memories did funny things, and J.T. waited while Leigh checked every room in her house. She wandered back to the living room and sat on the floor in front of a collection of CDs.

"Too tense to rest?" J.T. understood completely.

"Most of these are Ethan's. Kid tunes. Ever heard 'The Wheels on the Bus'?" Her voice had tears right on the edge.

"Not that I remember."

"I was so afraid Ethan would wake and come to my bedroom." She fidgeted with the different CDs. "Worse, I was afraid of what would happen to Ethan if he killed me."

"But he didn't. You should rest." God, he wanted to find the son of a bitch and beat him within an inch of his life.

"You're leaving?"

His blood flashed hot when she raised her wide-eyed gaze to his face. Her swollen cheek was already multicolored and matched the bruising on her neck.

"Hell no. I'm sleeping on the couch. Tomorrow, we'll get you a new door with deadbolt locks."

"Thank you."

He had to figure a way to comfort her without scaring the hell out of her. He sat on the floor behind her, placed a hand on each side of her narrow waist, and slid her into the juncture of his thighs. Her back went rigid at his touch, so he did something he'd wanted to do since they'd met. He removed the rubber thing that had failed to keep her hair under control and released her golden locks. He finger-combed them as they fell down the middle of her back.

"That was a mistake," she sighed, her bunched shoulders relaxing a little.

"Why?" J.T. forced his hands to his sides because she was right. Jesus Christ, he wanted to bury his face in her curls, feel the softness against his bare skin. Most of all, he wanted to tell her everything was okay.

"Turned loose, my hair goes wild. In the bun, at least one thing in my life is under control."

He felt her first tremble. Her shoulders shook. "Leigh," he whispered. "I'm sorry he hurt you."

"When I think about Ethan, helpless, sleeping down the hall, I . . ."

A mixture of fear and fury boiled up in him when she released a sob. J.T.'s anger and need to do something spun his mind in circles.

"Damn it, it's my job to protect him." Leigh's anger poured out. "What if he'd been taken or killed? I wouldn't survive that." She dropped her head into her hands and cried.

J.T. had never heard such a gut-wrenching sound. Her tears weren't for herself. She hurt for what might've happened to her son. The lump in his throat, the one growing with each of her sobs surprised him. He massaged the ridged tendons and muscles between her shoulder blades because he had to touch her, to comfort her. She didn't pull away, so he increased the pressure.

He tried to imagine being helpless, to be at somebody else's mercy. To have no control over a situation didn't compute and refused to process in his brain.

Finally, she straightened her back, drying her cheeks with her hands.

"Better?" He wanted to drag her into his arms and kiss away the aches and pains. To make her forget, to feel safe and cared for, but she was too vulnerable. He wasn't what she needed.

Leigh was sure her ex-boyfriend was responsible, and J.T. had no reason to doubt her. His palms itched to wrap his fingers around the bastard's neck.

"Better. You're a man of few words."

"I talk when I have something to say." The bruises forming on her had his temper ready to burst into flames. She didn't need him to blow up, so he kept his thoughts to himself.

"I can't thank you enough. Twice you've stepped up on my behalf."

"Not a problem. Now, I want you to do something for me." J.T. hated to put her through any more tonight, but memories dimmed. He needed her to concentrate.

She shifted, looking at him over her shoulder. "Okay."

"Think back. You were down for the count. Why didn't he finish you off?"

"He was sending a message. Give him what he wants."

"How'd you get mixed up with this jerk? Never mind. The question's out of line and none of my business."

"You deserve an answer." She reached up and patted his hand resting on her shoulder. "Jason and I had a few dates. He's an expert at pretense. When I saw what he was really like, I broke off with him. His reaction was off the chart. He wouldn't hear of it. I was his. Plain and simple."

"Well, you're not his," J.T. said, sliding his arms around her.

Leigh cried out then slapped a hand over her mouth. His gut bunched, and he moved back in a hurry.

"I hurt you?"

"Wait here." She stood. "Please." With one hand over her breast, she walked down the hall into her bedroom and closed the door.

J.T. didn't stir from his position. The hug from behind had been a friendly gesture. He hadn't touched her in a sexual way. Shit. He'd like nothing better, but he wasn't a complete jerk. Her eyes were rimmed red when she returned and sat on the floor. This time she faced him.

She swallowed hard a couple of times. "He squeezed my breast and twisted my nipple. You bumped me with your arm." Tears rose back to the surface. "The ER doctor said it would be painful, but he saw no permanent damage. I've been afraid to look."

"And?" J.T.'s chest was on fire. His hands rolled into fists. The sorry bastard who hurt her deserved more than a good beating.

"Tender. Bruised. I don't know what I expected." She wiped the tears hanging on the edge of her eyelashes. "Ethan will be up in a few hours. We'd better sleep while we can."

The desire to gather her close and comfort her hit J.T. hard. He'd never wanted to hold anybody as badly. Instead, careful not to hurt her again, he helped her up. A joke felt more appropriate for the situation.

"If you're scared, I can be convinced to sleep with you."

The corners of her mouth twitched, and J.T. waited for her answer.

"I appreciate the offer, but all I'm taking to bed with me is an icepack."

"Would you feel better with me asleep on the floor next to your bed?"

Finally, he got a light chuckle out of her. "Wait here, I'll bring you a pillow and blanket."

Soon, J.T. had stretched out on the too-short couch. Would Leigh rest? He couldn't. She had a lunatic on her hands, and they had to be ready for his next move. He pushed himself up, walked to the window, and stared out into the darkness. Carrington laying his hands on Leigh in anger revved J.T.'s heartbeat too high for sleep.

She'd flip out if she found out he'd dug around in her personal life, but, damn, he wanted to know more about Carrington.

He'd stood in her living room contemplating having a relationship with her, knowing he'd hurt her when the time came for him to walk away. What kind of bastard did that make him? The worst kind.

Chapter Ten

Doyle's eyes opened with a snap. Unfamiliar surroundings and the hand on his thigh sent his body rigid. The panic was fleeting. Last night, after a few drinks, he'd learned why Ellen lived alone. Five years ago, her long-term, cheating boyfriend had ended their relationship. To fill her lonely hours, she'd dedicated herself to her career and a local women's shelter. Until last night, she hadn't trusted another man enough to allow him in her bed.

Doyle didn't know or care why she'd welcomed him into her life and body without a lot of romance. He'd never been good at putting his emotions into words. Had fate been kind and sent him another woman who didn't need mushy talk?

Ellen would fill a void in his heart, and she had access to valuable data he'd never obtain without her help. She'd unknowingly provide information from the hospital and the women's shelter. With her help, he'd continue his work. His accomplishments would be legendary.

****

J.T. opened one eye and stared into two small, blue ones. There was a question coming. Like why he'd slept on the couch. Other than "go ask your mother," he had no clue what to say. He rolled off onto the floor to straighten out his bent, cramped torso. He groaned into a stretch. Ethan landed on top of J.T. with a giggle.

"Easy," J.T. pleaded. "Is your mom up?"

"No. Wanna play?"

"Not really."

The kid jumped up and down a couple of times.

"Don't bounce," J.T. warned.

Ethan turned his head sideways and studied J.T.'s face. Wide-eyed, the kid pointed at the scar with his index finger. J.T. wasn't surprised the kid was curious.

"How'd you get that?"

"A piece of shrapnel—" He paused and considered Ethan's age. "I was in the war. A bomb went off and a piece of metal smacked me in the face."

"Does it hurt?"

"Not anymore." J.T. marveled at the innocence in Ethan's eyes.

"Can I touch it?"

"I guess so." J.T. breathed in and waited. Ethan hesitated, leaning closer.

"I'm not supposed to talk about your scar."

"Who said?"

"Mama."

"It's okay. I won't tell."

J.T. turned his head to the side. No one had outright asked to touch the constant reminder of the day when his best friend had caught the worst of an IED. Hell, people shied away from his right side. Except for Leigh, she looked him square in the face. He lay still while Ethan poked a finger into the scar a couple of times. After a few seconds of investigation, the kid cupped the scar with his small hand and patted lightly. The oddest thing happened to J.T.'s heart. It swelled inside his chest and then clenched.

"Mama said you were a brave soldier."

Alien emotions swirled through J.T. and an unexplained urge to hug Ethan put a weird lump in J.T.'s throat. Unable to cope or understand, his mind raced for an idea, anything to end the moment. He growled, turned his head, and snapped as if he were trying to bite. Ethan shrieked with laughter and resumed his bouncing.

"Easy, kid." Thank God, the strange tightening of his heart ended. "Let me hit the bathroom, and then we'll fix coffee."

"I'm not allowed to touch stuff in the kitchen." Ethan slid to the floor and stood next to the couch.

"Okay. You'll show me where everything is. I'll take care of the rest." J.T. hurried to the bathroom, anywhere to regain his bearings. He stuck his head under the tap to wash away the unrealistic emotions he'd experienced, finger-combed his hair, and rinsed his mouth out with Scope. More than enough grooming for a Sunday.

Ethan, wearing gold and black Falcons pajamas, his blond hair wild and curly like his mother's, waited in the kitchen. He pointed out the correct cabinet and within minutes, Mr. Coffee was doing its thing. J.T. felt the tug on the leg of his jeans.

"Why did you sleep over?" Ethan asked.

J.T. looked toward the hallway, willing Leigh to materialize and provide answers. "Because your mom had an accident after I left. She's got some bruises on her neck and cheek. I came back to take care of her." J.T. braced himself for a barrage of questions or at least a child's version of a panic attack.

Ethan's brow furrowed, and he started moving toward his mother's bedroom.

"She's fine," J.T. added. "Maybe we should let her sleep."

Ethan considered the suggestion for a second. "I'm hungry." He opened the refrigerator. "Do you know how to make cereal?"

"Cereal, I can handle."

Ethan wandered back to the living room and turned on the TV while J.T. fixed two bowls of Fruit Loops. They sat on the floor, ate breakfast, and watched *SpongeBob SquarePants*.

J.T. was in the kitchen when he heard the *snick* of the lock on the bathroom door. He rinsed the dishes and then poured two coffees. The window over Leigh's sink looked out on a small yard, complete with a swing set. A lifetime ago, he'd had a truck tire hanging from a tree next to Nana's garden. He didn't do domestic, yet here he was, playing nursemaid to a six-year-old and worrying about the kid's mother.

"Is one of those for me?" Leigh asked.

"Shit." His effort to maintain a straight face failed. Her swollen cheek was already turning bluish purple. His blood spiked and his fingers coiled.

"Exactly. Standing in front of the mirror, the same word crossed my lips," she whispered. She tiptoed to the door and peeked into the living room. "Thanks for keeping him occupied."

J.T.'s hand shook when he carried the coffee to her. A fire raged through his veins, and he kicked himself for his shocked expression. "No problem." He tried to keep the sympathy out of his tone. He failed.

"You've seen worse. Right?"

"Never on somebody I cared about." He cupped her un-bruised cheek with his hand. She'd left her hair loose and an explosion of long, wild, blonde curls hung across her shoulders. The same hand touching her face itched to tunnel through the tangled silk.

She stepped away from him, glanced toward the living room, and then back at him. "What will I tell Ethan?"

"He's already asked why I was here."

"Oh, crap. What did you say?"

"The truth. You had an accident, and I came back to help. Didn't seem to faze or surprise him."

Her back straightened, and she moved closer.

"To correct any assumptions—he's never gotten out of bed and found a man in the house."

"Easy. Don't get pissy with me. I wasn't insinuating anything." Her statement pleased him, and, because it did, it confused him. His gaze drifted down the front of her shirt and stopped on her breasts. Had she been hurt worse than she'd admitted? "You sure you don't need to go back to the doctor?"

"I'm sure." She flushed pink, grinned, and turned away.

"Just checking."

"Ethan," she called over the TV. "Come in here, please."

J.T. pulled out his cell and carried his coffee to the backyard. The upcoming conversation between mother and son was no place for him. He'd find someone to install better deadbolts and check out prices on an alarm system. It wasn't his place to tell her what to do, but he could arm her with good information.

****

Leigh sat down at the kitchen table, closed her eyes, and relished the silence. After she'd called her mother with the news, the day had been a blur of activity. Her dad and J.T. had morphed into *Property Brothers* wannabes. Between them and the locksmith, her Dad had insisted on calling out, they'd accomplished a lot.

She'd agreed to their suggestion of a second set of deadbolts, window locks, and the installation of a burglar alarm. Even then, she couldn't relax. As long as Jason Carrington was a free man, she'd never feel safe.

She wanted to shower. Again. Wanted to wash away the memory of him on top of her. Wanted to know what he had planned next. Wanted to be ready. No doubt, this was a prelude to much worse. He was toying with her, taunting her.

Her mom had insisted Leigh needed recovery time before reporting to work Monday morning, so Ethan was going to Peachtree City for the night. Leigh walked to the front door and waved at her son one more time, wondering why they hadn't insisted she accompany them.

J.T. stood in the yard until they'd driven out of sight. Being the protector suited his personality, although, he'd probably be pissed if she told him so. She liked his quiet confidence and his stringent belief in right and wrong. She corralled the warmth spreading across her chest and the tightening around her heart. Allowing her emotions to take off to parts unknown was a huge risk. He was a short-term colleague, a loner, who, from what she'd seen, didn't allow people to get close. A woman with a son? Good luck finding the welcome mat to his heart.

"Your dad's knees were hurting," J.T. said as he stepped on the porch. "He limped all

afternoon."

"Bicycle raspberries take forever to heal." She shifted nervously, propping her hip against the doorframe. "You've been so helpful. I appreciate everything you've done."

"You've already said thanks." He raised his eyebrows. "You barricading the entry for a reason?"

"Oh." Leigh moved to the side and let him enter. "I figured you'd leave right after Mom and Dad."

"Nope." His chest rose as he inhaled a deep breath. "We can do this a couple of ways," he said in a formal, facts-only manner. "Until the alarm system is operational, either I stay here, or you come home with me."

"Not necessary. You've done enough." J.T. staying last night had made sense. What he'd suggested for tonight was entirely out of the question. Her pulse accelerated every time he got near. Geesh. She was a mother, not a young girl looking for a prom date.

"It's either me or your Dad. We made a pact." He spread his hands out like the scales of blind justice, moving them up and down.

"So, this is why Mom and Dad didn't insist I go home with them. Where was I when you men had this summit meeting?"

"There you go, getting pissy. Again." J.T. sat on the couch and folded his arms across his chest. "Your dad was in a state, muttering all day about what he wanted to do to Carrington. I convinced him I'd protect you."

"That's twice you've accused me of getting 'pissy' today." She purposefully narrowed her eyes and returned his scowl. Her pride wanted to tell him she could take care of herself. Her bruises said she couldn't.

"Must mean there's merit to my 'accusation.' " The corner of his mouth twitched.

"No, it doesn't and don't you laugh at me. The two of you should have consulted me."

J.T. lifted a shoulder. "All's left is for you to choose where to sleep. Either way, we make a run to my place; I need clean clothes."

"Folding your arms over your chest and staring grimly probably scares criminals, old ladies, and small children. Doesn't work on me." Sleeping in J.T.'s house had her hormones screwing with her normally logical thinking. "Relax. You and Dad won this round."

"Just as well. He needed a break from the tension. He mumbled something about how he wished he'd killed the SOB. If he's going to, and I might do it for him, he shouldn't talk about it out loud."

"Jason needs to go back to prison. Dad's being an overprotective parent. He'd never hurt anybody."

She hoped her dad hadn't slipped and told J.T. about the rape. She'd had enough of people's pity and condemnation. She didn't want that from him. But, sometimes, what you want isn't always what you get.

"As long as you're being cooperative, my bed's more comfortable than your couch." He stood and rubbed his lower back. "And Ethan's looks to be about a foot too short."

"Exactly how big is your place?"

"There are two bedrooms if that's what you're asking."

"I'll pack an overnight bag."

Leigh closed the bedroom door behind her, leaning her head back against the cool wood. Jason had almost destroyed her life once before. His time in prison had made him meaner, crueler, and more cunning. She had to put him back behind bars for the rest of his twenty-five-year sentence. In eighteen years, Ethan would be grown.

Bringing herself back to the job at hand, she pulled a bag from the closet. That simple movement caused an explosion of lightning strikes in her breast. Carefully, she filled the suitcase and then rejoined J.T. in the living room.

"I could've come after this." He took the roller bag from her, pushed the handle down, and picked it up. He raised and lowered his arm a couple of times. "Damn. You plan on staying for a long time?"

"My gun lockbox is in there." She chuckled on the way to the car. Laughing felt good but having that pistol within reach felt better.

****

Jason shifted in the seat and met Vick's gaze. "He wore the cologne?"

"Yeah. Trust me."

"I don't trust anybody. I need details."

Vick breathed out, filling the car with a disgusting odor. "He knocked the shit out of her a couple of times before he choked her." Vick snorted a laugh. "Tried to pop her nipple like a pimple."

"Damn, I bet that hurt." Jason got hard listening to the events of last night's visit.

"Yeah." Vick's voice got low and husky.

"Tell me what else you learned about Leigh then get out of my car. I hate Woodland Park and this part of town."

"We can meet at your fancy apartment."

Ignoring the wisecrack, Jason asked, "How long did you watch her place today?"

"Off and on, four hours. I moved around, parked in different places. It didn't take long for the guy to change out her locks, maybe a couple of hours. The old couple spent the day with her. Her boyfriend was there this morning when I made my first pass. They left together. I got a look at him when he carried a suitcase out to his car. Big fella." Vick drew a line down his cheek. "Scar."

"You followed, right?" Jason's blood stirred, heated inside his veins. So, she thought she'd sneak off and hide. Let her try. "Find out everything you can about this bastard."

"I followed." Vick nodded at the envelope in Jason's hand. "That mine?"

Jason passed it to Vick. "You took care of the guy who broke into Leigh's house?"

"Yes." Vick got out and slammed the car door.

****

J.T. unlocked his apartment and let Leigh inside. The second she crossed his threshold, it hit him. Alone, without the kid around, she was too much temptation. Smart and quick-witted. Beautiful and way too sexy. J.T. had nothing more to offer her but a good time, and she wasn't the type to use for sex and then move on.

Especially not tonight though. Not in her condition, hurt and scared.

"Do you rent or own?"

"I bought during the market downturn. For an eighth-floor, two-bedroom home in an old refurbished office building, the price was right."

"The view from the wall of windows makes the place."

"Yeah. Sold me. Most of the furniture Nana donated from her storage shed." That Leigh liked the place pleased him for some dumbass reason.

"I'm going to hit the shower."

Dressed in jeans and a T-shirt, he spread the barbeque they'd picked up on the drive over across the breakfast counter. When she padded down the hall barefoot, dressed in warmups, his appetite spiked—and not for food. Her long, blonde hair hung down her back in silky waves. Her satiny skin begged to be touched. She was completely unaware of the effect she had on him.

For the next couple of hours, they ate and talked about work, never touching on anything personal, mostly because when he'd broached the subject of her attack, she'd quickly changed the subject. Staying out of her business was getting difficult.

He stood and hit the light switch, throwing the room into darkness, so the city lights shined from below.

She quietly moved to stand beside him. "Ethan confessed he asked about your scar."

"So much for the kid keeping a secret."

"He thinks it's cool to have a friend who survived a bomb blast. I hope he wasn't rude."

"He wasn't."

She raised her hand, and for a split second, J.T. thought she was about to touch his face. Part of him ached for her to reach for him. Though, God only knew how he'd react if she did. Disappointment slid across him when she dropped her hand to her side.

"Well, I apologize for his behavior. He knows better."

She turned back to the window and away from him. J.T. had spent the last few years accepting his looks. So why did he wonder or care if the scar made her turn away? He administered a mental slap to his head. After what she'd just been through why was he even going down that road?

"The view's breathtaking."

"Yes, it is." If she figured out he was referring to her, she ignored his remark.

"You ever been married?" Her gaze stayed on the horizon.

So, she'd known he'd commented on her beauty. She wanted to change the subject.

"No. Never wanted to." He had to be honest with her. It wasn't his intention to mislead her. The quick straightening of her back said she got the message.

"Never is a long time."

"We Nobles are better left unwed."

"I should turn in." Her voice sounded distant and withdrawn. "We've got a sniper to catch tomorrow."

She'd taken a couple of steps toward the hall when he realized how badly he wanted her to stay. "What about you? Any ex-husbands I should know about."

She'd showered with his personal soap, and the scent filled the air behind her. The effect was more powerful than the usual hint of citrus in her hair. She was hurt, and tonight she was vulnerable. Taking advantage of her fear and insecurity was out of the question. However, his dick had no conscience and hardened with need. He clamped his teeth down, ignoring his desire.

"No. I never married." She stopped but didn't face him. "When I was seventeen, my uncle was killed in a drive-by. Boys and dating didn't seem so important afterward. His death helped me decide my major in college."

"I'm sorry."

"Me too."

"Leigh." She glanced over her shoulder, eyes full of questions, sending his blood pressure over the moon. "You'll get through this."

"I know. I have before."

She crossed the wide expanse of the apartment, hesitating at the turn long enough for him to hope she might come back. He held his breath. She moved, and seconds later, he heard the *snick* when the spare room door closed.

Another long fucking night.

Chapter Eleven

Casey held up a finger, keeping Leigh in her seat when the meeting ended and the team filed out. She'd explained the break-in and her bruised face, including her belief the attacker was an old boyfriend from years ago. Had her explanation not been enough? She'd left out the fact he was her son's father. If Casey wanted her to confess more— too bad.

Cramps hit her stomach, rolling through in waves. After her prior conversation with him, he must've dug into her background. If so, he'd learned about the rape and trial. Was he going to send her back to CID? Was she being paranoid?

"Leigh." His eyebrows dipped as he leaned forward, resting his forearms on the table. "I have to consider—"

"No need to explain," she interrupted. "I'll give my notes to J.T. and leave right away." She swallowed the knot wedged in her throat. She didn't like his reasons for sending her back to CID, but she understood.

"Did I say your assignment's been terminated?" He stopped her from interrupting again with a wave of his hand. "I asked you to stay behind because I sensed you're troubled. Telling the team about your attack was difficult. No need to deny it, your face told the real story."

"I'm trying to protect my son." Her temper flared. How could he not understand her motive? "No one here knows I was raped or that I got pregnant, and I'd like to keep it that way."

Casey's head moved back slightly. His eyes flashed with surprise. That expression quickly disappeared.

"You didn't know." Leigh sunk lower in her chair, drowning in her own stupidity.

"I didn't, but nothing you've said will leave this room. You're the only person who can decide when or if to share that information. Listening to you talk, I hear recrimination in your tone. You can't possibly believe being raped was your fault."

Leigh's back was against the wall. "I didn't realize the man I dated was a psychopath until it was too late. By the time I broke it off, he'd decided I was his property and wouldn't let me walk away. My poor judgment came close to getting me killed."

"By being so secretive, aren't you selling yourself, and the people around you, short?"

"You weren't around after the trial. Didn't hear the wisecracks, the suggestions, the innuendoes." Hurtful words from the past flashed through her memory. "People think women are catty bitches. Let me assure you, men can be damn cruel. A few insinuated I'd brought the rape on myself. When they learned I was pregnant, several cops in my unit who I worked with came right out and said I should have an abortion. Took years of hard work to earn back the respect of my peers. My promotion to detective transferred me into a new division. I'm sure the new guys don't know, but, if they do, they're too smart to mention the past when I'm around."

"How many people turned their backs on you, Leigh? It must've been a lot since you expect the same treatment from everyone. Someday you'll be forced to trust somebody. For now, you'll continue as a liaison." He rose and walked around the desk. "J.T.'s probably waiting on you."

Leigh pushed out words. "Thanks for understanding."

"Now go stop that damn sniper."

"Yes, sir." She hurried out of his office. The weight on her shoulders seemed a little lighter.

Leigh joined J.T. in the small conference room where he'd moved the files from the New York vigilante case. The first few of what had to be over twenty cartons were open, and he'd stacked folders on the table. She grabbed a box, opened it, and then stopped.

"How are you sorting?"

"Concentrate strictly on any reference to sniper assignments. We don't have time to tackle anything else."

"Got it." Leigh rubbed her hands over her eyes. Time to focus on the job. "Preston's police file with pictures is supposed to be right on top of one of these boxes."

"Yep. Keep an eye out for it. Romeo's getting copies faxed from New York. It doesn't mean we skip reviewing Preston's personnel file. After we separate all the information, we'll read and catalog by relevance."

J.T. took the heavy box from her and lifted it to the top of the table. He looked down at her.

"This is only until your bruises go away. Then my gentlemanly manners vanish."

Leigh refused to look at him, knowing he'd try to talk about her assault, which was the last thing she wanted to do at work.

She and J.T. fell into an easy silence, working through the morning. The stack with references to the sniper continued to grow. Occasionally, he let out a deep sigh. Leigh seconded the feeling and kept sorting. She welcomed the interruption when Olivia stepped in and broke the tedium.

"Along with the trust fund, Angie Preston had a safety deposit box at her bank. As the deceased wife of our suspected sniper, if the bank still has it, I've got enough for a warrant and a look-see inside."

"Interesting." J.T. looked up from his file. It varied by state, but some banks were allowed to sell the contents to pay for delinquent fees. Any money found is turned over to the state as unclaimed property.

He leaned his head back against the wall, his gaze aimed at the ceiling. Leigh could almost see his mind working. She and Olivia waited, letting him mull over the news.

"It's Angie Preston's attorney we need to locate. Maybe he can tell us if there was money in the deposit box and, if so, what else." J.T. jotted down a note. "Preston may already know his wife is dead. We have to think about this, maybe a waste of time, but if he doesn't know the bank has the rights to the contents of that box, he might check on it."

"We should check with the police department in that state. See what they know. Doyle is legally dead. I don't see how he could pull that off." Olivia asked.

"Me either, but we're desperate enough to ask." J.T. laid his hand on the stack of files. "It's possible Preston has numerous identities, money stashed, and contacts to help him in case of an emergency. We get those questions answered; we'll understand more about the man. He may not need anything his wife left behind."

"Alone and desperate is a hell of a place to be," Olivia said on a sigh.

"We'll set this up so Angie Preston's attorney notifies us if anyone contacts him about the trust." J.T. stood, stacked another empty box in the corner, and then rubbed his lower back with a groan. "I'm starving."

"We goin' out or ordering in?" Olivia asked.

"Makes no difference to me." J.T. shrugged. "Long as it's in volume."

"There's nothing sexier than a hungry man. Don't you agree?" She jabbed an elbow in the direction of Leigh's ribs. The blow landed against bruised breast tissue.

A zillion razor blades shot through Leigh. She folded over and dropped into the nearest chair.

"Oh, shit! What did I do?" Olivia knelt, her eyes wide.

"Nothing. I'm fine." Sweat popped out on Leigh's face while she fought back the urge to vomit. J.T. knelt beside her. His large hand splayed across her back.

"I'm sorry." Olivia clasped Leigh's arms and squeezed.

"I'm fine. Really." Leigh tried to laugh off the fact her nipple burned like a blowtorch from the inside. She stood and hurried to the restroom. The minute of privacy she wanted wasn't to be. Olivia followed.

"Talk to me," Olivia said. Her lips formed a thin, grim line. "Did that happen during the break-in?"

"Bastard tried to pinch off my nipple. Any bump triggers a firebomb."

"How do we make the son of a bitch pay?" Olivia asked.

"We don't." J.T.'s deep voice rumbled and bounced off the tiled walls.

Leigh blinked back tears. There he stood again, feet apart, arms folded across his broad chest, prepared to protect her. His body, from head to toe, screamed, "I'm in charge so don't fucking mess with me."

"Why not?" Olivia took a step back.

"Leigh will ask for our help if she wants it." His tone left no room for argument.

"What the hell are you doing in here anyway? Didn't they test your reading skills at Quantico?" Olivia's shoulders squared. He'd encroached on feminine territory and, clearly, he didn't intimidate her.

He sidestepped Olivia, ignoring her outburst, unfazed by his surroundings. Deep green eyes softened as they searched Leigh's face. He reached for her, his fingers hovering over the bruise on her cheek. J.T. standing so close seemed to have settled her stomach instantly.

"You sure you're okay?"

She worked to find her voice. Other than her family, no one had ever rallied to her defense as he did. "I'm better for having you two around. Let's order in and keep working." She hoped the change of topic would end the discussion about her injuries.

"Works for me. Olivia, if you'll order, I'll pay." J.T. walked to the door and held it open.

"I'll call out for an assortment of Chinese." Olivia turned to Leigh, raised an eyebrow, apparently waiting for approval.

"Sounds good." Leigh headed back down the hall to the conference room only to be stopped by J.T.'s hand on her shoulder.

"Why don't you call your dad? Check on how the installation is progressing," he suggested.

"Good idea. Maybe I can sleep in my bed tonight."

"Hello." Olivia whirled, her gaze darted from Leigh to J.T. and back. "And whose bed were you in last night?" Her eyes flared wide, full of curiosity.

"Nowhere juicy." Leigh prayed her face didn't turn beet red. "Staying at home is off-limits until the alarm system is installed. Dad's making sure the job's finished today."

Leigh had danced around the truth and half-expected Olivia to push for more details. Thank God, she accepted the explanation and returned to her desk. When she was out of earshot, J.T. leaned down close to Leigh's ear.

"Nice save," he whispered.

"Too nice." She'd lied to Olivia without thinking, stunning herself. The answer had popped out of Leigh's mouth with no effort. She hated liars.

J.T. fell in step with her on the way back to the conference room. After they were inside and alone, he put his hands on her shoulders and turned her around. "That's what you wanted, right? For us not to interfere?"

She grasped his forearm, felt the muscles twitch. "I don't want anyone here involved."

"Except me." He smiled down at her. "By the way, I was way off base when I offered to sleep with you the other night. I apologize for being a smartass. I just wanted you to smile."

"I like some smartasses," she said, unable to concentrate on anything except him standing inches away. His hands gripped and released her shoulders, the gentle massage telegraphed hormonal shocks to regions left untended for too long. The same breast, which felt pain a minute ago, now ached with desire. The faint scent of his cologne drifted into her nostrils. Woodsy, musky, and all man. Leigh held back the sigh riding at the top of her chest.

He tilted his head sideways with a cocky, lopsided grin. "But I stand by my offer."

"Stop that." She laughed as the tension between them thickened. He stared at her mouth for a second then abruptly turned away.

J.T. rolled up the sleeves of his shirt, lifted another carton of files onto the conference table for her, and then returned to his stack. The muscles in his forearms rippled and flexed with the movement. The innocent baring of skin hit her as sensuous and personal. The severity of his daily attire, the starched, snowy white shirt, and black slacks set all her womanly nerves sizzling. She'd had the privilege of seeing how he looked in the mornings, unshaven with dark stubble and uncombed black hair hanging across his forehead. All disheveled, J.T. fired her imagination and sent images of naked, sweaty bodies to her brain. Lord have mercy, shave him, dress him in the standard FBI outfit, settle his weapon over his right kidney, and she went weak in the knees. He took her breath away. No doubt, he'd deny his good looks. He'd be wrong.

Poor Ethan had been hurt badly when one bastard had dropped her after learning the truth about her rape and pregnancy. Would J.T. react differently? Dare she put him to the test? No. He'd been clear when he said he'd never marry. Tonight, she'd sleep in her bed. She needed to clear her head and get her priorities, such as Ethan, back in order.

Chapter Twelve

"Talk to me, goddamn it," Jason demanded.

"Wait a minute," Vick spit out the words. "I'm trying to take a picture with this piece-of-shit phone."

Jason tightened his grip on the receiver. Soon . . . very soon, the ex-con's services wouldn't be needed. Then he'd kill the son of a bitch for speaking to him in that tone of voice. There'd be no witnesses. Vick wouldn't be around to talk or blackmail.

"I'm sending it right now," Vick said. "Got a good shot of her and her boyfriend."

"Boyfriend? The guy you saw at her house?" Jason's blood pressure shot higher. "He's there?"

"Yeah. And he's with the FBI."

"Fed or not, he won't be able to keep her alive. Stay with them."

"How long?"

"Stay low-key and call me when you start recording."

"We should've bugged her place before that fuckin' alarm was installed. Dude says the job's more expensive now."

Jason bit back a comment about disrespect. "You're sure this electronics guy's good enough to bypass the new system?"

"He's robbed fancier places than hers and didn't set off the alarms. He's the best."

"Has 'the best' done time?"

"Once. He learned a lot of cool stuff inside."

"I'll bet." Jason's gut tightened. He remembered all too well the shit that went on "inside."

"How are you with money?"

"Gettin' low."

"Call me when everything's set up. I'll drop off extra cash then. See how much time Leigh and her boyfriend spend together."

"Why? What're you thinkin'?"

"That he may need to die too."

"You fuck with a fed, you're asking for heat. You'll have to do that deed."

****

Doyle held the door open and followed Ellen into the neighborhood café. Once seated across from her, he covered her hand with his. "The past few days have been wonderful. Thank you."

Ellen's cheeks flushed. "You made them special. Not me." She wound her fingers through his. "I wish I could call in sick tonight."

"Me, too." Doyle had business later, and he'd miss her warm body next to his.

"No one's ever made me feel the way you do." Her gaze met his. "I'd like to stay this happy forever."

"Nothing's stopping us." He filled his lungs with air and steeled himself for possible rejection. "I may be jumping the gun. If it's too soon, tell me; I'll understand if you don't want to spend all your time with an orderly, but I've fallen in love with you."

"Not too soon for me. I'm fifty-four years old, and it's high time I had love in my life." Tears welled in her eyes. "A few months ago, a battered woman came into the emergency room. I fell in love with you when I saw the pain and compassion in your eyes. You hurt for her the same way I did. I don't care what you do for a living. I love who you are inside."

Ellen's love filled the empty space left in his heart.

"Don? Where'd you go? Is something wrong?" Her hand tightened on his.

"No. Something is right. I'm thinking we should get married." His decision to propose surprised even him. The idea came from nowhere.

"I'm thinking you're right." She checked the time, and pink rushed up to her cheeks. "I have an hour before I have to report to work."

"What did you have in mind?" He loved the way she blushed.

The waitress set two glasses of water and the menus on the table. Ellen smiled up at her and said, "We're not staying. We're going home."

****

"The house is better secured," J.T. announced. He'd walked through the alarm set up with the installation guy. After he'd left, J.T. had retested the windows and doors. Over and over. His disappointment that she wouldn't be going home with him tonight drove his need to keep busy.

"I'm sure my neighbors are happy you've stopped testing." Leigh handed him a glass of tea. "You sure you won't stay for supper?"

"Some other time. It's been a couple of days since I checked on my grandmother." He leaned against the kitchen counter next to her.

"She lives in Atlanta?"

"In Newnan."

"You grew up there?"

He nodded. "Yep."

"You don't have an accent."

"Too many years living in Chicago. I graduated from the same high school as Alan Jackson. Although, he was several years ahead."

"The country singer?" Her eyes widened.

"The same. Don't be too impressed. I never met him."

"Do your parents also live in Newnan?"

"No," he snapped, hating the bitterness in his tone. She appeared to be genuinely interested, but his parents weren't a subject he wanted to discuss. What he wanted stood right in front of him.

Leigh had swapped the khaki slacks, blue blouse, and sensible black shoes she wore to work for jean shorts, a tank top, and sandals. The knot at the back of her neck was driving him crazy. He set the tea glass down and stepped in front of her. The noticeable stiffening of her back said she was unsure what to expect. "That's too tight."

He turned her around, smiling to himself when he heard the sharp intake of air. He removed the hairpins, unwound a thick rubber band, and tossed the lot on the counter. Thick, soft curls tumbled into his hand. He tunneled his fingers underneath those curls and rubbed the base of her neck. Her soft moan sent a jolt of fire to his groin.

Leigh turned slightly. Her mouth opened, and the tip of her tongue slid across her bottom lip. If he didn't kiss her now, his head would explode. He spun her to face him, dragged her against his body, and covered her mouth with his.

Her gasp put a knot in his gut. He jumped back, gripping her arms. "I hurt you."

"I'm okay," she murmured.

She cupped his scar with her soft hand, apparently unafraid to touch it. It crossed his mind she'd never asked about it. The always-present tightness vanished as he lost himself in her tenderness.

She rose onto her toes and kissed him. Her lips were soft. Warm and sweet. Hot and hungry. Her free hand slid under his shirt, stroking up and down his back. The room shrunk. The world faded away. Nothing existed except the softness of her skin, the gentle curve of her hips, and the heat from her body. He lowered his hands to her ass and lifted her higher, against his growing erection. She whimpered and ground into him.

"Mom!"

Ethan's yell and the door slamming jerked J.T. from his web of lust. Startled, he jumped away from Leigh and whirled toward the noise.

"In the kitchen," she answered on a nervous laugh.

J.T. grabbed his tea, sat at the kitchen table, and scooted the chair forward as close as he could. A blind man would've noticed the bulge about to rip the zipper from his slacks. He closed his eyes against the sound of the rapid pounding of Ethan's feet running across the living room floor. J.T. glanced at Leigh while she struggled to wipe the smile from her face.

"Not funny," he whispered. She gave him a yes-it-is nod.

Ethan burst in at a run and launched himself at his mother. She winced but caught him, sending J.T.'s respect for her higher. Damn, he hoped he hadn't hurt her when he pulled her against his body. Leigh nuzzled the neck of the small boy in her arms. J.T.'s chest walls clenched.

Leigh's mother entered the room and smiled when she spotted him at the table. Her presence certainly eliminated any residual erection.

"Hello again."

"It's hello and good-bye." He stood, walked over, and ruffled Ethan's curly mop of hair. "I've got to run. Monday hasn't been a good day for the taskforce."

"We're having a picnic at Olympic Park on Saturday. Why don't you join us?" Sara asked.

"Yeah." Ethan seconded the invitation before J.T. could open his mouth to refuse.

"I'd like that." The aroma of citrus must've blocked J.T.'s reasoning powers. "Should I bring something?"

"An appetite," Sara quipped.

"Even better, bring your grandmother," Leigh chimed in.

"What a great idea. We'll plan on two more." Sara carried a full laundry basket down the hall.

"Go help Mimi put away your clothes." She put Ethan down and pointed him toward the hall.

J.T. crossed the room in two strides. He cupped the back of Leigh's neck in his hand. "Me coming to a family picnic is not a good idea."

"Too late. Ethan's expecting you," Leigh whispered with a grin.

He exhaled a sigh of surrender. She kissed him on his lips, causing him to damn near swallow his tongue. "Fine."

J.T. made his way out of the house and drove to the corner, where he stopped and scratched his head. What the hell had he just agreed to? His brain told him one thing and his mouth said the exact opposite. Yet, he felt a buzz of excitement at the prospect of spending the day with Leigh and her family.

Yep, he was nuts.

****

Leigh dreaded answering her cell. The hang ups had worn her patience thin. She considered not answering when the caller ID came up blank. "McBride." She disconnected and then slammed her cell down on the conference room table.

"How many of those have you had today?" Olivia asked.

"Four."

"You think it's the bastard who broke into your house?"

"It's him. I just can't prove it."

"Did the cops question him after the break-in?" Olivia asked.

"Yeah. He had an alibi."

"Can we get back to work?" J.T. scowled at them. Leigh knew he was protecting her from questions.

"I'm all ears." Leigh smiled her thanks and returned to her seat.

"These men were murdered by a sniper in New York. Each had a history of spousal abuse." He tapped the top of a stack of pictures, frowning when Romeo entered. "This was a young policeman. The chief of police's son. Accused, never charged with the beating death of Doyle Preston's daughter."

"You've been invisible. What've you been doing?"

"Working on something for Casey. I did get you pictures of Preston while he was on the NYPD force."

Olivia took the pictures from Romeo. "Why didn't you do your photo magic and change his hair color or add a beard. I'll bet he's changed his appearance."

"Your attitude is precisely why we'll never be a couple." Romeo gave Olivia a wounded face. "You're never satisfied."

"Please. Your young heart would give out on the first go-round."

Leigh laughed, enjoying the camaraderie.

J.T.'s gaze locked onto hers. Heat charged around inside her lower belly. A picture of him kissing her and holding her against his body flashed in her memory. Then he broke away, turned his back, and ignored the banter between Olivia and Romeo. What made him withdraw?

Leigh's cell vibrated again. Olivia and J.T. both reached across the table. He moved faster.

"Caller unknown." J.T. handed the phone to Romeo. "Find this son of a bitch. I want a name and address. Don't tell me you can't because it's a burner."

"Does this happen a lot?" Romeo asked Leigh.

"Yes. I'm not answering anything without an ID."

"Want Romeo to get you one of our cells?" J.T. asked. "You can turn yours off and throw it in the desk drawer."

"No. Atlanta CID uses this number as well as the school and my family."

J.T. dropped another stack of files on the table. Romeo left and the rest of the group dug into their respective stacks.

"Here's something. Phone bills with calls from New York to Atlanta. Holy shit. The New York vigilante group had ties here in Atlanta." She passed the pages to J.T. to look over. "Preston's coming here was no accident. He thinks he's righteous."

Slowly, J.T.'s head moved in a nod. "Work with Romeo. Get names and addresses to go with these phone numbers. Leigh and I will run background checks. One good lead is all we need."

****

Rushing in with an apologetic look, Romeo shoved Leigh's phone in her hand. "Sorry, I answered without thinking."

Leigh checked the readout on her cell. It was Karen Parker, her attorney. "Excuse me." She stood, leaving the room.

"What's up?" Leigh held her breath hoping this was good news.

"If I'm interrupting—"

"Not at all. One of the FBI geniuses was trying to trace my hang ups. You have news?"

"Jason Carrington's attorney contacted me this morning with an offer. He claims he's found a judge who'll hear the paternity plea—"

"You're kidding."

"I wish I were. He's offering you the chance to keep the case out of court. He won't pursue if you'll agree to the test."

"Can you block the motion?" Lunch threatened to revolt. She wanted to run. Fear her legs wouldn't hold her weight kept her rooted to the spot. Nobody was drawing blood or plucking hairs from her son. "What honest judge would agree to listen to this monster?"

"I don't know. Morgan Anderson assures me Jason's attending counseling sessions, taking all the right steps to show the court he's remorseful."

"You're warning me, aren't you? Bracing me for the possibility of him winning." Leigh's voice rose and shook. She pulled in a quick breath to compose herself. She had to calm down unless she wanted everyone in the office to know her problems. "How does he benefit by knowing if he's Ethan's father? He wants something."

"There's no court date set, and months may pass before the case comes up on the docket. This action is a maneuver to scare you into complying. I recommend you refuse his offer. Remember, the final decision is yours."

"Tell the bastard I said no." Leigh fought to keep from saying something a lot stronger.

"One word of caution. The longer this drags on, the more time Carrington has to establish himself as worthy of a chance to know his son."

"Then I'd better prove he's the one harassing me."

"What? When did this happen?"

Leigh went through every detail. She described the bike being delivered from nowhere, the break-in, how he'd pinned her body to the bed, and the punches the bastard had thrown. "That's all, you already know about the hang ups."

"You can't keep this kind of information from me," Karen admonished, a hard edge to her voice. "Call me with the smallest invasion of your privacy. Nothing is insignificant."

Leigh ended the call and stared into the distance as she tried to regain composure. "Where's Romeo?" She needed to give him the phone back.

"I sent him to his desk. You okay?" J.T.'s eyes softened.

"I'm beginning to wonder if anything will ever be okay again. Romeo couldn't trace the calls either, could he?"

J.T.'s expression confirmed what she'd expected.

"Occasionally, after somebody says something can't be done, Romeo works a miracle. But not this time."

Her phone buzzed. J.T. rose, leaned over her shoulder, and they both read the words on the caller ID aloud. "Caller unknown."

She punched the silent button, refusing to answer.

"I'm going to catch this bastard alone and stomp him," he growled his words.

Leigh put her hand on his arm, feeling the tense muscles. "Please don't. You have to leave him alone or things will look worse for me."

Chapter Thirteen

A slight breeze told J.T. she'd walked up behind him. Leigh's scent was out of place, considering he stood over a man with more than half his head missing and blood spattered everywhere. J.T. turned away from the macabre, dark scene, and yellow tape toward her.

"Hey." She smiled up at him. Even with the floodlights casting shadows across her face, she was stunning.

"Hey, yourself." J.T. froze in his tracks when her hand brushed across his back as she stepped around him to view the crime scene. Lightning streaks trailed her fingers.

"Charlie," she addressed one of the techs.

"Detective McBride. Long time no see." The tech closest to the victim gave Leigh a wide grin. "You're looking good."

J.T. stared at the guy in disbelief. Bent over a dead body and he still found time to flirt with Leigh.

"I could say the same about you."

A flash of heat hit J.T. when she favored Charlie by returning his silly grin.

"He's been killing his victims in the daylight. There's a reason he changed." J.T. moved around the perimeter, speaking to no one in particular.

"You ID the victim?" Leigh asked.

"Dr. Nathan Holibeck," Charlie said over his shoulder.

J.T. ignored the tightness in his chest at the familiarity Leigh and

Charlie displayed. She leaned down, walked under the tape, and stood close to her friend, who'd squatted next to the body. J.T. clenched his jaw while the word *mine* cycled through his brain like a revolving sign.

"A doctor this time. What else can you tell me?" she asked.

"He was dead the second the bullet hit him." Charlie looked directly at her. "I'd say the shooter was on the top of a building, but I'm only guessing at this point."

J.T. shook off his irritation. "ID clipped on his scrubs says he worked at Piedmont Hospital."

"Took one hell of a shot to be this accurate at night." A second tech stood and turned in a circle, studying the tops of the buildings in the cluster of high-rise apartments. "Wonder if he sticks around to watch the aftermath."

"Don't know." J.T. glanced at the tech. He moved around behind Leigh, her gaze remained on the dead man. Not once had she flinched at the face of death. Had she ever taken a life? He'd taken his share in Afghanistan. He carried no regret and no remorse for doing his job. The faces he remembered late at night were his friends; the ones who hadn't come home.

"Do we know if he lived around here?" she asked.

"According to his driver's license, he's in the Emerson Towers," Charlie answered.

"He was almost home." She pointed to the apartment nearest them. "Expensive digs. This area is known for families, I'll bet he had a wife."

"My money's with you." J.T. slid his hand around her bicep. The hit of pleasure at her slight shudder pleased him. He led the way across the parking lot into the building and waited for the elevator.

"You and Charlie are—what?"

Blue eyes shimmered like the sun bouncing off the ocean when she leaned back against the handrail. "Cousins."

Her one-word delivery made J.T. wish for a rock to crawl under as he followed her into the elevator. "Looked like kissing cousins, the way he drooled over you."

116 |

Her smile broadened. She flashed enough pearly white teeth to make any dentist proud.

The damn elevator stopped. With a swish, the doors opened, and she was gone. He caught up with her in front of the dead man's apartment.

J.T. gave the ringer a push and held his ID up to the peephole.

A dark-haired, middle-aged woman opened the door. Eyes wide, she clutched the tie on her yellow terrycloth bathrobe with both hands. J.T. identified himself and Leigh.

"What's wrong?" Her lips trembled.

"Doctor Nathan Holibeck live here?" J.T. asked, sliding his ID into his back pocket.

"Yes. He's not home. I'm his mother."

"May we come in?" Leigh's tone was soft and soothing.

The woman steadied herself by resting her hand on the doorframe before she waved them inside.

"Ma'am, are you alone?"

"No. My grandson is sleeping. I stay with him."

"Maybe you should sit." Leigh followed the woman to the couch.

"It's my daughter-in-law, isn't it?" Her gaze shifted from Leigh to J.T. and back, confusion clouded her eyes.

"Why would you think that?" Leigh asked.

"She's in Piedmont Hospital. She tripped and fell."

J.T. felt Leigh's gaze on him even before he glanced in her direction. The older woman's face paled. She moved down the couch, away from Leigh, and glanced at the door expectantly. "My son's a doctor at Piedmont. He should be home soon."

Leigh spoke first. "I'm sorry to inform you Nathan won't be coming home."

She handled the situation with ease. Her gentle approach led the woman through the routine questions and answers. Standing by her side while she called her husband and broke the news.

The trip down the elevator was somber. "How does the sniper learn about these battered women? Is he a doctor too?"

"Could be." J.T. rested his hand on Leigh's lower back. "Olivia's interviewing a witness. Let's check in with her."

"I hope she's got something that will help." Leigh fell in step with him, her strides too short to match his so he slowed down.

They stopped next to Olivia and listened as she wrapped up an interview.

"Thanks, I appreciate your time." She gave her card to the man and sent him on his way.

"They were no help," she said without waiting for J.T. to ask. "The stories were the same, they heard the gunshot, hit the ground, and stayed down for a few minutes. None of them could say where the shot came from."

"The victim's wife is in Piedmont Hospital. Leigh and I are going to head over there."

"I'll interview the last witness and then head home."

"Good enough." He turned to Leigh. "Do you want to ride to the hospital with me? I'll bring you back to your car."

"No. I'll meet you at the front entrance."

****

Jason's eyes opened fast when he realized the burner cell was ringing. He rolled to the side of the bed and answered. "This better be important," he whispered.

"She's on the move and alone," Vick spoke rapidly. "She just left a murder scene."

"And?" Jason glanced over his shoulder at the sleeping woman in his bed.

"Some guy got his head blown off."

"You imbecile. I don't give a shit about the dead man. Talk to me about Leigh."

"She left the crime scene, but she ain't headed toward her house."

"You followed her?"

"Yeah. I'm about half of a mile behind her on Peachtree Boulevard. The road is deserted."

"Is your shit together enough to test her driving skills?"

"Fuckin' A. Long as you pay to fix any damage done to my pickup."

"Just don't kill her. And don't call me back. I'll be busy." Jason ended the call, took a leak, and went back to bed. He slid in behind his secretary, reached around and squeezed her plump tit.

"What time is it?" she mumbled as she rolled to check the clock on the nightstand.

"Time to party." He wanted her wide-awake in case he needed an alibi. He pushed his rock-hard cock against her ass. "I've got something for you."

****

Leigh sipped the strong Stop-N-Shop coffee. She'd taken the side streets while J.T. had roared full speed onto I-85 toward the hospital. She needed to think. Why had he called Olivia? Leigh had worked the previous crime scene with him. Had she not been good enough? Was she being overly sensitive? Shit. What was she thinking? She wasn't a real member of the team. She was Atlanta CID, the liaison, an outsider. She wasn't a part of the federal family. J.T. could call in whom he wanted. Period.

A light rain had started, not heavy, just enough that she turned on her windshield wipers. The streets were slick and deserted. The usually busy hospital district seemed to have bedded down for the night.

Leigh turned the radio up when she heard the announcer break in about tonight's sniper attack. Bright headlights came out of nowhere, blinding her vision in the rearview mirror. The vehicle streaked past and then pulled right in front of her. Red brake lights flashed. The pickup cut too close. Leigh hit her brakes and cut to the right to move into the empty lane. Her left front fender clipped the truck's rear bumper. Leigh's tire traction broke on the wet road and the rear of her car swung around. Fear and hot coffee exploded simultaneously. She took her foot off the brake and tried to steer into the skid. The seatbelt tightened, preventing her body from slamming against the door. The steering wheel jerked out of her hands. The car careened out of control.

Seconds became eternity as life shifted to a crawl and the world moved in slow motion. No! Her mind raced, her thoughts turning to Ethan.

The airbag exploded in her face when the car slammed into a streetlight. Coughing and gasping, she pushed at the already deflating bag. Her pulse hammered against her ribs. Air burst in and out of her chest in gasps. She hit the seatbelt and let out a sigh of relief when the buckle released. Freedom. She pushed to open the door and failed. Terror clawed through her brain. The other half of her car was bent around the lamppost, and the bow in her car had messed up the driver's side, too. Trapped. She fought back the panic pulsing through her veins. No hysteria. Not now. Get to safety.

"Are you hurt?" A man's voice said.

Startled, a scream released before she could stop it. She shook her head. "I don't think so."

"Stay calm. I'll try to open the door."

She pushed with her shoulder while he pulled. The lock gave, and the door moved. The opening wasn't big enough for her to slip out.

"We need help. My cell is dead, if you'll loan me yours, I'll call 9-1-1."

She reached for her phone in the drink holder but it wasn't there. "Hang on." She tried to do as the man suggested and stay calm. She found it where it had slid between the seats. "Got it."

He placed one foot against the car and tried again. Groaning, as if in pain, the metal surrendered a few more inches. Leigh sucked in a deep breath and squeezed through. She put her feet on the ground only to find her knees had turned to rubber.

The stranger's arm wrapped around her. "Here, now. Can't have you falling."

Maybe fifty, he wasn't a lot taller than Leigh. He shouldered her weight and helped her to the curb, easing her down. He knelt in front of her, and his kind, brown eyes did a quick visual inspection.

Thunder shook the pavement. Lighting shattered the dark, racing through the sky. Leigh and the stranger looked to the heavens as the rain came down in buckets.

"You've got a few scratches, and you'll be stiff in the morning."

"I'll bet." Leigh welcomed the wetness on her face, hoping it would help calm her mind.

"Nothing appears to be broken." He frowned and leaned closer. "Your face and neck are bruised."

"Yeah. It's beginning to look like I have a target on my back." She offered him a trembling hand. "I'm Leigh."

His grip was strong and steady. "Doyle. And I might be able to help you."

****

Doyle's frayed nerves and fractured thoughts bounced all over the place. His hands trembled as he parked in the employee lot at the hospital. Had fate sent him down the back roads after the execution? The driver of the pickup who'd caused the accident hadn't stopped to render aid.

He hadn't recognized the woman at first. Not until he noticed the bruises. She'd been in the ER not too long ago where he'd overheard her conversation. Hadn't concerned himself because she was a cop. He'd thought she could take care of herself. Well, maybe fate had just proven him wrong.

A cold knot formed and settled in the pit of his stomach as he hurried inside. What if Ellen had gone looking for him? Or the night housekeeping supervisor? He frantically tried to think of a viable excuse for not being on the job. Lies on top of more lies. His relationship with her complicated his missions. Keeping Ellen innocent would take a lot of work.

Could he keep up the façade? For the abused women, he'd try.

Chapter Fourteen

Sitting in the back of the ambulance, Leigh's anxiety eased when J.T. parked and stepped out of his car. Again, he'd responded to her call for help without question. Long, deliberate strides brought him closer and closer through the torrential downpour. His dark expression dared anyone to stop him. Rain-soaked, his white shirt clung to every sinew and muscle. J.T. stopped two feet away, his breathing harsh and uneven. His gaze scrutinized her body. Satisfied she wasn't injured, the lines on his beautiful face relaxed as he extended his arms.

Leigh slid from the back of the ambulance into the safety of his powerful grasp. His head bowed and rested on top of hers. She leaned into his chest, listened to his heart pound, and drew from his strength while rain sluiced over them.

"Thank you for coming," she said, pressing her face harder against him.

"Count on it." His words were thick and husky. "What happened?"

She repeated everything she'd said to the patrolman, adding how the accident had felt deliberate. When she'd told him about the man who helped her, J.T.'s gaze never left her face. She babbled, unable to stop, and he listened patiently.

"My memory's a little fuzzy, and I probably sound crazy. I'm sure he said his name was Doyle." She shoved the wet hair off her face. "And he favored the pictures of Doyle Preston. Or did the name association screw with my mind?" She blinked her eyes, tried to clear her blurry head. "My Good Samaritan paled at the sight of my badge and gun. Suddenly, he needed to go. He stood and jogged toward a car parked down the block. I yelled for him to wait." She shrugged a shoulder. "He didn't."

"Then you called me?"

"Yes."

"Maybe the guy did look like him. You were shaken up and weak, no way you could have stopped him." J.T. tucked a dripping strand of hair behind her ear. "Short of shooting him in the back." His eyebrows went up, he grinned, and his dimple sunk in.

Leigh laughed at his out-of-character attempt at humor. "I'll admit my knees gave out. I couldn't stand, much less aim."

"Let's check with the EMTs. If you don't need to go to the hospital, I'm taking you home."

"I need a wrecker to pick up my car."

"I'll get one of the cops to call one." J.T.'s arm slid around her. "Put your weight on me."

He returned her to the waiting medical technicians and the Atlanta patrol officers. Within minutes, she'd signed a release for the ambulance driver and thanked everybody for their help.

Snuggled tightly against him, their shoes squished as they crossed the street on the way to his car. Leigh stopped him when they reached the sidewalk. "We can't get in your Corvette like this."

"As much as I love my car, the other option is against the law." His deep-throated chuckle vibrated his ribcage against her.

"I wasn't suggesting we get naked," she quickly added. The heat from his stare seared right through her.

"Come on." He looked down at her through wet eyelashes and stepped closer, resting her weight against him.

"But . . ." She felt protected with his arm around her.

"Stop worrying. The seats are leather, and you're shivering."

"Nerves. Reality's setting in." Her teeth chattered.

"Hang on," He reached behind her and retrieved a windbreaker from behind back seat. "Put this on."

Leigh wrapped his jacket around her and huddled in the seat. He started the car and shoved his wet, black hair off his face. Despite the warm night, J.T. turned on the heater full blast, and then shifted the Corvette into supersonic. Highway signs whizzed by while Leigh did her best to stop shivering. The interior temperature of the car had to be frying his brain, yet her bones were still cold. Weird, because it was warm outside. He'd shot down an off-ramp before Leigh realized they were in the parking garage of an apartment building.

"Why did we come here?"

"My place was closer. You're freezing. One way or the other, those clothes are coming off."

His argument sounded reasonable, so she didn't protest. He parked, and Leigh tried to get out on her own. The world spun. She reached behind her, searching for something to grab. What she found was J.T.'s strong, firm hand.

"I shouldn't have let you refuse a trip to the hospital."

"Don't like hospitals." Leigh rested her head on his shoulder when he lifted her in his arms and hurried for the elevator. He put her down long enough to unlock his door, walk her inside, and kick it closed.

"I can stand," she protested.

He ignored her by scooping her up again and carrying her straight to the bathroom, where he turned on the shower one-handed.

"I'm putting you down. Get under the warm water. Don't make me undress you."

"I can do this. Go." If she hadn't been so shaken and cold, she might've accepted his offer.

"I'll be right outside the door." He kissed her on the forehead and left her with the memory of his warm lips on her skin.

Leigh struggled with her wet jeans. Her strength had vanished. Damn, she'd had a wreck, not major surgery. She stripped, opened the glass door, and stepped into the heat. Leigh sank on a bench seat, thankful his shower had one, and let the water flow over her body.

Slowly, the tension and terror subsided. Had she let her imagination get out of control? How crazy did she sound insisting her crash wasn't an accident? Had the Good Samaritan said his name was Doyle? And why hadn't he hung around unless he'd wanted to avoid the police?

J.T.'s voice snapped her out of her deep thoughts. "I'm leaving dry clothes on the floor by the door." He was silent for a minute. "Leigh. Say something, or I'm coming in."

Another time, she might've considered his words a dare. "I'm okay. I'll be out in a sec."

"Yell if you need me."

Her fingertips had wrinkled by the time she turned off the shower. She grabbed the towel hanging on the nearby hook and dried off. She'd been trying to remember everything the man who'd helped her had said. It nagged at her while she ran a comb through her hair. She opened the door, gathered the clothes off the floor, and dressed quickly. They swallowed her, but at least they were warm and dry. And his. She tightened the drawstring on the running shorts and slid the baggy Falcons sweatshirt over her head.

She found him at the kitchen stove stirring something in a pan. She slid onto a swivel barstool while he poured soup. Her eyes followed the movements of his hands. Strong, long fingers carried a bowl and napkin to the breakfast bar. Safe inside his apartment, she was glad he'd brought her here. Seeing him wearing camo pants, a black T-shirt, and no shoes, he made her forget she ached all over. He scanned her from head to toe, nodded approvingly, and handed her a spoon.

"Nice outfit." His eyes grew dark and sultry.

"Thanks." Leigh stared into the bowl of chicken noodle soup. She wanted to ask him to wrap those bare, muscular arms around her. To put his hands on her. To touch her. Skin to skin. Instead, she rolled her sleeves up then stabbed the spoon in her bowl and stirred. "I seem to be thanking you a lot."

"Feel free to stop. It's not necessary." He tossed the empty can in the recycling bin. "Although you do seem to be a trouble magnet."

Her breath caught. "I'm sorry."

J.T. walked to her and swiveled the stool around. He wedged himself between her knees and bracketed her body by placing his hands on the counter. "You can stop saying that too. It so happens, I like trouble."

The vein in his neck throbbed with the rapid rhythm of his heart. She boldly opened her thighs wider to better accommodate his hips. The air crackled with an electrical charge, heat raced up her legs, and she sighed. "You do?"

"Yep." He tucked her damp hair behind her ears, stepped back, and spun her back to her soup. "Now eat, before I forget you were just in a car wreck."

Leigh waited for the blood in her veins to cool while she tried to steady the spoon enough to get a bite to her mouth. Her breasts were swollen with need. Not to mention the rapid pulsing between her legs. Geesh, she'd been seconds away from ripping the shirt off his back and tasting every inch of his bare flesh. She finished eating and pushed the bowl away. "That was good."

"I'm available for weekend work," J.T. said, his gaze locked on her mouth. "I left Casey a lengthy update on his voicemail. Told him we'd be in the field and not to look for us tomorrow."

"Ethan is with his sitter so he's fine until tomorrow. I'll call Mom in the morning. She'll take charge of him. I need to stop by my house before we check in with the hospital."

"Works for me. Your wet clothes are in the dryer. I'm going to clean up and change while you make your phone call. Make yourself at home."

"Thank you. I'll see you in the morning."

"No problem." He pointed at a door. "Your room."

Under different circumstances, she might've invited him to join her in the shower earlier. Fear of having sex with him wouldn't keep her out of his bed, the danger to Ethan would. He'd fall in love with

J.T., and his heart would be broken when the temporary fun of playing daddy wore off and J.T. moved on. She slid off the stool, walked to the spare room, entered, and then closed the door behind her.

****

Leigh was sitting at the breakfast bar with two cups of coffee in front of her when J.T. removed her wrinkled clothes from the dryer.

Last night he'd wanted to kiss her until she begged him for release. No, he wanted to devour her. Repeatedly. If he didn't get her naked and under him soon, he'd be the one having an accident. J.T. looped the lacy, beige bra over his finger, and gathered the rest in his arms. Her panties fell off the stack and landed on his foot. His moan echoed off the washer and dryer. He snatched them up and stuck them on the bottom of the pile, out of sight. He adjusted himself, willed his aching hard-on to go away, and went to join her. He plopped her things on the breakfast bar and pointing to one of the cups. "Is that for me?"

"Good morning to you too." Leigh smiled, pushing the mug in front of him." Dark circles under her eyes reflected a lack of rest. He'd been lusting over her underwear while she'd tried to recover from a car accident.

"We need to interview Mrs. Holibeck."

"Give me ten minutes to dress."

J.T. drank his coffee, his thoughts on Leigh's car wrapped around the streetlight. She believed the pickup driver had deliberately cut in front of her and caused the accident. Her instincts were good, and sometimes your gut was all you had to go on. He needed someone to gather information without drawing attention. He dug his old friend's card out of the catchall drawer and punched in his number.

By the time Leigh came back to the kitchen, J.T. had arranged a meeting with David Campbell tonight. Prying into her background went against everything he believed in, but Leigh needed help.

"After we stop at my house for me to change clothes, and we leave the hospital, will you drop me at a car rental agency?" She placed his

128 |

neatly folded running shorts and sweatshirt on the end of the counter. Then all that's left is the insurance company."

"Of course." J.T. took their empty cups to the kitchen and set them in the sink. "Ready?"

Leigh picked up her phone off the breakfast bar. She stopped in the middle of the room, staring at her cell with a puzzled expression.

"I turned it off last night while you were in the shower. You needed some peace and quiet to recover from the accident."

"What the hell were you thinking?" Color rushed up her neck, across her face, and disappeared into her hairline. "What if there'd been an emergency?"

"You can 'what if' all you want. Somebody would have taken care of it." J.T. walked to the door, opened it, and waited.

Leigh's face turned bright red. She stormed across the room and stopped in front of him. "That's the most irresponsible thing I've ever heard. I'm not only a law enforcement officer, I'm a mother." She was in his face yelling and couldn't stop. "The psycho father of my son is out there. He broke into my house and assaulted me. I don't doubt that he ran me off the road. There's no such thing as somebody else taking care of my life."

"Leigh," J.T. was confused. "What the hell?"

" 'Hell' would be if something happened to my son!" Her eyes closed while her chest rose and fell rapidly.

The emotional bond she shared with her parents and the love she showed for her son was way past J.T.'s level of understanding. His grandmother had never clung to him. She'd pushed him out into the world and encouraged his independence. Except for his grandmother, the devotion and commitment gene didn't run in his family's DNA.

He reached out and cupped her cheeks. "I'm sorry. Maybe I'll never understand, but I won't do it again." He didn't wait for a response. Instead, he walked down the hall and pushed the call button.

The elevator arrived, saving him from more of her anger. The trip to the ground floor was silent as was the walk to his car.

"I want to change clothes before we go to the hospital," she said before she pulled the car door closed.

"Okay." J.T. drove through a fast-food restaurant and picked up breakfast on the way to her house. He followed her inside and spread the food out on her kitchen table while she changed clothes. Before her egg and bacon croissant had cooled, she sat across from him, polished and professional. The guilt-ridden mother, along with the frightened woman, he'd held in his arms last night, had been replaced by the cop. She hadn't complained about being stiff or sore, but the fact she moved slower didn't escape him.

"You up to this? It's okay if you take the day off." J.T. gathered the trash when they'd finished and tossed it in the garbage.

"I'm fine." On her way out, she leaned down, picked up a plastic baseball bat, and dropped it in a toy box.

The sight of her heart-shaped ass bent over in front of him flooded his groin with blood. Christ, her taut, firm cheeks would fit perfectly in his hands. "Yes," he said mostly to himself. Had he missed a chance to make love to her last night? If so, it was a chance he might not get back. "You are fine."

She straightened her shoulders and tossed him a frown over her shoulder. He waited for a comment that didn't come.

****

"She ain't hurt, but she needs a new car." Vick's lips curled into something he'd probably call a smile.

"Good. If anybody questions my whereabouts, I have an alibi. Too bad you couldn't stick around and take pictures." Jason pushed the plate with his uneaten meal away. Vick's putrid breath wafted across the table, polluting the air and Jason's food.

Vick picked up a fist-full of fries and stuffed them in his mouth. "I got the hell away from there. Wasn't taking a chance on getting questioned. Besides, the bitch tagged my rear end. You owe me a taillight."

"What else?"

"She didn't go home last night. I was listening when she showed up with her boyfriend in tow. Stayed long enough for her to change clothes."

"She spent the night with him?"

"How the hell would I know? I followed him but didn't introduce myself."

"Find out this bastard's name and where he lives. If you can't do it, I know a PI who'll be happy to take my money."

Vick leaned over the table. "You gonna kill her soon?"

"Shut the fuck up." Jason looked around to see if anyone had overheard Vick. "Not yet. Keep the new guy you hired close by. We'll use him again. Soon as I pick the right spot and time."

"He's up for anything we need."

"I'll be in touch." Jason dropped a twenty on the table.

****

Nana surprised J.T. and accepted the invitation to the picnic with the McBride family. She not only wanted to go, she intended to bring a covered dish. He'd been counting on her for an excuse to get himself out of attending. Instead, they'd talked through her entire list of recipes before settling on banana pudding. Hell, a trip to the park would do her good.

"Supper was delicious." J.T. patted his full stomach. "I'm miserable."

"I'm glad you enjoyed the dumplings. I need to get a new housekeeper because Elva wanted me to use store-bought biscuits. Can you imagine a more disgusting idea?"

"Walk me out." He ignored her question. She and Elva were exactly alike, bullheaded, and opinionated. J.T. knew better than to take sides.

"No need to eat and run," Nana protested.

"I have an appointment."

"You mean a date?"

"No, an appointment. I'm meeting David Campbell." He extended his hand and helped her stand. "Saturday may be warm. I can offer our apologies."

A sparkle lit up her eyes. "Come down here."

J.T. bent at the hips and lowered his face to hers. "Ma'am?"

Her eyes narrowed as if she were looking for clues or an untruth. Nobody on the planet made him squirm, except her. She had this uncanny ability to see right through him. Nana was the reason he'd understood Ethan's story about his mother having a third eye.

"Why don't you want me to meet your new girl?" She cupped his cheek to ensure he didn't look away or pull up where she'd have to crane her neck.

"She's not my girl. You're my one and only." He wanted Leigh in the worst way. The urge was physical, sexual, But not in a long-term way. And nothing to be thinking about while he was with his grandmother.

"But she could be." Nana nodded her head, passing judgment before she met Leigh. "I feel it. She may be the one."

"Don't start matchmaking or I'll cancel for sure." Damn, he wished Nana would give up on him. "You know how I feel about marriage, passing on bad genes, and parenting. We Nobles are a bunch of drunks who never cared about anybody but ourselves. How long do you think I'd last before I ruined her life? A year? Five? Besides, she's got a kid to raise."

The instant hurt in Nana's eyes ripped a chunk out of his heart, and a shot of remorse burned through him. He covered her small hand on his face with his. "You're the exception. You got all the good stuff. All the virtue and decency are in you."

"Why do you talk such nonsense? You're a good man." She patted his cheek firmly. "God and I made sure of that."

"If you say so." He straightened his spine and led her to the backdoor. "I'll call you with a time for Saturday."

"Teddy?" she called from the porch.

"Ma'am?" A sharp pain stabbed the base of his skull. If she called him Teddy on Saturday—

"You're still looking for your mother, aren't you?"

"Tonight, Nana. I promise. I'll look tonight."

****

"Do you think J.T. plays football?"

Leigh worried about Ethan getting attached because he'd talked about J.T. all through supper. Tucked in bed, Ethan's mind had drifted to the upcoming picnic.

"He's not coming to entertain you. His grandmother will be with him, and he'll want to spend time with the adults." Leigh stood and pulled the sheet up to his chin. She smoothed Ethan's curly hair off his forehead, clearing a spot for one more kiss. "I love you. You know that, right?"

He snuggled down under the sheet. "Right."

Leigh backed to the door, taking one last look at her son before flipping the light switch.

"I love you more," Ethan called out.

Leigh heaved a sigh. J.T. was already on her mind too much. Wednesday night he'd left no doubt he wanted her, and she'd almost gone to his bed instead of the guestroom. Would the world come to an end if she spent the night in his arms? She wanted him to satisfy the pulsing sexual need he generated way down deep inside her. Could she have sex with him without emotional ties or expectations?

She tested the locks on the doors and windows and double-checked the alarm before she headed to bed. She'd scrimped and saved to buy this house. She'd researched carefully and had selected this neighborhood especially for her son. Tonight, she slid between the sheets and listened to the sounds of the night. Every rustle of the bushes made her jump. She snapped off the bedside lamp and willed herself to relax. Leigh rolled to her side, slipped her hand under her pillow, and found comfort in the cool handle of her pistol.

Chapter Fifteen

J.T. scanned the nightclub to get his bearings. His stomach lurched at the smell of cigarettes and stale beer. Famous for hundreds of different brands of beer, the Kegger had been a favorite hangout of law enforcement for years. Knowing his mother wouldn't be caught dead in a place full of cops didn't keep him from looking. A young couple and two men sat at the mahogany bar, which ran the length of one wall. The small bandstand was dark and empty as were many of the tables.

A loud crowd had bunched up around the pool tables. Tournament night.

"Over here."

David Campbell met J.T. halfway, grabbed his hand, and pulled him close for the mandatory shoulder bump. J.T. snagged a waitress and ordered a rum and coke without the rum. She frowned, taking a second to get his meaning. She laughed with a slight nod of her head.

"Thanks for meeting me."

"Anytime, man. Looks like the sniper is leading you feds around by your dicks. Any way I can help?"

"No, but I do need your help with something personal."

"Sure! Since the wife left, I'm at loose ends. So, what's this personal thing I can do for you?"

"I need information."

"Let's hear it."

J.T. gave David a brief overview of Leigh's break-in, attack, telephone hang ups, and car wreck. Hell, after he'd told the story out loud, the conspiracy theory didn't sound farfetched at all. "I can't prove Carrington's harassing her. However, this shit didn't start until after he got out of prison."

"He'll be easy to check out." David drained his beer and waved at the waitress. "Let's get out of here and walk down to Harriman's."

J.T. had several places to hit before he looked Nana in the eye and honestly said he'd hunted for his mother. None of them as nice as where he and David were headed.

They walked a few blocks and stopped on a corner. While they waited for the light to change, J.T. checked out every female coming or going.

"Still looking for your mom?"

"Off and on." The question caught J.T. off guard. "My grandmother keeps the pressure on. I have no idea why."

"The hell you don't." David chuckled. "You don't turn your back on family."

"When did you get promoted to shrink?"

David's laugh lines disappeared. "Your mama's sick, man. And you know it."

"I won't find her in this neighborhood." J.T. stayed on the sidewalk when the light changed. "I'm going to pass on Harriman's. There are a few places I need to check out."

"Next time you go barhopping, change out of your FBI clothes. The natives will be more cooperative."

****

J.T. surprised her by walking around the conference table and plopping down next to her. Casey was waiting for a briefing from the team on what progress, if any, they'd made on the sniper case.

Leigh sat quietly while he and Olivia gave their findings on Dr. Holibeck's murder. J.T. turned the reporting on their interview with the doctor's wife, Carla, over to Leigh. Without looking at him, she flipped open her notes and brought everyone up to speed. "Mrs. Holibeck had been sedated so we were unable to interview her. The report from the doctor stated she was hysterical and incoherent when she was brought into the ER. She has multiple contusions on her face, her bottom lip is split, and she has a nasty cut on her cheek."

The muscles in Casey's jaw twitched. "What we have is one more dead man and no clues. The press is eating us alive. Somebody had to have seen something."

"Every crackpot in Atlanta's called us or the TV station." Romeo patted his stack of notes. "We need help if we plan on interviewing all these people."

Casey ran his fingers through his hair. "Then we'll add a team to conduct them." He leaned forward and rested his arms on the table. "Romeo, run the names against the system and identify the people who sound legit. Send them and we'll assign the rookies to Olivia. Leigh and J.T. you two continue working the boxes from New York."

J.T. held a hand up to stop anyone from leaving after Leigh pushed back from the table. He turned and looked at her for a long moment.

"You wanted to tell the team about the accident?"

Leigh blew out a breath. Everyone in the room leaned forward, so she described her wreck. "The odds must be astronomical against him being our sniper, but my hero's name was Doyle," she said, wrapping up her comments. "And he looked like Preston."

"Stranger things have happened," Casey said. "Don't blame yourself for not stopping him. Sounds like you're lucky to be alive."

Leigh left the meeting wondering if she'd overreacted to Olivia being at the crime scene. What was with her paranoia? Lack of sleep? Worry? Fear for Ethan?

J.T. bypassed his desk and headed for the smaller conference room housing the case files. "Leigh, let's keep digging."

"Right behind you."

Romeo caught up with her. "Don't forget this."

Leigh recognized the folder containing the phone contacts she'd found in the boxes from New York. "Thanks, Romeo. Did you locate anyone?"

"But of course." Romeo handed Leigh the list. "You doubted me, too?"

"If she didn't, she should've." J.T. sat and scooted an unopened box in front of him.

"You'll appreciate me someday," Romeo said. Wiping fake tears from his eyes, he left the room.

J.T. dragged a chair over next to his, patting the seat for Leigh to join him. She breathed in the air around him. Images of the great outdoors and clean mountain mornings played with her senses. "I'd like to ask you something."

"Shoot." He faced her, his green eyes looking into hers.

"Why'd you call Olivia to the crime scene?"

"I called her to give you time to get Ethan squared away. Why?"

J.T. being thoughtful wasn't one of the possibilities she'd considered. Her pride couldn't allow it though, even if she appreciated his intention.

"I've never asked for favors or special treatment. Don't assume I'm less of a law enforcement officer because I have a child."

His gaze hardened. "Nobody gets 'special treatment' when I'm working a murder."

Leigh had to be honest. "I'm not a permanent part of the team. I assumed her presence was your way of reminding me."

"Were you jealous?"

That he stared at her openly and lustfully, made her squirm in her chair.

"In your dreams."

"You're in them frequently."

All the blood ran from her head and flooded her lower belly. Moisture dampened her panties. The only way out was to laugh. "Okay, I'm glad we cleared up my misunderstanding."

She handed him the folder Romeo had given her.

"What did he find?" J.T.'s eyes sparkled like a kid on Christmas morning.

Leigh cleared her throat, shifting in her chair. No doubt about it, he enjoyed making her uncomfortable. "Two telephone numbers, one address."

"That's all?"

"Which is more than we had." She scolded him to get her mind off the heat rushing south. "You want to call or go?"

"Go. Hanging up on me is easy. Slamming the door in my face . . . not so much."

"Let's go." She bravely accepted his hand when he offered to help her stand. She wasn't prepared for the tenderness when he gently squeezed. His green eyes shimmered, and the solitary dimple flashed fleetingly.

"If it made you unhappy I called Olivia, I'm sorry. Know this. I'll never intentionally hurt you." He released her hand and walked out the door.

"But I'm afraid you will—unintentionally—someday," Leigh whispered to the empty room.

****

Jason leaned back in his office chair, closed his eyes, and pictured Leigh's car crashing. Adrenaline rushed through his system. The bold knock ruined his daydream. He snorted a light hit, dropped the small vial in his pocket before he stood, and opened the door.

His father stormed into the room with fisted hands and teeth clamped shut. "Why was the door locked? I don't appreciate having to knock like I'm your lackey."

"Sorry, Dad." Jason laced his tone of voice with contrition. Daddy needed to be careful; the posturing old fool didn't intimidate Jason. Tragic accidents happened all the time. "I didn't want office gossip started if someone overheard my phone conversation."

"What conversation?"

Jason's mind whirred as he searched for a believable lie. "With Morgan." He was smarter and faster on his feet than the old man had ever been. "No one seems to care my son is being kept from me."

"Do I need to get involved?"

"No, Dad. You have to let me handle this."

"Good enough." He dismissed the topic with a wave of his hand.

"What can I do for you?"

"Your mother wants you to join us this weekend in the Hamptons."

"Absolutely." Could life get any easier? With his alibi buttoned down tight, he'd finalize his plans. He had something special in mind. Something to remind Leigh that no matter where she went or who she was with he could get to her. Of course, she'd try to tie it back to him. Soon he'd prove she was a neurotic liar who blamed him for all her bad fortune.

He'd come up with many different ways for her to die. His latest idea made the most sense. The Carrington name and money would get the hearing moved up. After the court ruled in his favor for the paternity test, and the results came back proving he was the father, he'd file for visitation rights. High-strung, unstable Leigh would hang the boy and then herself. Watching them both swing was barely enough payment for the time he'd spent in prison. Jason would watch her horror as the boy's life left his body. Then he'd watch her legs jerk, tongue swell, and eyes bug out.

****

J.T. stood in his kitchen and spun the swivel seat of the stool around. Jesus Christ. He remembered Leigh opening her thighs, making room for him to get closer.

"Oh, hell." He snatched his cell off the counter and called her.

"J.T.?" The sound of Ethan's laughter in the background brought instant regret. J.T. had interrupted something. Had he gone too far? Goddamn, he wanted her. Maybe one taste would be enough. Maybe,

140 |

she'd turn him down. Maybe, he'd lost his fucking mind.

"Has there been another murder?" she asked.

"No. I was wondering if you'd eaten." The next few seconds of silence made him wish he could turn back time. Calling her was a mistake.

"We're fixing to wash supper dishes."

"I see. My bad luck." He smiled at her use of the southern slang. He'd made her nervous.

"I haven't had dessert," she said on a soft sigh.

The undercurrent in her voice blasted through the line. The bulge in his pants grew harder. "I can pick you up in thirty . . . no, twenty minutes."

"No. I'm at Mom and Dad's. I'll come to you."

J.T. stared at the cell in his hand. A hot Lamborghini on the open highway would struggle to keep up with the fire racing through his veins. If she drove fast, she'd be standing in his apartment in thirty minutes. He spun on his heel and conducted a mental survey. Damn, he didn't own a bottle of wine or have a beer in the fridge to offer her. He scrubbed his hand across the stubble on his chin, a shower and shave were definitely in order.

Halfway down the hall, J.T. stopped dead still. His insides were jumping all over the place. The Iceman, a nickname his Marine buddies had given him, was nervous as hell, and rightfully so. A relationship with Leigh was an active minefield. He had to be careful where he stepped, or the affair would blow sky high. She could wind up a casualty. He didn't like the idea of causing her pain.

Almost two hours after his shower, J.T. accepted the fact she'd changed her mind. Something between anger and relief stirred under the surface. She'd simply come to her senses. He clicked on the TV, found a baseball game, and kicked back in his recliner. Okay, maybe he was pissed. How the hell was he supposed to act tomorrow at the picnic?

At the sound of a knock, he bolted from his chair and hit the off button on the remote. Without checking the peephole, he opened the door. "I was worried."

"I should've told you I had to go home first."

His concern for her safety disappeared. Everything, including his name, disappeared as his eyes feasted on her. She wore a blue dress with tiny straps. No knot tonight, she'd left her hair down. Blonde curls cascaded over her shoulders and down her back. A weird pain stabbed his heart. Her blue eyes seemed wider than usual and uneasiness radiated from them.

Leigh's eyebrows quirked up. "May I come in?"

"Oh, yeah." J.T. swung the door wide and ran his hand across his eyes. "My God, you're stunning."

She walked straight to his wall of windows and looked out over the city. "I love this view. You live in the perfect location."

"I like it." He shut the door and flipped the deadbolt without taking his eyes off her. Her flinch when the lock snapped didn't escape him. He closed the distance between them and stood behind her, giving himself a minute to breathe in her presence. God, he'd wanted her since the first time he'd laid eyes on her. An image of her with her legs wrapped around him never strayed far from his mind.

"I'm glad you're here."

"Back to using four-word sentences. I'm nervous enough without you not talking to me."

"You render me speechless." He placed his palms on her arms. Soft, supple skin yielded to his grip.

She leaned her head back against him. "Still with the four words."

He slid one hand to rest on her stomach and smiled at the slight tremor of her muscles. She turned and looked up into his eyes. He covered her lush lips with his. Slid his tongue inside her mouth to sample her sweet taste. Repeatedly, he dove deep into the wet, warmth, and drew from her. When her knees buckled, and she leaned into him with a moan, he moved back.

"What would you like me to say? Want me to say you blew my

mind by coming here? Or how I was scared shitless you'd decided against it? Or how I want you more than I want to breathe?"

Her breath hitched, and her eyes darkened to that need-you shade of blue. The air around them filled with her scent rolling through his senses.

"All of the above," she whispered.

J.T. moved his hands to her ass and lifted her against his erection. She ground her body against him with a moan. He leaned down, his face inches away from hers. "Kiss me."

****

Leigh cupped the back of his neck, pulling his head down. She nipped at the corners of his mouth, breathing in his woody cologne. Tracing the inner edges with the tip of her tongue, reveling in the intense heat coming from his muscular body, she covered his lips with hers.

His grip tightened as he angled his head and returned her kiss. Hard and hot. Hungry and fierce. Their tongues fought for dominance. She moved her hands to his hips and pulled him tighter. She needed more. Needed to touch his skin. Needed to feel the fire.

She tore herself away from the kiss and looked into his green eyes, glistening with desire. Swallowing hard, she found her voice. "Show me you're glad."

"Hang on." J.T.'s breath was raspy. He lifted her and headed for his bedroom.

Barely aware of her shoes hitting the floor, Leigh's dress rode up, leaving nothing except thin lace protecting her hypersensitive skin from the rock-hard ridge pushing at his jeans. She locked her legs around his hips and dug her fingers into his shoulders. She groaned in pleasure and ground into him, desperate for more, the friction sending shock waves through her body.

"Clothes," she complained, tugging at his shirt.

He deposited her on the bed, stretching out next to her. Garments were peeled off and tossed aside. His hungry, predatory eyes seared her naked flesh. Then his mouth was on her, and his hard, muscular frame stretched next to hers. Moving, tasting, licking, sending her higher as pressure built inside. She floated on sensation, arching into him while his hands, large and possessive, touched, caressed, and stroked. Leigh completely surrendered to her body's frantic needs and cravings. His long fingers blistered a line of heat up her thigh. So near. So close.

"Please." Leigh wasn't sure she'd spoken out loud until J.T. pulled his mouth from her breast and pushed himself up on one elbow. His palm rubbed in a circle above her pubic bone.

"Talk to me." His words were thick and husky with desire. Emerald fire danced in his eyes.

"Touch me."

"Here?" His hand slipped between her legs.

"God, yes," she cried out.

His fingers stroked her center. Leigh closed her eyes and lifted her hips in hunger. She whimpered a frenzied plea for more. She stripped her soul bare and asked for what she wanted. "Inside me. Please."

She felt the momentary loss when his hands left her body. He grabbed a condom from the bedside table, and seconds later, his weight hovered over her. His knee nudged her thighs apart, and he pressed into her. Slowly, farther, until she was full, and he was buried inside her. The connection stirred something deeper, something stronger.

"Jesus Christ. Finally." His gaze bore into hers.

His thrusts, timed and measured, drove her wild. Years of denying herself, refusing to trust, rejecting her emotions and sexuality vanished. She matched his pace until the past disappeared. Only the two of them existed.

Fire streaked through her, pushing. Pushing her closer to the edge. His hand slipped between them and his fingers found her clit.

"Oh. God."

"I want it all, Leigh. For me. Come on me."

His words broke down the last barrier keeping her from coming completely undone. Her world shattered. Pressure rushed from down deep, exploding into pleasure.

****

J.T. dug deep and held himself together until she gave him everything. Her legs tightened around his waist. Her gaze met his, her eyes darkened to midnight blue, and she climaxed. Lost in the heat of her eyes, he ground his hips against her, relishing her release. When she pulsed, clenching around him, and drew him deeper, he lost it. With a groan, he came to the rhythm of her orgasm.

Gasping for air, he rolled to his side and pulled her close. She'd completely surrendered and given him a precious gift. He knew this one night of passion wasn't enough. He'd never get enough of her. He was close to surrendering his soul.

He propped up on one elbow. She'd trusted him. Opened herself to him. Given freely. A heavy weight wrapped around his shoulders. He had to be honest about his feelings on marriage and family. Tears glistened in her eyes. A hard punch surged inside his chest.

"Crying sort of hurts a guy's ego." He brushed his thumb across her damp eyelashes. "Can you tell me?"

"It's been . . ."

"A long time." He tried to help when her words trailed off.

"Yeah."

"If it makes you feel any better, I'm not in the habit of hopping from bed to bed. It's been a while for me too." He confided, honestly.

"Almost seven years?"

Reality struck like a bolt of lightning. She'd given him way more than her body. She hadn't had sex since before Ethan was born. Coming to him tonight was more special to her than he'd imagined. His heart slid up to the back of his throat and wedged. For the next few hours, he intended to show her how much he appreciated her honesty.

"Don't look so stricken," she smiled. "It was my choice. Until you came along, no one stirred my hormones. You were wonderful by the way."

"*We* were wonderful," he corrected. Her smile broadened, and his heart spun in rhythm with his mind. "And nowhere near finished."

His cell buzzed. He kissed her swollen lips, palmed her breast, lifting it to taste her sweet nipple. God, she was beautiful. "I've imagined you naked in my bed, but the real thing is so much better."

She raked her gaze down his body, hunger in her eyes. Blood rushed to his cock. His cell vibrated again. J.T. ignored the interruption.

She licked her lips. "Could be important, you should answer."

"Nothing's more important than this." He tongued a rosy, beaded nipple. Jesus Christ, her breasts were soft and silky. A few fades bruises lingered but nothing could mar their beauty.

The insistent buzzing forced his attention away from her luscious body. A dark cloud formed above his head when he saw the caller ID. He answered the call with two words. "I'm busy."

"How busy?" David snapped back. "Because I'm sitting here looking at your mama."

Chapter Sixteen

"Damn it." J.T. swung his feet to the floor. Holding the phone close to his ear, he turned his back to Leigh. His mind raced in a dozen different directions. Why now? Why tonight? "Talk to me."

"Your mama is sitting in my cruiser, drunk and madder than hell. She pissed off her boyfriend and he dumped her."

"Where?" Without looking back, he reached for Leigh. His heart tumbled to his feet when her fingers wound around his, and she scooted close enough to rest her head on his back.

"Entrance to Woodruff Park."

"She picked a nasty part of town." Shit. No options. Promises made to Nana were kept. If he didn't go get his mother right now, no telling when she'd turn up again.

"What do you want me to do?" David asked.

J.T. turned and stared into Leigh's blue eyes. Open and trusting, she waited quietly. Fuck. He had to go get his mother. The die had been cast a long time ago.

"Can you hang on to her until I get there?"

"I can't make her stay, short of arresting her. Didn't think you'd want her hauled downtown."

Fuck. In an instant, J.T.'s plans for the rest of the evening collapsed. He ended the call and tossed the phone on the nightstand.

"I'm sorry, Leigh. I have to go." He dropped his head into his hands.

A chill skittered across where her warmth and gentle touch had been when she moved away. Shit. When he raised his eyes to her, she'd already slipped into her underwear.

"I understand." She lifted one shoulder.

She stepped into the dress he'd casually tossed across the room and glanced up at him. The embarrassment on her face stunned him, turned him inside out. Jesus Christ, just shoot me.

"It's not like we're involved or something." She shrugged but didn't look at him.

J.T. slid on his jeans. He'd hurt her, yet she held her expression, giving nothing away. What the fuck could he say to make her understand? He'd never been good at lying. But to blurt out he had to go pick up his drunken mother wasn't something he wanted to do. His family history wasn't something he discussed.

"Leigh, come here." He caught her by the arm. "Please."

She allowed him to wrap his arms around her only after he tugged. Her spine felt rigid as a steel rod under his hands.

"I shouldn't have come." Her body shifted away from his.

"You can't mean that, not after what just happened. I've wanted you from the first day we met, and I'll never regret tonight." J.T. cupped her face in his hands, leaned down, and kissed her soft lips. He thumbed away the smudged mascara under her eyes.

All the air left his lungs when she politely nodded and backed away. He had to tell her the truth. Had to trust her. Pride be damned. "It's—my mother." Damn, doing the right thing shouldn't be this hard. Leigh deserved to know, even if telling her wiped out any chance of a relationship between them. He couldn't remember regretting anything this much. "She's drunk and needs my help."

"Oh." Leigh's tone had a distinct surprised ring. A slight smile appeared before she walked over and slid on her shoes. "Then why aren't you dressing? We need to go."

She had that stubborn look she got when she wasn't taking no for an answer. He formed a time out sign with his hands. "There is no 'we' when the subject is my mother." J.T. jerked his shirt over his head to find Leigh holding his socks and his tennis shoes. "You have no idea how ugly this could get."

"Doesn't matter. You've been there for me."

"One has nothing to do with the other." Damn, he wanted to drag her back to bed. The way she stood nose-to-nose when she argued was one hell of a turn on. Her chin jutted forward, and her gaze locked on him.

"I'm going with you." She cupped his jaw, stroking his chin with her thumb. "Don't argue."

A twinge of regret and disappointment zinged him. After tonight, after she met his mother, he doubted she'd want to continue whatever it was they were doing. "Then saddle up."

She led the way to the elevator and pushed the button. J.T. spun her around and kissed her, pinning her body to his with his hands. Before this night was over, he'd lose her. For now, he'd take what he could—while he could. The doors parted, and, without breaking the hold, they boarded.

"Maybe we are involved," she breathlessly retracted her earlier comment.

J.T. tightened his grip around her waist and mentally prepared for the mother he hadn't seen in . . . funny, he couldn't say how many years for sure.

"Or something," he agreed.

****

They'd decided it made sense to take her rental since three people wouldn't fit in his Corvette. The nerve in his jaw twitched. His muscles tensed, tendons bulged, and heat boiled off his body. His reaction to helping his mother was more than unsettling.

He knew far more about her personal life than she'd intended to reveal. It was time he shared. Leigh looked forward to learning more about him. Judging from his behavior, she was about to be privy to things he didn't want her to know.

Unable to resist touching him, she reached across to stroke his cheek. He cocked his head and rested the scar in her hand. Allowing her this peek inside his private life meant he trusted her. Warmth surrounded her heart. Tears swirled, blurring her vision.

He glanced at her and then quickly looked away. Realization slammed into her. Why hadn't she noticed it before? Sure, he appeared to be angry with his mother, but his eyes, oh, God, his eyes told a different story. Buried beneath the surface, he struggled to mask intense pain.

J.T. left the freeway and drove into an area Leigh recognized as one of the roughest neighborhoods in Atlanta. Homeless people, drunks, and junkies hung out there. He parked behind a patrol car. A burly cop got out and walked back to them. His shoulders were as wide as his smile.

"You know him?" Atlanta was a big city, and Leigh wasn't surprised when she didn't recognize the patrolman.

"We grew up together," J.T. explained while he rolled down his window.

The patrolman leaned down and reached across J.T.'s chest, ignoring him completely.

"David Campbell, ma'am. Pleased to meet you."

She returned the warm grasp. "Leigh McBride."

"Where is she?" J.T. pushed David's arm away.

"She walked down the block to the Cycle House."

"Why the hell didn't you hold her?" J.T. demanded.

"I did you a favor by not arresting her for public intoxication."

A few more pieces of the puzzle fell into place for Leigh.

J.T. stabbed his fingers through his hair and shook his head.

"Prying her out of the bar may take a wrecker."

"It's lucky I spotted her. I don't usually work on this side of town."

"I wouldn't call it lucky, but I appreciate you calling."

"I've got to get back into service. Nice to have met you, ma'am."

David's arm stretched inside again, and his hand clamped on J.T.'s shoulder. "Be aware—you'll be dealing with a rough crowd."

"And the good news keeps coming," J.T. muttered.

He drove two blocks and parked across the street from the run-down building. Dark of night didn't hide the peeling paint or the pitiful condition of the bar. Burned out light bulbs on the sign provided very limited lighting for the four motorcycles and three cars in the small lot. A hard chill rolled down Leigh's spine. She'd patrolled the streets for years before her promotion. A joint like this spelled trouble.

"If your mom's in that dump, we need to get her out." Leigh reached into the back seat for her purse to retrieve her badge and gun.

"There you go using the 'we' word again."

Leigh winced at his cutting tone. "I may not be dressed like one, but I am a cop."

J.T. blew out a breath, unbuckled, and turned to face her. The staggering expression of defeat in his eyes ripped her heart to shreds.

"I wasn't challenging your ability." He reached over and tucked her hair behind her ears, his touch soft and caressing. "Look at you, beautiful with your hair down, wearing a dress. I take you in with me, I'm asking for trouble. Bottom line, I'm trying to spare you from what may be an ugly scene."

She slid across the seat and wrapped her arms around his broad shoulders. He leaned into her, buried his face in her hair, and held on tightly. She wouldn't force herself into something this personal. If he wanted to shield her from meeting his mother, Leigh would back off. They both had parts of their lives tucked away in private. Tears welled for the man in her arms.

"Okay. I'll wait here for you."

"Leigh, I can't deal with my mother and worry about you out here alone." He held his hands up in surrender. "I need you to trust me. I want you to go home."

"No." Shocked at her quick refusal, she scrambled for a reason. "I can't leave you here without a ride." His warm lips covered hers and silenced

151 |

her argument.

"I'll call a cab. We'll talk tomorrow." He glanced at the clock on the dash. "No, today at the picnic." One eyebrow lifted. "That's if I'm still invited."

"Ethan's looking forward to seeing you there. And so is his mother."

Leigh drove away slowly as J.T. crossed the street. No way was she abandoning him. She'd honor his request and let him handle his mother. Nothing said she couldn't park down the street and wait until he was safely on his way home.

****

The aroma of coffee woke J.T. from a deep sleep. Bright sunlight streamed through the window and across his grandmother's living room. He pushed himself up, remembering why he'd spent the night on Nana's sleeper sofa. Mother.

He'd never forget the sympathy behind Leigh's eyes before she'd driven away. How many times had he seen the same expression when he was a kid? Local people knew Roxanne Noble was his mother, and they'd taken pity on him. Like when he was seventeen and the cop yanked him out of class because she'd passed out in the women's restroom of a bar. The principal had allowed J.T. to leave school, go get her, and drive her home.

Had he agreed to answer Leigh's questions today at the picnic? It might've been easier to have taken her inside the bar with him. One good dose of his mother and he wouldn't have to explain anything. Leigh would gather her son close and run as fast and far away as she could.

Dressing meant slipping on shoes and a shirt since he'd slept in his jeans. He secured the last button on the way to the kitchen to join his grandmother. Going topless was begging for an ass chewing at Nana's house.

"Hello, gorgeous." He spoke from the doorway.

"Good morning." She filled a mug and carried it to him, holding her face up for a kiss. "Sorry if I woke you. I wanted to let you sleep a while."

"You didn't get back to bed until after four either. You're the one who should be resting." Nana had insisted on her daughter bathing before getting into J.T.'s old bed.

"I'll bet I slept better than you did."

"The couch was fine." He turned a kitchen chair backward and sat facing her.

She took her apron from the key rack he'd made in woodshop and tied it around her waist before joining him at the table. Her eyes were bright and full of excitement. Hell, she looked rejuvenated.

"You do glow this morning."

"My daughter is home, thanks to you."

"You wanted her here. Here's where I brought her." J.T. cast an irritated glance down the hall toward where his mother slept.

"This is where she belongs."

"Nana," he disagreed with a shake of the head. "She needs another stint in rehab."

"You know how well the last time worked."

"When was the last time she tried to get sober?"

"What time do I need to be dressed and ready?"

J.T. laughed at her blatant attempt to change the subject. "You're not seriously considering leaving Mother here with Elva?"

"She's a retired nurse. She understands the situation." She waved her hand as if his concerns were unfounded. "We're keeping our commitment to your lady friend's family. What's her name again?"

"Leigh McBride. Don't try to change the subject."

"McBride's a good Irish name. Besides, Roxanne will sleep all day."

"When she sobers up, she'll be gone. She doesn't want to be around us." Nana was setting herself up for another heartbreak. Her ability to forgive time and time again boggled his mind.

"Teddy," Nana said in her don't-argue-with-me tone. "Roxanne is aware of how much she put you through. She needs my help."

"Put me through? That's nothing," J.T. scoffed. "You've got your hopes up, and she'll disappoint you. Again. Maybe, you should stay here today. Keep an eye on the silverware, because she'll clean you out and never look back."

"Now you're talking nonsense, she's in no condition to go anywhere." She stood and pushed her chair back in place. Her lips drew into a thin line, and she stabbed her hands on her hips, sending a clear message. She was through talking. "I have to get ready."

"Yes, ma'am." He surrendered, knowing he'd been defeated.

"I hope we're stopping by your apartment so you can clean up before we go to the park."

"I will if you won't call me Teddy."

"James Theodore is a perfectly good name. What's your problem?"

"That's the deal." He stood and grinned down at her, determined to win at least one argument. "Take it or leave it."

"I'll take it."

"We should go as soon as Elva gets here to babysit Mama. Lunch is at one."

J.T. poured a fresh cup of coffee and carried it outside to wait while Nana dressed. He wandered over to his grandmother's favorite chair next to her flower garden. Maybe the fresh air would weaken the odors from the bar that had permeated his skin. No shower or clean clothes would get the stench from his nostrils or his memory.

Last night, his mother had put on one hell of a show when he'd walked into the bar. She'd jumped out of her chair, run to him, and then thrown her arms around him. Her performance had been a ruse. Her sallow skin, coated with makeup and smudged red lipstick, gave her a ghoulish appearance. The stale smell of body odor and urine coming off her had slammed into his senses and brought back memories he wanted to forget.

He'd called a taxi and then he'd alerted his grandmother they were coming. Caring for a drunk put a huge strain on a person, and J.T. worried about his grandmother. His biggest fear was the aftermath and if she'd recover from her broken heart when his mother left again.

At least Elva was around during the day to be his eyes. Once again, Nana would try to reform his mother. Once again, Mama would take advantage of the one person who'd protect and give in to her. Years ago, he learned change couldn't be forced on another person, and his mother was no exception.

He dreaded seeing Leigh today. Dreaded the pity in her eyes. Refusing to feel or deal with emotions, he pushed them to the back of his mind.

****

The tension in Leigh's neck eased when a car pulled into a parking spot next to hers. Ethan would've been crushed had J.T. changed his mind about coming.

Sex with him had been wonderful, but the episode with his mother had been on Leigh's mind since he'd ushered the woman into a taxi, and Leigh had driven away. She'd been unable to sleep. Her thoughts moved back and forth between remembering his hands on her body to the hurt in his eyes when he'd spoken of his mother.

"He's here." Ethan jumped to his feet. His voice reverberated through the park.

Her dad chuckled. "Take my hand, kiddo. Let's go greet him properly."

J.T. waved, walked around to the passenger's side, and then helped an older woman out.

"Holy cow," her mother whispered. "Even in jeans and a pullover, he's beautiful."

"Mother," Leigh playfully scolded.

"How'd it go last night?"

"What?"

"You left my house to go out with him. So?"

"I can't believe you asked such a question." Leigh put both hands on her cheeks as if she could hold off the blood rushing to her face or the smile spreading across her face.

"Why wouldn't I ask? He's drop-dead gorgeous. And look—" Her voice turned syrupy. "He's kind to his grandmother."

Leigh remained at the picnic table, determined not to rush to J.T.'s side. Her heart stuttered when Ethan extended his arms. His little face turned up to his hero. She held her breath, watching closely. How J.T. treated her son meant more to her than he could imagine.

He lifted Ethan in the air, tossed him over his head, settled him on his shoulders, and together they joined the party. The small woman next to J.T. shook hands with everyone while Leigh introduced them. The older woman's emerald green eyes twinkled, and a single dimple dug deep in her cheek when she smiled.

"Mrs. Noble." Leigh warmed to her immediately. "I'm glad you came."

"So am I. Everyone calls me Nana." She took Leigh's hand and patted. "Unless you already have one in your family."

"Nana it is. I'm Leigh."

"You're tall. I like that. You'd better be strong if you're going to hold your own with Te—"

"Nana," J.T. interrupted. "Come sit in the shade and watch us play football. Unless you want to quarterback." He swung Ethan down to his side. "You used to have a good arm."

"I'll be fine right here with Sara and Leland."

"Looks like Leigh will have to call the plays." J.T. offered his hand to Leigh.

She welcomed the jolt of heat as he tugged her to the open area in the park. His dimple winked, and his gaze softened. He squeezed her hand, sending her heart into its cartwheel thing. Last night, Leigh had finally gone to sleep after her heart had convinced her brain J.T. was worth taking a chance. They'd talk about the dynamics of him and his mother later today. Her alcoholism was troublesome and something to be considered because of Ethan.

Today they'd enjoy life. Enjoy spending time together.

Chapter Seventeen

J.T. hated the conversation he was about to initiate. His lunch swirled, moving slowly upward. Leigh deserved better, and he'd end this before she was hurt. While Ethan played, J.T. guided her to an empty table, sitting next to her.

"This is probably as close as we'll get to being alone today. I need to thank you for last night."

"Thank me?" Leigh's cheeks flushed. Her chest and face had turned the same shade when she'd climaxed. Pink was now his favorite color. "Do you always thank women for having sex with you?"

"That's not what I meant." He slid his arm around her waist. "But speaking of sex, the first part of the night ended way too soon." Jesus Christ, his sex drive was out of control. In a public place with family on all sides, all he could think about was being inside her and making her cry out in pleasure.

"I agree. To be honest, I'm curious." Her gaze locked on his and held. "Was last night a one-time-only thing or what?"

"Leigh." His stomach knotted. Damn, she didn't pull her punches. "I'm not the kind of guy you should allow into your life. As you learned last night, my family's not the typical happy-ever-after bunch."

Her shoulders stiffened, and her blue eyes turned icy. The last thing he wanted was to piss her off. "I appreciate your concern. But what's your family got to do with us having sex?"

"We Nobles hurt people who care about us. We screw up other

people's lives and then walk away. Disappear. It's in our DNA. Hell, my old man couldn't be bothered to marry my mother. If the guy was even my father."

"Please. You're saying if you break my heart, it won't be your fault. We'll blame genetics?" She seared him to the soles of his shoes with a blue-fire stare.

Damned if he wasn't tempted to check for blisters.

"You're nuts if you expect me to buy into this psycho-babble. That's pure crap," she said, her tone laden with disgust. "DNA? Fuck you. You're responsible for your actions."

"That's not what I meant." Damn, he'd hurt her by running his mouth. Maybe he had been hiding behind his parents. "Ethan has you for a mother. I believe in nurture versus nature, too. I'm high risk."

"Getting out of bed is a risk. Life is a risk."

"Leigh, I—" He couldn't. Wouldn't walk away. He hadn't been this fucked up over a woman since he was sixteen. And that had ended badly after his mother had shown up at school drunk, needing money.

"Why are you here?"

"I wish the hell I knew. There's a difference in what I want and what's best for you." He studied her face, memorizing every inch of creamy, soft skin.

"I don't appreciate other people deciding what's best for me." Her eyes moistened. She blinked rapidly and turned her gaze toward Ethan, who'd run to the swings. Thankfully, he appeared to be oblivious to their conversation.

"Please don't cry."

"Do not misunderstand." She spoke through narrowed lips. "I have a bad habit of crying when I get mad, and then I get pissed at myself for appearing weak."

"I wasn't trying to piss you off. I'm telling you how it is."

"I'm not sure you know what 'it' is."

"Like I said last night, my mother's a drunk." He spit out the words. "A-fall-down-in-the-street—sometimes she doesn't recognize

159 |

me—never-to-be-recovered-lush."

"You're not your mother. Alcoholism happens in the best of families." Her words were rapid-fire, clipped, and sharp as a scalpel.

His chest squeezed, registering her words. Then hope hit him. Hard. She hadn't lumped him into the same category as his mother. But maybe Leigh didn't understand how hard this disease was on a family.

"We're not talking about your run of the mill alcoholic family. She's exactly like her father, and their blood runs through my veins. She's an alcoholic who dumped me on her mother's doorstep when I was seven. She drifted in and out when she got in trouble or was broke. One day I discovered she could come or go because it didn't matter to me anymore."

"Had to be hard on a young boy." Her gaze full of compassion searched his face.

He'd known this picnic wasn't a good idea. And now more than anything, he wanted to drag her into his arms and tell her he was sorry he'd never be the man she expected him to be.

"I had my grandmother." J.T. would've preferred Leigh stayed pissed. Anger was much easier to deal with than the expression of sympathy on her face.

"What about your dad?" Her tone softened.

"Lives in Macon." He forced himself to answer. Her questions opened doors he kept locked. "He found somebody worth marrying. They have a son."

"Leaving no room in his life for the old one," Leigh said softly. "Is that why you don't want anyone to get close to you?"

"What?" J.T. regretted following this line of conversation. Talking about personal shit was not his idea of fun. Leigh's words hit sore spots and raw nerves. She was way too deep inside his head.

"Don't play dumb with me. You keep people at arm's length, protecting yourself from being hurt when they leave." She sucked in a deep breath and continued. "It's not your fault your parents left you."

Bitterness rolled up in the back of his throat. He didn't want or need her pity. And he didn't think he was to blame that neither of his parents cared enough to stick around. Did he?

She glanced at Ethan, who waved and kept swinging. "Why did you go to your mother last night?"

"My grandmother asked me to find her and bring her home." Thank God, she'd changed the subject. "Mission accomplished."

"You still love her. You must."

With such a tender heart, Leigh obviously couldn't comprehend that sometimes, shutting down your feelings and emotions was the only way to survive. Coming from a close family, she'd never understand his dysfunctional one. "Love? That's a stretch. Because she gave birth to me, I guess, maybe so. I have no respect for her. None."

"Yet, you and your grandmother have a great deal of affection for each other. She beamed with pride every time she looked at you today."

"It was me and her against the world. I owe her a lot."

"You're a lot like her. Aren't you?"

"No. I take after my grandfather and mother."

"Nonsense." Leigh's eyebrows drew together. "I heard Nana talk at lunch. You two deliver phrases the same way. You have the same stubborn jaw line and forest green eyes." She ran a finger across his chin. "And when she smiled, I saw where your dimple came from."

"Her looks are the only markers we share. She's forgiving and trusting. I'm nothing like her." Leigh's eyebrows dipped. She wasn't running scared, and he tamped down the pleasure that gave him.

"Are you trying to chase me away?" Hard lines formed around her mouth. "If so, be a big boy and spit it out. Don't use your family as an excuse."

He stood, gripped her by the arms, and pulled her to her feet. Truth was, he wanted nothing more than to kiss her, but there were things he needed to say.

"I'm giving you options. Information you can use to make decisions. My mother's supposed to be sleeping off her hangover at my grandmother's. In reality, she's probably searching for anything valuable she can steal and sell."

Leigh's gaze never faltered. Never darkened as others had when they'd learned about his family. She stood her ground, and his respect grew immeasurably.

"For a guy who doesn't talk in long sentences, you're on a roll today. You've said a lot, but not enough to make me run into the street shrieking at you to stay away from me."

Ethan came charging across the playground at full speed, ending their discussion. Leigh would have to decide whether she'd accept what J.T. had to offer or walk away. Could she settle for a relationship in which there was no future, no permanence? God in heaven, he hoped so.

"I need to go." Ethan danced from one foot to the other.

"Then I guess we'd better hurry."

J.T. followed along behind as Leigh held Ethan's hand on the walk to the picnic table where J.T.'s grandmother and Leland sat.

"Where's Mom?" Leigh asked on the way past.

"Rinsing off a few dishes in the restroom." Leland glanced at his watch. "She's been gone a long time."

"I'll help her," Leigh answered over her shoulder.

J.T. sat on the bench beside his grandmother. Her gaze tracked Leigh as she and Ethan kept walking. Nana patted his knee and beamed up at him.

"She's a beautiful young woman, your Leigh."

J.T. stifled a laugh when Leland cocked his head sideways with both eyebrows raised in question.

"Nana, Leigh's not my woman." *Sure, she is. I'm just too fucked up to admit it.* "But she is beautiful."

"Dad, the lights are out and Mom's not answering," Leigh yelled.

Leland stood, the color draining from his face. "I'm coming."

J.T. grabbed the flashlight from his car and rushed to Leigh. "Where's your dad?"

"Around back looking for the main switch. The lights are out

162 |

inside and it's pitch dark. If Mom's in there, she's not answering." Relief filled her eyes when Nana walked up and took Ethan's hand.

"We'll find another restroom."

J.T. followed Leigh into the darkness, sweeping the flashlight beam back and forth across the cement floor. Sara lay crumpled in a heap next to the far wall, still as death.

"Mom." Leigh dropped to her knees, pushing her mother's hair off her face. "She's unconscious."

"Don't move her." He squatted next to her, placing two fingers on Sara's neck. "Her pulse is strong." He dialed 9-1-1 then succinctly gave the operator the necessary information. Light flooded the room and, shortly, Leland ran in wild-eyed, full of worry and concern.

The room closed in, and he needed air. Felt out of place. He couldn't forget for a minute he was an outsider. "I'm stepping out to check on my grandmother and Ethan."

Leigh wiped her hand on her shorts. "Go ahead."

Outside, he scanned the area. No Nana. No Ethan. Sweat popped out on J.T.'s forehead. Nana wasn't in the best of health, and Ethan could be a handful.

"We're here," Nana called from across the playground.

The raging fire of panic subsided as relief rushed across his damp skin. He jogged to where she and Ethan played on the swings.

"You scared the shit out of me," he grumbled, wrapping his arms around her.

"Teddy." She stood up tall and blistered him with her "now-you've-done-it" look. "Watch your language. We took a potty break. Afterward, our young friend gave me a grand tour of the park. We decided to let you grownups take care of business."

"You always know the right thing to do."

"What happened? Is Sara okay?" she whispered.

"Don't know, but she was unconscious when I left. Leigh had blood on her hand from the back of her mother's head." Distant sirens screamed in the background. "Police and ambulance will be here soon."

163 |

Ethan moved closer, taking in every word. J.T. knelt and ruffled the boy's curly hair. He kept his voice low and calm. "Your grandmother bumped her head, and I called the paramedics. Those guys know their stuff. They'll take good care of her. No worries, okay?"

"Can I see?"

"Probably best if you wait for your Mom to decide. Why don't you hang out with Nana for a while, okay?"

Ethan's little face scrunched up into a series of wrinkles, his mouth pursed for a second. "Okay." He ran off after a grasshopper, unaware of the seriousness of the drama unfolding around him.

"We're going to swing for a while," Nana said.

Her easygoing confidence concerned him. With her stubborn streak, she'd do too much. "Nana, if you start getting tired or too warm—"

She silenced him with her hand on his arm. "Go. Come get us when you're ready."

J.T. jogged back to Leigh, who hovered over her mother. "How's she doing?"

"She's coming around," Leigh said, looking over her shoulder at him.

Her blue eyes, filled with anguish, ripped out his heart. God, he wanted to take her pain from her. He'd never felt this helpless.

"Dad, I'll be right back." She rose and walked outside. "Ethan?" Her eyes widened while she searched the park.

"Still with my grandmother, I'll have to take her home. There's no way Ethan can stay with her. Not as long as my mother's at Nana's. And I've never kept a kid before."

Leigh faced him. Her lips tightened, dipping at the corners, and the color drained from her cheeks. "Ethan goes with me."

J.T. recognized that look all too well. Back when he was a kid people looked at him with pity. No more. He accepted sympathy from no one. Not even Leigh. Especially not Leigh.

He shifted the boulder sitting on his heart and stepped out of the way. She went to meet the EMTs and a squad car. J.T. walked to where Nana and Ethan played. Together, they went back to the McBride family.

Sara was awake when they wheeled her out and loaded her gurney for the trip to the hospital. She'd remembered a voice whispering, "This is for Leigh."

That memory would bring a rush of cops to the scene. The stress on Leigh's face pulled at him. He understood how badly she wanted to stay and take part in the investigation, yet she had to leave. She gathered her son and followed the ambulance with her dad.

As suddenly as it began, the flurry of activity was over. The little corner of the park the McBride's and Noble's had filled with laughter was eerily still and quiet. J.T. and his grandmother were alone. Strangely enough, alone felt normal.

Maybe alone was the way he'd always be.

****

Doyle's heart damn near popped like a balloon pierced with a pin. He faced the wall, ducking his head. The lady cop walked right past him. Thank God, no one paid attention to the man scrubbing the floor. He hurried after his cleaning cart, which he'd parked in the hall. No doubt, if her mother was in the ER, the family would talk. He'd keep his back turned, continue cleaning, yet be close enough to listen.

He'd caught a glimpse of goodness in the young woman's eyes the night of her accident. Something about her had struck a chord in him and reminded him of his daughter. The fading bruise on her face and her frightened blue eyes had upset him. Instinct told him this particular cop was good people. Her situation intrigued him.

A little boy bounded into her arms. Doyle wrung out the mop and kept working.

"Mom?" The kid's eyes were wide as saucers, and a frown marred his face. "Is Mimi gonna die?" His voice shook, and his bottom lip trembled.

"No. The doctors will fix her right up. She'll be home playing with you in no time."

She cuddled him close, reminding Doyle of when he used to hold his daughter the same way. Curiosity moved him closer. A man stood and joined her, sliding his arm protectively around her waist. Doyle noticed the way the man stood, with his hip turned slightly, always keeping the bulge under his jacket within reach. Another cop?

The little boy wiggled out of his mother's arms when another woman entered the room. "Look. DeeDee's here."

"There's my buddy." She perched him on her hip and bounced her way across to the young cop. "If it's okay with you, Ethan and I are hitting the snow cone stand. Then he can come help me figure out my new video game. Pick him up whenever."

"Can I, Mom?" the boy pleaded.

"I guess so."

She moved aside to let Doyle get his mop-bucket past them. He held his breath that she wouldn't notice, but he couldn't mop the same square tile over and over. He relaxed when she walked out of the room with the boy and another woman.

Doyle was covering for one of the other porters. The nurses in the ER were used to him being underfoot. Nobody would give him a second glance when he went through emptying all the trash receptacles. Locating information on the middle-aged woman tended to by the trauma team would be easy. Fate pushed him to help the lady cop. Not right away, but he intended to look into her troubles.

Chapter Eighteen

Jason's day was about to get a whole lot better. The burner in his pocket vibrated again. Leigh should be sporting a few new bruises after the picnic, and Vick would have all the details. "How'd your trip to the park go?"

"Nothing like you wanted." Vick babbled like an old woman.

As always, Jason's temples pounded while he endured Vick's lame excuses. The imbeciles had attacked Leigh's mother. Jason didn't give a flying fuck about her. She wasn't the target. Vick's friend was to beat the shit out of Leigh again. "You're saying the whole thing turned into a clusterfuck."

"Well, maybe you should've checked out that park before you sent us out there. The bitch was never alone. The boyfriend was in her ass pocket all day. I changed the plans before somebody got curious about two men hanging around the swings."

He closed his eyes as anger morphed to rage. He imagined cutting the idiot's throat. "You still there?" Vick asked in a meeker, more subservient tone.

"I'm listening. Go on." Jason swallowed and kept his voice level because Vick had to believe all was forgiven.

"The mother spent the night in the hospital. My guy told the old woman the beating was a special delivery for her daughter. Your girl got the message."

Jason smiled at that. "What else have you learned?"

"That every morning the boyfriend stops at a corner newspaper stand after he picks up his coffee."

"So?" Jason scrubbed a hand over his face. He didn't give a shit about reading habits.

"I'm gettin' there. I talked to the old man at the newsstand. Cost me a C-note to learn the fed's name is J.T. Noble. Ain't got his address yet."

"Good. Stay close. I'll swing by tonight. I want to hear more about the park."

"Okay." Vick cleared his throat.

"And, Vick, I want your helper taken care of. Today."

"No problem."

Jason leaned back in his chair. A surge of adrenaline rushed through his body faster than a hit of cocaine. Killing Vick wouldn't be a major setback. After all, men like him were plentiful. And expendable.

The Carrington wealth far surpassed what Jason could spend in a lifetime. For a company whose worth ranked in the top four-hundred in *Forbes* magazine, dear old dad was extremely lax in controls and careless where he placed his trust. The money Jason filtered to an offshore bank in his name was his little secret.

****

J.T. turned toward the sound of Leigh's footsteps. He'd recognize them blindfolded. Her purposeful strides and sensible low heels made their distinctive sound. Damn, he liked the way she moved. The gentle sway of her hips, her narrow waist, and curvy hips, reminded him of when those long legs had clamped around him while he'd carried her to bed.

Forcing his attention back to his computer didn't stop him from wondering if he'd blown his chances with her. Exposing her to his family hadn't been easy, but she'd deserved to hear the truth. A relationship with him would be a temporary situation, nothing more.

"Good morning. Did I miss anything important at the meeting?" She slid into her chair, her face unreadable.

"Not much," he answered. "Olivia made notes. They're on your desk."

Leigh waved a silent thank you. "Thanks for sitting with me at the hospital. And the texts you sent." One hand went straight to her head, patting an imagined stray hair back into place, but her eyes were the biggest tell. Tired with a hint of hurt.

"How's your mom?" he asked.

"The doctor insisted she stay in the hospital overnight. She went home Sunday with a shaved circle and a couple of stitches in the back of her head. I'll tell her you asked. How about your mom. Did she have a rough weekend?"

Her tone was formal, like when she'd first been assigned to work with him. Maybe he should've gone to the hospital Sunday, but by the time he'd left his grandmother's, he wasn't fit company. "According to her, she's dying." He waved off any impending questions. "She's not. It's part of the drying out process."

Forcing himself to concentrate on the case, J.T. plotted out their next move. He was getting tired of running in place where the sniper was concerned.

"Hunting for Doyle Preston's old contacts is getting us nowhere. Let's concentrate on how he obtains current information. Who knew about the widows' recent abuse? Those wives talked to somebody."

"Let's find out." Leigh pushed away from her desk and stood, sliding her purse strap over her shoulder.

He followed her to the elevator. As soon as the doors slid closed, his resolve to keep his hands off her began to slip. The need to touch her, to hold her in his arms went to war with his common sense. By the time they arrived at the car, he caved. The door handle was in her grasp when he reached around her, covering her hand with his. She turned. Tired blue eyes looked up at him.

He crushed her lips under his, feeding like a starved man. He swallowed her gasp, taking the opportunity to plunge his tongue inside her velvety, hot mouth. When she moaned and grabbed a handful of his hair, pulling his lips tighter to hers, he was lost.

Her tongue stroked across his, pushing right and wrong to the far recesses of his mind. He cupped her breast, relished the hard nipple against his palm, pulling her body closer. With a deep sigh, he stepped away and then opened her car door.

That she'd kissed him back put a smile on his face as Leigh sat, straightened her blouse, and then buckled her seat belt. The walk around the car took an eternity. He slid behind the wheel. Waited for her to tell him off.

"That's better." Her voice was barely a whisper.

"Come again?" J.T.'s head whipped around to find her gaze locked on his.

"You heard me. Don't make me repeat myself."

She was right. He'd heard. His brain refused to process her statement. "Better for me. How is it better for you?" He started the engine.

"I thought maybe you were pissed." She reached across, resting her hand on his shoulder.

"Not at you." He breathed out a sigh, cursing his weakness. His guilt worsened when she massaged the rigid tendon in his neck with her thumb. "Not you."

"Talk to me. It's hard to communicate via text messages, and we left a lot unsaid in the park."

"I'm a selfish, thoughtless son of a bitch who's no good for you. Remember?"

"Nobody makes decisions for me. Remember?"

"Yeah, I do." He liked that she stood up to him. "And I'm also selfish enough to not walk away from you."

"Great. We can debate your selfishness later. Where are we headed?"

He struggled to keep a smile from breaking out. "Pull up directions to Juanita Ortega's house for me"

He ran his tongue across his lips hoping for a remnant of her taste. He shrugged away a hard wrench to his heart. She deserved Christmas carols, family vacations at Disney World, Sunday mornings in bed, and, hell, maybe a sister for Ethan. Things he couldn't give her.

His cell vibrated. A glance showed an email from David Campbell with an attachment. J.T. would read the file on Leigh's ex-boyfriend later when he was alone. She hadn't asked for his help, and, no doubt, she'd be pissed when she learned he'd intervened. He'd deal with her wrath after the fact. She'd convinced him who was behind the attacks, the break-in, and the phone calls. Carrington's background and current activities were about to be ripped apart.

He drove through town to the upscale suburb and parked in front of a manicured lawn typical of the Atlanta well-heeled. Huge magnolia trees shaded the front of the two-story colonial style home. Nothing on the outside indicated the widow of a wife-beating attorney lived there. They got out of the car, and Leigh joined him on the sidewalk.

"Think we should've called first?" Leigh tucked her jacket behind her badge, making sure her ID was in plain sight.

"Why give the widow a chance to think about her answers?" J.T. rang the doorbell, stepped back, and waited with Leigh.

The housekeeper escorted them into the living room, where they were joined by Juanita Ortega. A pretty woman around forty with dark hair and eyes. Her makeup couldn't hide the evidence of abuse. The split lip would leave a permanent scar.

"We have a few follow up questions," Leigh said.

Mrs. Ortega waited while the housekeeper placed a tray with coffee on the table and left the room. "I saw on the television the FBI was involved."

Leigh leaned forward. "We asked for their assistance. Their knowledge in catching serial killers will help us get the man who shot your husband."

"Who knew your husband abused you? In particular, did you tell anyone about the last occurrence?" Always best to get to the point; J.T. pulled no punches.

She sighed. "Very few people knew how he acted when he was drunk. He reserved those moments for me. The kids and my housekeeper witnessed some of the beatings." She paused and blinked rapidly. "The people at Piedmont Hospital have pictures and documented details."

"Who else? Friends? Relatives? Neighbors?" J.T. prodded.

"I'm sure the people next door heard. The only person I ever talked to is my sister in Birmingham. You don't want to talk to her, do you?"

"We might. I'd appreciate you writing down her name and phone number." He handed over his pad and pen and waited for the information. J.T. glanced at Leigh and accepted the slight shake of her head to mean she had nothing to ask. "We'll get out of your hair."

The widow escorted them back to the front door, waiting on the steps until J.T. drove away. "Anything, in particular, you want for lunch?"

"I'm open to anything that doesn't include sauerkraut or anchovies."

J.T. silently debated restaurants. "I know just the place."

****

Leigh read off a text message while J.T. drove. "Other than the abuse, Olivia and Romeo didn't find a link to connect the widows."

"There is one. And that's what sent the sniper calling. We just have to find it." J.T. stopped at a local restaurant with a metal chicken sitting on top of the building.

After carrying their lunch to a corner booth, Leigh considered his earlier comments. He'd kissed her and then reminded her that he wasn't good for her. Why did he pull her to him and then push her away? Shame because of his mother? His gruff persona, perpetual frown, and short sentences didn't fool her anymore. She'd bet he intentionally stopped all relationships just short of intimacy. Not the sexual intimacy they'd shared, the kind that would open him up to falling in love. The wall he'd built around his heart was thick and high. Maybe even impenetrable. Her brain warned her not to get her hopes up. Her heart refused to give up on him.

"The sniper hasn't struck since last Wednesday. We may not have long before he kills again," he said.

"Maybe we should check in at Piedmont. Ask if any abuse cases came in over the weekend."

"Works for me. You finished?"

He reached for her trash, and his hand brushed hers. A jolt of heat rushed up her arm. His gaze met hers, sending a second spark. He'd felt something too. He tossed their empty sacks, opened the door, and waited for her to exit.

After she'd settled into the car, Leigh studied the map and addresses. The dead police officer's home was between the café and the hospital. "Let's swing by the widow Slocum's in Smyrna and finish the day at the hospital."

"Good idea."

"How's Nana dealing with your mother?" Leigh had broached this subject before, and he'd shut her down. Something compelled her to get inside his injured heart.

J.T. kicked the car's speed up a notch when he hit the freeway and headed toward Atlanta. "She's been through this many times. Nothing pleases her more than holding her daughter's hair off her face while she pukes up her guts."

He glanced at her, and the cold detachment in his eyes startled her. Leigh's arms ached to hold him. She refused to believe his indifference was real. "Give me a break. I know you care. It's not necessary to be pissed all the time."

"Sorry. I do worry about my grandmother, and I never chitchat about my mother."

Brian Slocum's grass needed cutting, the blinds were open, and a week's worth of newspapers indicated nobody had been around for a while.

"Hey. You okay?" The worried look on J.T.'s face touched her. He gave her a full-face, light-up-the-day smile. Finally, he'd relaxed the bad-boy attitude. How brave or bold should she be?

"I love it when you give me that huge smile of yours."

"Are you trying to be funny?" His eyebrows dove together.

"No. Why would you think that? We haven't talked about your scar but you know Ethan and I did. When he looks at you he sees a hero. When I look at you I see a man, a gorgeous man."

The emotion on his face was a mixture of distrust and pain. He clamped both hands on the steering wheel. "Are you sure you don't pretend I don't have one?"

"No." A pain ripped through her. "It's part of you. A very small part."

"You told Ethan not to question me about it."

"I told him it might be something you didn't want to discuss. Curious children can be unintentionally cruel. Don't be angry with me for teaching my son manners."

J.T. cleared his throat. "I don't discuss my time in the military."

"That's another reason I haven't asked. Can we move on?" She wasn't sure whose feelings were hurt, hers or his. Either way, he'd open up if and when he wanted.

"I'll have Romeo track down Mrs. Slocum." J.T. headed toward the freeway.

"Maybe I should ask to return to CID," Leigh blurted the words out after what seemed like miles of silence.

"What would you accomplish by leaving the taskforce?"

"I'm afraid my personal life is interfering with us as partners," she admitted.

"Do you hear me complaining?"

"All I hear from you is 'stay away.' " Her words landed, bitter and harsh. Damn, she wanted them back. "That was uncalled for. Forget I said anything."

"It's forgotten." He shot down the exit and within a few turns, he'd parked close to the same spot where they'd started the day. This time he didn't pull her into his arms and kiss her until she forgot her worries. Instead, he got out and walked straight to the stairs.

"Leigh McBride?" A young woman in jeans and a T-shirt stepped out of the shadows.

"Yes?"

Handing Leigh a manila envelope, her pleasant smiled changed to a smirk of arrogance. "You've been served."

Chapter Nineteen

J.T. closed the door to his apartment. The place was graveyard quiet, and the silence drew a sigh of pleasure and appreciation. Being alone didn't bother him. He enjoyed having a chance to chill after a day at work, and he was past ready for this day to end. They'd made zero progress on the sniper case, which meant another person could be hours away from getting his head blown off. The time he'd spent at Nana's tonight hadn't improved his mood, but no way could he turn his back on his mother during her drying out process.

Sobering her up was never a pleasant experience. After she passed the hating everyone who came near her stage, she entered the nausea and self-pity mode. Everything she put in her stomach came right back up, except for one thing, and for days the house smelled of canned cream of mushroom soup. One sniff of the stuff sent J.T.'s gut into revolt.

Tonight, his grandmother's housekeeper had stayed late and had whisked Nana away for a few hours of shopping while J.T. took his turn waiting for his mother to need something. She'd emerged from her room, pale and gaunt, wearing her poor-pitiful-me expression. She'd had the nerve to ask him to go buy her a six-pack of beer—to settle her stomach. When he'd flatly refused, she'd asked for that God-awful soup. There was an outside chance he'd never be able to face food, in general, again.

J.T. stripped, showered, and slipped on a pair of warmups. He wanted to be sharp and wide-awake when he opened the file on Leigh's ex-boyfriend. He'd just clicked on the email when the doorbell rang.

He wasn't in the mood for company. Sliding the peephole cover aside, he saw the one exception standing in his hall. Eyes narrowed and lips drawn to a thin line, Leigh looked like an electrical storm ready to explode. She'd left without explanation that afternoon after a process server had handed her a manila envelope. No doubt, her bastard ex-boyfriend had delivered another crushing blow. J.T. closed his computer before opening the door.

"Come in."

"I had to talk to somebody." She stormed by him without waiting for an answer, babbling her words out all in one breath.

"I'm glad you came to me."

She whirled and faced him. A wildfire raged behind her eyes. "The bastard got a judge to issue a demand for a paternity test. I'll kill him before I allow him access to Ethan."

J.T. closed the door. "Not sure you'd look good in handcuffs unless they're velvet lined."

She shot him a scorching look, leaving no doubt his attempt at humor was a mistake. "He'll never get near my son." She ground out her words. "I'll go underground. Pack my car and hit the road. Ethan and I will disappear."

J.T. silenced her the only way he knew how. He bracketed her face with his hands and covered her mouth with his, swallowing her gasp of surprise. For a split second, she stiffened against him. Her fingers clamped down on his wrists. Then she simply detonated in his arms. Her tongue streaked across his. Her hands slid up his arms, threaded through his hair, and clenched, holding his lips against hers in a death grip. Heat lashed through his blood, surging inside his veins, racing straight to his groin. She stroked his back. Fierce and demanding, she dug trenches in his flesh.

He wanted inside her. To hear her cry out his name while he thrust deep into her again and again until he satisfied his insatiable need to possess her. From somewhere deep in the recesses of his humanity, a voice reminded him he'd intended to calm her down, not take advantage of her. Her emotions were running wild. He had to stop this. Reluctantly, he pulled his mouth from hers, gripped her by the arms, and put some distance between them.

Breasts heaving, lips swollen and wet, desire shining from her eyes, she lifted one eyebrow. Desire obliterated his common sense, making the need to drag her to his bed almost overwhelming.

Truth was, she hadn't come to him for sex. He stepped back and released her. She might not admit it, might not believe it, but Leigh didn't want to make love. She wanted to make hate. He understood. She wanted to pound something, anything, until she couldn't think, didn't hurt. She'd regret her behavior afterward, and he never wanted her to suffer a minute's remorse. Certainly not because he hadn't controlled his selfish desires.

"Better now?" Trying his best to sound casual, he walked across the room. The heat boiling off her was too tempting. He was having a hell of a time keeping himself in check. His raging hard-on had developed a mind of its own and demanded satisfaction.

"Oh. My. God." Pink raced up her neck and settled high on her cheeks. "I lost my mind for a second, didn't I?" She ran her hand across her face, and a nervous laugh rolled from her swollen lips. "I can't believe I attacked you."

"You can attack me anytime. I'm available all hours, but sex isn't why you came here tonight." More under control, he crossed to her and caught her hands in his when she reached up to pat down a stray lock of hair. "Don't. It's a dead giveaway that you're nervous. When you fight this bastard in court, you can't give him or his attorney any help."

She dropped down on the couch, her gaze never leaving his face. The look of despair emanating from her eyes reminded him of a wounded animal. One thing for sure, whether it was for help or comfort, Leigh had come to him tonight. Now, he was involved, and when he went in, he went all in.

"I'm sorry I rushed off today without any explanation."

"None needed."

"You're thinking he bought a judge?"

"I don't know what to think. His family can certainly afford one." Her blue eyes clouded. "They want Ethan's toothbrush or a hair with root intact. Before we go that far, I'll acknowledge Jason is his father."

"What happens then?"

"Who knows? My attorney has the subpoena. She'll contact Jason's lawyer tomorrow."

"Then what?" He held up a finger to qualify his question. "Since killing him is out." His second attempt at humor worked. At least he'd gotten a small grin from her.

"That horse left the gate seven years ago. What if he wants visitation rights?" She made a move to smooth out her hair, stared at her hands for a second, and then dropped them to her lap with a grimace. "What do I say to Ethan if this winds up in court? He's too young to understand."

J.T. shoved the laptop aside and sat on the coffee table in front of her. "What does Ethan know about his father?"

Her gaze broke with his, and she studied the floor between them. He pulled her hands from her lap. They were cold and trembling. Anger boiled up into his chest. She was a walking bomb with a lit fuse.

"I told him his father moved away."

She scooted to the edge of the couch. Her gaze flitted around the room, landing everywhere except J.T.'s face. He expected her to bolt for the door any second.

"I'm sorry. My question was too personal."

"It's late. I should head home."

"Have you eaten?" J.T. couldn't let her leave feeling like the weight of the world sat on her shoulders. Food was the first thing to pop into his mind. He wanted her to stay. He wanted to hold her and calm her fears.

"No. Ethan and I went out to have supper with my folks. Just the thought of food turned my stomach."

"He's staying the night with them?" When she nodded, he took her hand and led her to the kitchen. "How about an omelet?"

"You cook something other than soup?" For the first time since crossing his threshold, her smile reached her eyes.

"If it's eggs or in a can, I'm your man." He dug out a carton of eggs and a bag of wilting spinach from the fridge.

When he turned, his blood rushed south. She'd sat on that stool, his favorite ever since he'd wedged himself between her open thighs there. Need flooded his groin as her eyes scrolled across his bare chest and back up to his face. Oh, yeah. She remembered too. Maybe, she wanted more than talk and food.

"Omelet sounds good." Her smile deepened, as did the color of her eyes.

She'd paid no heed to his warning she shouldn't get mixed up with him. Truth was, neither had he. He wasn't the right man for her in the long run, but for now, he'd be there for the short haul.

He was toast. Literally. He grabbed the bread from the cabinet.

First, he'd feed her and let the night progress. His cell buzzed. If the sniper had killed again, J.T. was going to be seriously pissed. He leaned over the back of the couch to where the phone lay on the coffee table and read David Campbell's name on the display. J.T. hit the silent button.

"You're not answering?" She raised one brow in a teasing question.

"Nope. Not important." He tossed her the loaf of bread. "You're in charge. Toaster's right there, butter and jelly are in the fridge."

She looked good in his kitchen, not quite as good as she looked in his bed. They worked well together there, too. He caught her by the hips and reached around her to get two plates from the cabinet. She leaned back against his chest and tilted her head, giving him an open invitation to taste the sweetness of her neck. Her scent washed over him. Instantly, he was hard again. He licked the soft spot behind her ear. She moaned, pressing her ass against him. It was his turn to moan when she rotated against his erection. Sweet Jesus. The kitchen counter was beginning to offer great potential.

"Did you say something?" The laugher in her voice said she'd forgotten her troubles, at least for a while.

"You're killing me." The toaster popped, reminding J.T. of the eggs in the frying pan. He turned down the burner, realizing he was still bare-chested. "I'll be right back." He jogged down the hall to his bedroom and slipped on a T-shirt.

"Not fair," she complained when he returned. "I love to look at your chest."

"My grandmother would skin me alive if I showed up at her table half-dressed."

She smoothed the front of his shirt, flexing her fingers on his pecs and sliding down to his abs. "But I'm not your grandmother."

He leaned down and kissed her, lightly, because anything more and supper would burn, and he wouldn't give a damn. "You're not standing around topless." He offered a dare, praying she'd accept the challenge.

"Touché." She patted his chest and went back to buttering the toast.

Soon the kitchen smelled of omelets and strawberries. Watching Leigh eating painted erotic pictures in J.T.'s mind. She captured a drop of errant jelly with a flick of her tongue and it sent an electrical pulse through him, strong enough to power the lights in the entire complex.

His relationship with her had started as fun and games. Now he found himself on a trip down a dead-end road. One he couldn't turn back from. Eventually, she'd figure out she needed a family man. Then she'd turn a critical eye toward him, forcing him to walk away.

"I had no idea I was hungry." Leigh pushed her empty plate back with a moan. "You'd make a great chef. Or somebody a good husband."

"I do make a mean waffle." No way was he touching the husband comment. Instead, he started gathering the dishes. Leigh pushed him aside, insisting she rinse and put them in the dishwasher.

While she busied herself at the sink, J.T. entertained himself by taking her hair down. Pin by pin, he loosened the twist and carefully removed the rubber band. He threaded his fingers through the blonde silk and held the curls to his right cheek, letting the softness warm his scar.

"Nice," he whispered. "You should wear it down more often."

"Doesn't fit my daytime persona." She turned into his arms and looked up through long eyelashes. "I'm glad you like it. Oh, I can't have you thinking I don't believe in equal rights." In one motion, she whisked her blouse over her head and tossed it toward the bar.

Without hesitation, he shed his shirt. She stood on tiptoe and covered his lips with hers, sliding her tongue across his. Sugar and strawberry swirled inside his mouth. J.T. reached behind her, unhooked her bra, and pushed the straps off her shoulders, tossing the piece of beige silk on top of her blouse. Her arms slid around him, tugging him closer. Bare flesh touched. Fire flashed. Skin seared. He lifted her higher. Heartbeat against heartbeat. She pressed against his bulging erection and made a low guttural sound. His heart stumbled.

Their tongues dueled for dominance. He wanted her naked, spread out under him, begging for release. Tonight, they'd finish what they'd started. With no interruptions.

He'd discover all her secret places, where and how she liked to be touched. He'd find her sensitive areas and pleasure her. He needed to do these things for her. Judging from the heat rolling off her body, she wanted the same from him. Time stopped. Nothing mattered except her wants and needs.

J.T. picked her up and hurried down the hall, her soft laugh reverberating against his chest. He gently put her feet on the floor, and they finished undressing. He drank in the sight of each satiny, smooth inch of her bare skin. J.T. caught her hand and stopped her when she hooked her thumbs in her thong. This, he wanted to do himself. He dropped down on his knees and removed the flesh-colored strip of lace with as much reverence as his shaking hands would permit. The nearness of her proved too much, and he had to taste her.

He slid his tongue across her soft skin and found her wet with desire. She thrust her hips forward with a startled cry. He thumbed her delicate folds open and took one long, hard lick, her flavor flooding his mouth.

"Jesus, I'm in heaven," he whispered against her tender flesh, nudging her legs farther apart. Over and over again, he stroked and licked with her hands buried in his hair holding him in place.

"Oh," she murmured. "My. God. I'm. I'm."

He moved to her clit, lashing the erect little nub. "Come for me." Her legs trembled. She cried out his name. It was a beautiful sound. Her knees buckled, and he caught her, gently moving her backward until he lay next to her on his bed.

Leigh stretched, arms overhead, back bowed, her smile one of sated passion. A sexual kitten with wild, blonde hair fanned across the pillows. Her gaze drifted down his body, stopping at his raging hard-on.

She reached for him, wrapped her fingers around his shaft, and, with a feather touch, traced the length. Up and down. Her gaze, intense, wanton, slid up his body and locked on his eyes. When she pulled his hand to her breast, he felt his heart stumble.

"More. Please." Her legs spread in invitation.

Her actions were carnal, erotic, and damn powerful. With a herculean effort, he kept himself from coming in her hand. Instead, he slid down, kissing the inside of her thighs, pausing for one more taste of heaven before licking his way back up. Her soft, creamy breasts were beautiful. Rosy nipples waited for him to kiss. He wasted no time pulling one into his mouth.

****

Leigh arched her back and willingly surrendered all control. On fire, her body teetered on the verge of incineration. Heat licked through her flesh with every touch of his tongue, his mouth, and his hands. Self-combustion was near. She tunneled her fingers in his hair and held him to her breast. The tug of his mouth sent shards of lust rocketing through her.

He lifted up on one elbow, his dark green eyes clouded with need, and the lone dimple winked at her with his smile. The yearning in her body spread to her heart.

"You are beautiful," he whispered.

"You make me feel beautiful." Tomorrow, she'd deal with whatever life threw at her, face criminals, and fight for her son. Tonight, she needed the man making love to her. She needed him to end the throbbing between her legs.

Leigh covered his hand with hers and slid it down across her stomach to the pulsing center of her body. "I need you. All of you. Inside me."

"Have I ever refused you anything?"

"Don't start now." Anticipation burned through her while he ripped open a condom packet and then covered himself.

He entered her with a single solid push. Filled her, stretched her, belonged inside her. Strong hands slid under her, angling her hips upward. She locked her legs around him, matching his moves, thrust for thrust. Again and again. Over and over. Leigh didn't know where she began and he ended. The lines blurred. They became one, racing toward the same plateau, barreling end over end. She didn't want the feeling to stop, but the pressure building in her core was too great to hold back.

His lips covered hers, taking her breath away. He pulled back a few inches and whispered, "I've got you. Let go."

His hips pistoned, causing an explosion deep inside her, rolling like a tidal wave. Unstoppable. Heaven and hell converged at the juncture where their bodies joined. Shattering, she convulsed around him, pulling him deeper inside her.

He hovered above her, his face taut and dark, a study in passion, his breathing, quick and shallow. His hands held her tightly against his body as he ground his hips hard against her skin. When he came with a groan, Leigh marveled at the ecstasy on his face.

Chests heaving, bodies glistening with sweat, he rolled to his side and turned her with him. He flashed his incredibly sexy dimple at her, liquefying what was left of her heart.

"Amazing." He leaned over. His lips covered hers in a tender, lingering kiss.

"Yes. It was." Leigh laid her hand over his right cheek, covering his scar. He closed his eyes and leaned into her palm.

"I'm so very sorry," she whispered, afraid if she spoke louder, she'd sob.

"For?" He frowned over closed eyes.

"For the war. For your injury. For your pain." She swallowed the lump in her throat.

"I was lucky. An inch higher, I'd have lost an eye. A couple lower, my head. The surgeons did their best, considering where we were." His eyes opened, his gaze raking across her face for a second before he closed them again.

"I'm grateful to them."

He huffed out a grunt. "Me too."

A painful contraction squeezed her heart and slammed it hard against her chest. When had she fallen in love with him? When had being in his arms, touching and being touched by this man, become her life's breath? She tried to put into words what was in her heart. A lump in the back of her throat stopped her. Did he want to hear them? Did he truly believe she shouldn't get mixed up with him? Or was it the other way around? Perhaps he didn't want to get mixed up in the drama of her life.

She savored the nearness of him, swallowing back the building emotions. They lay in each other's arms, quiet and peaceful. His chest rose and fell in a steady rhythm.

"I'm thinking about asking for a leave." She kept her words low in case he'd fallen asleep. Sleepy green eyes opened and met her gaze.

"Don't. You're too strong to quit."

"I wish I knew what to expect. What if Casey gets cornered by the media and is bombarded with questions?"

"He's a big boy. I pity the reporter who corners him."

Leigh snuggled closer to his strong body. Tomorrow was soon enough to make decisions. Tonight, the man lying next to her was wide-awake. She leaned over and traced a line down to his nipple with her tongue. Her gaze stayed on his face. She closed her teeth and bit down, and a moan rumbled from deep in his chest.

A second later, she found herself flipped onto her back with J.T. sliding on a fresh condom before settling between her thighs, his erection already renewed, the glow in his eyes was unmistakable.

"Whatever happens, I'll be right there with you. Never doubt that."

Leigh gave herself over to him, relishing the first thrust. The slow and steady rhythm of their joining set a pace of leisurely give and take. She tilted her hips to take him deeper into her body.

Chapter Twenty

Doyle turned off his headlights before pulling into the driveway. Ellen wanted him to give up his apartment and live with her. For the past few nights, they'd slept in her bed, but he hadn't committed to the move.

Had he made a mistake? Not about his feelings for her, making her happy gave him a second purpose. No matter how much joy she brought into his life, living with her presented a completely new set of problems. His stomach was in a constant state of flux. A headache lived at the base of his neck. He'd lied to her about tonight. Now, he had to sneak in without disturbing her. What would he tell her if she woke?

Sweat coated his skin by the time he closed the front door. Stepping lightly, he made his way across the living room, undressing while he moved to the bedroom. He placed his clothes on the chair by the bed and slid between the cool sheets.

He'd had a tough time getting Sara McBride's address and still hadn't identified the name of her daughter's tormentor. He'd taken chances at the hospital, asking more questions than Don the orderly normally would. This case was proving to be more difficult than he'd expected. Doyle needed to know the name of the bastard who'd beaten the young cop's mom.

He lay next to Ellen's warm body and tried to figure out why he was drawn to Leigh McBride and her family. The night of the accident, he'd helped her get out of her car, and they'd connected on a level he didn't understand. Then while her mother had been in the ER, Leigh had comforted her father and son. Doyle had enough evidence to convince him of her loyalty and love for her family. He'd be patient. She'd lead him to the source of her misery. Doyle had a bullet with the bastard's name on it.

****

J.T. sat in the silence of his living room. After Leigh had fallen asleep in his arms, he'd eased out of bed, curious about the file waiting on his laptop. David had sent information on both Carrington and Leigh. J.T. swallowed hard. Mixed emotions stormed his sense of right and wrong. She'd be furious if she knew. Yet, he couldn't look away. Like some sick voyeur, he stared at the screen and read every word.

The State of Georgia versus Jason Carrington read like a horror movie script. The pictures of Leigh taken by the rape unit while she lay in the emergency room ripped his pounding heart wide open. He memorized every cut and contusion. The wonderful woman asleep in his bed and the one on the screen bore scant resemblance to one another. Deep purple bruises had covered a face swollen to the point she was barely recognizable.

He'd killed men with his bare hands while in combat in Afghanistan. The Marines had trained him in the proficiency of silently dispatching the enemy. He'd never wanted to use those skills more than he did this second. J.T. wanted Carrington to suffer the same pain, the same fear, the same feeling of helplessness Leigh must've endured. His fists itched to make the son of a bitch beg for mercy. Death would be sweet justice.

Her love for her son amazed him. How strong did you have to be to love a child born from such an act? Yet, she did. He couldn't grasp how difficult the decision must've been to raise Ethan. Respect grew daily for the amazing woman in his bed.

J.T. shut down his laptop and walked down the hall to his bedroom. He stopped just inside the doorway and stared across the darkness. The pain in his chest for what she went through made him sick. He wanted to tell how sorry he was for what had happened but couldn't.

Leigh's slim body lay stretched across his sheets, her long, graceful arms flung carelessly over her head. Those same arms had wrapped around him last night. Those fingers had dug into his flesh while she came apart with him buried deep inside her body. For now, she slept, at peace with the world. He turned to leave the room, wishing for a way to vent his anger.

"Don't go."

Her voice, heavy with sleep and soft with emotion stopped him. His arms ached to hold and protect her. He went to her, determined to offer her comfort. His warmups hit the floor seconds before he slid in the bed beside her. She scooted against him. Her face nuzzled his neck. Heat shot through him when she held him tightly. She belonged there in his arms where he could protect her. Her strength and bravery humbled him.

"Sh." He moved a long golden curl off her face. "Go back to sleep."

Her soft breasts pressed to his body. He hardened instantly. Would he ever get enough of her? The curve of her hips, the softness of her skin, the taste of her; everything about her fueled his desire. Her fingers stroked down his ribcage, and he sucked in a breath.

"I will. Later," she whispered.

Her hand slid between them and trailed down to his erection. Warm fingers wrapped around him. He moaned a sigh of pleasure. With each movement, each stroke, his need intensified. Without a sound, she slid on top of him. Damn, he hated to stop her, but he grabbed her hip with one hand and fumbled with a condom. Finally, with a laugh, she took it from him, covering him herself.

"Now. Where were we?"

"Right here." She made a soft mewl and guided him to her. Hot and wet, she took him deep inside. In the darkness, with a sliver of a moon shining through the blinds, streaking across her naked shoulders, she looked ethereal. A silhouette of darkness and light, head back, curls bouncing around her shoulders, she rode him. Rising and falling, rocking back and forth. The urge to explode slammed into him. Not yet. Not yet. He dug deep and held off. She needed this release, and he'd give it to her. When she cried out his name, her contractions, clutched around him, pushed him toward the raging water, and under the rolling tide. One word reverberated in his mind as he followed her over.

Mine. Mine. Mine.

She collapsed, heaving, and spent. They rested in silence for a minute, before she rolled away from him onto her side, pulling his arm across her body. "J.T.?"

"Hmm?" He grabbed a tissue from the bedside table, wrapped the condom, and dropped it the trash can next to the bed. He turned Leigh over, cradling her in his arms.

Tears fell on his bare chest, searing a trail straight to his heart. His knowledge of a woman's inner emotions was zero, but crying was a form of release, and she'd been building toward this since she'd walked through his door. So, he held her until her sobs subsided. Then he placed the box of tissues on the bed.

"Thanks." She turned away to wipe her face and blow her nose. For a heart-stopping minute, J.T. feared she was leaving. Instead, she stretched out beside him again. She breathed in deeply and then blew out a sigh.

"He beat me, raped me, and left me for dead."

J.T. knew who "he" was. "Sorry bastard." He pushed the words over a lump in his throat.

This was her story to tell. He wouldn't interrupt, and he damn sure wouldn't tell her he'd read her file. He'd carry that breach of privacy to his grave. Instead, he smoothed his hand across her body and tried to convey with his touch what he felt down deep inside.

She pushed up in bed, pounded a couple of pillows into submission, and then slid them behind her back. J.T. propped on his elbow and waited.

"I met Jason at a department fundraiser. His mom and dad contribute lots of money to different charities. Handsome and charming, he invited me to dinner, but I turned him down. A few days later, he called me. That time I accepted. We went out a few times. I swear, he seemed normal at first—until he started getting possessive. All of a sudden, he wanted to know why I wasn't at home when he called, insisting I account for every minute of my time. I ended the relationship."

"But he didn't go away."

"No. He started sending flowers, showing up unannounced, and making demands. I threatened to file stalking charges against him."

Leigh reached for the sheet, dragging it to her chin. She flipped her hand through the air as if to shoo away bad memories.

"I woke up one night with Jason on top of me. He hit me in the face. Again and again. Then he raped me."

Her eyes closed. When she opened them, the tears were gone. J.T.'s eyes were damp, and his chest felt as if a hand was slowing tightening its grip, taking his breath away.

"Did you know it's possible to become numb and stop feeling pain?"

He nodded.

"I mentally shut down. Sort of had an out-of-body experience, like the attack was happening to somebody else." Tears returned and ran unchecked down her face. "I was stupid. I'm a cop and should've seen through him."

"Easy," J.T. whispered, struggling for something comforting to say. The pain in her voice hurt his heart. "You're not stupid."

She'd given him a second sacred gift tonight. One that caused her great pain to share. Her trust moved him beyond words. A weird sensation rolled into his heart and found a home.

He sat up, pulled her off the pillows, and into his arms. He then rocked her as he'd seen her do Ethan when he'd fallen off the swings.

"Nine months later Ethan was born." Her whisper came out raw and painful. Anger for what she'd suffered ripped him apart inside.

"Something good out of the bad," he whispered into her hair.

She didn't have to explain. He got it. Understood. Regardless of how Ethan had been conceived, her love for him was boundless. The boy would never understand how fortunate he was to have a mother like Leigh.

She blinked a couple of times like he wasn't in focus. Stared at him with wide eyes. A smile pulled at the corners of her mouth. No one had ever looked at him with such an expression—as if he'd invented the light bulb or walked on the moon. It hit him, smacked him square in the heart. She made him feel like a hero. Like maybe he could walk on the moon.

"Exactly." Her fingers dug into his arm. "I'm ashamed to admit my first thought was to have an abortion. I was so angry. At Jason. At myself. I got as far as the parking lot of a clinic. Couldn't go inside. So, I decided I'd go the adoption route. The first time the baby moved something funny happened. My anger vanished. He was a helpless little being who wanted nothing more than to be loved. When I held Ethan in my arms, I apologized for ever considering giving him away. How could I not love a blameless child?"

"He's a lucky kid and you're an awesome mother." Awed by her inner strength, J.T. didn't know what else to say.

"I don't know about that. Took lots of therapy to get past the fear Ethan would turn out like Jason. For the first few years, I watched every gesture, every move Ethan made. He's spent years with my father as a role model, and it's his mannerisms I see my son picking up."

"He's the perfect example to support the theory it's who raises you and the values they instill that molds a child's personality."

She turned her gaze toward him, studying him with an intensity that made him squirm.

"Like you."

"Me? What's one got to do with the other?"

"Your grandmother raised you. You live by her values. Not your mother's."

While spoken softly, Leigh's words struck him square in the chest. He swallowed hard, trying to wrap his mind around her statement. If only she were right about him.

"And Ethan will grow up with your values."

"I think so too. All I've ever wanted was to do the right thing by him."

"And you won't stop now."

J.T. wound a flyaway curl around his finger, and she rewarded his gesture with a full smile. When she lit up, she warmed places deep down inside him. Turned lights on in areas that had been dark. J.T. held her hand to his face and placed kisses on her warm palm.

She pressed her nose against his neck and sniffed.

"Know what I remember most about Jason?" she said, her breath warm against his skin.

He shook his head, unable to speak. He'd been through several rough patches in his life, but she'd lived through more hell than he could imagine. Yet, with all the ugliness she'd been through, her spirit was strong and unbroken.

"His cologne. I wake up sometimes and smell him." She pressed herself closer, held him tighter. "Makes me physically sick."

He buried his cheek in her silky hair, soft as angel's wings. "You can relax now. I've got you. He'll never hurt you again."

It was a promise J.T. intended to keep.

****

Leigh sat at her desk trying to concentrate on the notes from today's briefing. She glanced across the FBI bullpen. J.T. stood outside Casey's office, propped against the doorjamb. His white shirt hugged his broad shoulders and reminded her of the snowy sheets on his bed. Heat rushed to her face. She turned her chair around and tried to concentrate on reading.

Unable to stay focused, her mind wandered to the mad dash when she'd left J.T.'s apartment at a dead run. She'd barely managed to get home, shower, and change clothes before reporting to work. That led her to think about what had happened between them last night. She'd said things to him she'd never spoken to another human being, including her parents. Since the attack, she'd cut herself off from friends. Her instincts as a cop and mother had made her cautious, and her need to protect Ethan had made her leery of outsiders. J.T. inspired her to trust, to open herself for possible rejection. She'd looked into his eyes and found no condemnation or blame. His understanding meant more than she had words to describe.

Pulling her out of her thoughts, J.T. settled down in his chair, his long legs stretched out in front of him. The cup in his hand carried the scent of fresh coffee. Sultry, emerald eyes studied her.

Preferring to believe his sexy gaze stemmed from affection, her heart did its silly cartwheel spin. Had she fallen in love with him, or were her hormones totally out of control? "Stop undressing me with your eyes."

"I don't think so. Your blush is sexy."

"Don't start with the three and four-word sentences." She dropped her voice so only he heard. "You didn't have trouble talking in grownup terms last night."

He choked on a sip of coffee. When he stopped sputtering, both sides of his mouth lifted. "You bring out the poet in me."

"I wouldn't go that far." She loved it when he dropped his guard and allowed her inside.

He opened a desk drawer, pulling something out and tossing a neck lanyard to her. "Here, hang your badge on this."

"Wow. A gift. I'm touched."

He stood, rubbing his lower back, and then stretched his arms over his head. A soft groan drifted from him.

"Are you okay?"

"I'm not sure," he said, his voice low. "Sex with you is hard on an old man."

She clamped her hand over her mouth, but not in time to cover a burst of laughter, which drew attention from half the agents in the office. J.T. had walked away and left her sitting at her desk alone. She slid the lanyard over her head and resisted the urge to smooth down the hair she knew had escaped and hurried to catch up with him.

He waited by the elevator doors, holding them open with his foot. His dimple still dipped into his cheek. Reality slammed into her. She'd never known a man like she did him. He made her life better.

"Very funny. You caught me off guard." She backed against the wooden handrail as the elevator started its descent.

"I like hearing you laugh, and you haven't done enough of it lately."

"You're right about that," she admitted.

"Now who's talking in short sentences?" He moved closer and ran the back of his hand across her cheek. "Are you up to this?"

"I have to be able to do my job. It's important to me. Part of who I am." Of all people, he'd understand. "Besides, when you're with me, I'm up for anything."

Chapter Twenty-One

Because Dr. Eric Marsh didn't recall treating Juanita Ortega, Leigh reconstructed the night using details she and J.T. had obtained from the widow. Finally, Dr. Marsh raised his hand.

"I can't discuss her case. You've already spoken to the patient." Young, with steady brown eyes, the doctor folded his arms across his chest.

Leigh appreciated his discretion. "We don't want to talk about her medical condition. However, we understand you encouraged her to file charges against her husband. Is this correct?"

"I didn't suggest she go to the police or file charges. I talked to her about her safety. I gave her the name of a shelter for battered women." Dr. Marsh leaned forward in his chair, his brows dipped. "Has something happened to her?"

J.T. shifted in his chair, moving slightly closer to the doctor. "Are you aware her husband was murdered?"

Leigh studied Marsh as different emotions played out on his face. She believed he hadn't known about the murder until now.

"I had no idea." His gaze shifted to Leigh. "Why are you questioning me?"

"Who else heard your conversation with Mrs. Ortega?" J.T. asked.

"I don't know. Any number of people. Privacy curtains separate patients in the examination rooms. They're protected from prying eyes not eavesdroppers."

"Anything you remember could be important." Leigh pressed.

"You think one of the hospital staff killed Mr. Ortega?" His face paled as if all the blood had drained from his head. Leigh felt his surprise was genuine. "And you're looking at me?"

"We're asking questions. No one's accusing you." J.T. stood, dug out a card, and handed it to Marsh. "We'd appreciate a call if you think of anything."

The doctor walked them to the door. "You said Ortega was murdered. How'd he die?"

"Sniper's bullet," J.T. said over his shoulder. "Almost took his head off."

Dr. Marsh recoiled. "I never connected her name with the news story. It didn't click."

Leigh walked to the car, fully understanding why J.T. had been so blunt. She buckled up and waited until they were on the freeway to comment. "You're satisfied he's not involved. Right?"

"Yep. He's not our killer."

"You still think the sniper's an ex-cop or a member of law enforcement?"

"I do. The way he selects his vantage point, his weapon of choice, that kind of knowledge comes from training."

"You sound experienced." J.T. had mentioned his stint in the military but never talked about a tour of duty. "What did you do in the Marines?"

He made a combination laugh and scoff sound. "I followed orders."

"That narrows it down."

He'd questioned her, so she considered asking about his career fair game, even if sharing personal information was hard for him.

"I was part of a special unit skilled in various weapons and hand-to-hand combat."

"Did you want to be an FBI agent when you were a kid?"

"No. The military helped me decide. I liked defending people. When the FBI recruited me, the choice was easy."

"You made the right decision."

"I think so. Are we done with the Q&A?"

"One more." She chuckled when he shot her a frosty look. "You described the rifle you'd use if you were the sniper in great detail. The Marines teach you that, too?"

"You pay attention."

"To everything you say or do."

"I'm flattered you noticed me." He glanced at her with a devilish gleam in his eyes.

"No way not to. I thought you were pissed at the world in general." She cleared her throat. "And hot-hot-hot."

"Hot is a stretch but pissed is a fair description."

"But why? Being mad all the time can't be much fun."

"There's not much in the world to be pleased about. If we don't have a son of a bitch trying to bomb us into oblivion, we've got a lunatic perched on top of a building killing people. I get tired of being patient with the bastards."

"I get it. I do. I don't feel sorry for the men the sniper has killed." Leigh confided, glad no one else heard their conversation.

"That's because you don't know who the hell to feel sorry for. The wife who got the shit beat out of her, the kid who saw it all go down, or the sniper who thinks he's justified. There's a right and a wrong. I don't like it when the lines blur."

She didn't argue. He cared about people. A fact he'd deny if she called it to his attention. "Olivia's report this morning was good news. The hospitals didn't report a single spousal abuse case."

"Doesn't mean it's over. The sniper's due to kill tonight if he stays with the pattern. If he doesn't, we may have caught a break."

Leigh called her attorney's office for an update. Disappointment washed over her when she failed to reach her. Disconnecting the call, Leigh leaned her head back on the seat.

"I know it's prying but what's wrong?" J.T. rested his hand on her knee.

"Not at all. You've learned all my secrets." For all his hard edges, J.T.'s gentle touch stirred Leigh's blood. She twined her fingers through his and shifted where he was in her line of vision better. "I wanted to know if my attorney had been successful getting the subpoena set aside, but she hasn't returned to her office."

"She's probably working on other clients' cases."

"That's what her admin said." She'd trusted him last night, had cried in his arms, and not once had he pried or passed judgment. Funny, sharing the anger and pain with J.T. helped wash away her self-recriminations. She'd always be grateful for his understanding and compassion.

****

Doyle couldn't ask too many questions at work for fear of discovery. A home computer allowed him to research Leigh McBride in private. She'd been on the police force since graduating college, and her name had come up about a few cases she'd worked in the past.

Determined, he'd kept searching until he'd hit the jackpot. She'd been a victim. That set him back in his chair. The hair on the back of his neck rose, and his skin tingled. Had he found her tormentor? Detective McBride had testified against a man who'd attacked and raped her.

Doyle leaned closer to the computer screen and jotted down information while he read.

The story had splashed big in the headlines seven years ago. After the jury had found her attacker guilty, the sensationalism died down and interest in the case slowed to small blurbs. Doyle scratched his chin. Rack one up for the system.

Doyle changed his search to Jason Carrington and found his answers. Carrington liked to beat up his women.

"I'm home," Ellen called out.

"Crap." He hadn't heard the garage door open. "Coming." Shit, he'd forgotten he was supposed to run a load of clothes while she'd gone out for groceries. The continuous lies to Ellen were affecting his concentration. He closed the website, hid his notes, and walked to the kitchen.

"Are you okay?" She stood over the basket of laundry.

"I'm fine. I dozed off in the chair."

"You needed the rest. You've been getting in and out of bed at all hours. I worry about you not sleeping well."

"Don't." He scrambled for a new lie. "I've always gotten up a couple of times a night."

She tilted her face, accepting his kiss. He held her close, felt her trusting heart beating against his chest, and then hustled out to her car. He gathered an armload of grocery bags, wondering how to continue his investigation without alerting Ellen.

****

J.T. wasn't prepared for the scene in his Nana's backyard. The frail figure kneeling pulling weeds wasn't his grandmother. His mother's long, frizzy, blonde hair was now a short brown bob. He recognized the old, gray warmups as a pair Nana wore when digging in the garden. They hung on his mother's thin frame. The tug at his heart pissed him off. Too many times he'd fallen for her promises only to wake up the next morning and find her gone, leaving his grandmother to make excuses.

"Are you gonna stay in the car?" his grandmother asked.

"Shit." He swung his head around to the driver's side window. "You'll give me a heart attack sneaking up on me."

"Teddy," she admonished. She stepped back, allowing him to get out and kiss her cheek. "You're not in the locker room."

"Sorry." He ignored her use of his nickname. "How is she?"

"She's well. And she has a name. I expect you to use it when you say hello." She added, "Nicely."

Nana's last word resonated like the sound of a slamming door. The subject was closed. J.T. tucked her hand in his elbow and turned to face his mother.

A small smile lifted the sides of her mouth. "Hello, son."

"Mother." He waved her off when she stood. "Don't stop on my account." His muscles tensed at the pinch to the inside of his arm.

"It'll be dark soon. It's time I finished."

Her words were spoken softly, making him strain to hear them. She stood, slid off the cotton gloves, and took a tentative step toward him. Her hands trembled slightly. She was either nervous or still going through the tremors that came with sobering up.

He left his grandmother behind and walked to the edge of the garden. He extended a hand to his mother. She hesitantly wrapped her fingers in his, and he helped her step over the rows to the sidewalk.

She moved closer and tentatively slid her arms around his waist. His heart worked its way to the back of his throat. He swallowed hard and gathered her frail body close. They stood silently, holding each other for the first time in years. A sudden wave of remorse hit him. Caught him off guard. Slammed into him with such fierceness, he staggered under the weight. Years of lost time because of her drinking and his inability to stop her pulled him into deep water. He couldn't force her to do anything. Why did he feel so responsible?

"You two come in the house. I made peach cobbler, and it's cooled long enough." His grandmother opened the back door, waiting.

"Can you eat?" he asked, walking his mother into the kitchen.

"A little." She kept her gaze on the floor. "At least my food's not coming right back up anymore."

"That's gotta be a relief." He blocked old images from his mind.

"She's doing great," Nana announced, standing on tiptoe to pull bowls from the cabinet.

They sat around the table and made small talk about the weather and the garden. Nana's cobbler was his favorite, and when she offered a second helping, he didn't turn her down. She chattered away as if this little gathering happened all the time.

Her enthusiasm and optimism amazed him. The capacity for forgiveness in her heart was bottomless. Hell, he'd benefited from it as a kid more than once. He worried she was painting a happy family portrait in her mind, which he'd guarantee was fake. The colors would turn dark and run. How soon? That was a question nobody could answer.

J.T. made up an excuse to leave after they'd finished eating. He'd made nice like his grandmother had wanted while trying to get a feel for how his mother had progressed. Trust didn't come easy for him, and he doubted she'd stop drinking if she didn't get help. Part of him hoped she proved him wrong this time.

He kissed his grandmother good-bye and turned to find his mother's hand extended. An odd gesture, she seemed to be returning his earlier action of escorting her into the house by walking him to his car. He caught her small fingers in his, and they went outside. The night air hit the sweat forming on the back of his neck sending a shiver up his spine. She was still his mother, and he loved her despite all the heartaches they'd been through. Respect her? No. Damn it, hard as he'd tried, his heart had never been able to fully cut her out.

"Take care of yourself," she said.

"You too." He leaned down and kissed her on both cheeks. A single tear ran down her face, and his heart cratered. Imploded. He gathered her in his arms.

"Mama," he leaned down and whispered in her ear. "You can do this."

The nod of her head was so slight, for a second, he wasn't sure whether he imagined it or not.

He slid in behind the wheel and took one long look. "Call if you need me."

When he backed out of the driveway, he wondered if he'd seen his mother for the last time. If she left again, how long would she be gone? Years? For good? He hoped she'd at least try to stay sober. For Nana's sake.

Chapter Twenty-Two

Leigh reread the same paragraph for the third time before she realized her brain hadn't registered a single word on the page. She closed the book and lay staring at the ceiling. How could she have been so stupid? She'd walked right into a trap by acknowledging Ethan was Jason's son.

His attorney contacted Karen with a new demand—visitation rights or face a nasty court battle. In a fit of fury, Leigh had sent back the message that she'd see Jason in hell before she allowed him to get near her son. No doubt, her attorney had reworded the statement. She issued instructions to Leigh to control her temper.

Tonight, she'd decided to tell Romeo and Olivia about her past and Jason's demands. God, the idea of baring her soul and sharing the assault sickened her. And yet, she couldn't let them be blindsided when all hell broke loose.

She tried to relax. She pushed the negative thoughts from her mind by taking air deep into her lungs and then releasing the breath slowly. Her mind wandered to J.T. and how wonderful he'd been tonight. She'd worried needlessly about how he'd react around Ethan after she'd shared the circumstances of his birth. If anything, J.T. seemed more connected and openly demonstrative with Ethan.

Like a mother lioness, she'd paid close attention when Ethan had fallen into J.T.'s arms to say good night. She'd stood out of the way while her two guys exchanged a bear hug. After tucking Ethan in, she'd curled up on the couch in J.T.'s arms and requested a hug for herself.

Now, lying in bed all alone, she ran her fingers across her mouth, remembering the pressure of his lips against hers, his strong hands cupping her breasts, lighting fires with his fingertips. Neither Leigh nor J.T. wanted to test fate with a little one in the next room, so, reluctantly, Leigh had escorted him to the door and let him drive away. Her hormones were still running amuck, loudly protesting because she hadn't brought him to bed with her.

On the nightstand, her cell vibrated, and her cheeks heated when she read the caller ID. "Hey. Are you home already?"

"Yeah. Are you in bed?" His voice was husky. Thick. Sexy.

Her heartbeat relocated to the juncture of her thighs. "Yes. I can't seem to concentrate on my book." A tingle raced from her head to her toes.

"Why not?"

"I don't know." Should she tell him where she throbbed?

"Yes. You do. Tell me."

His low chuckle rolled through her phone touching off small tornadoes in her stomach.

"I wish you were here."

"Doing what?" He pressed for more.

"Stop it." A statement she didn't mean.

"In bed with you?" He growled. "Inside you?"

"God, yes." The throbbing intensified. "By the way, I'm a beginner at having phone sex." Easier to joke than admit how his voice had her aching for him.

"You're a quick learner."

"Hang on." Leigh put the book on the bedside table, slid her pistol under the pillow next to her, and snapped off the reading light. "Now. Where were we?" She closed her eyes and imagined his warm breath on her neck.

"Get naked."

****

Leigh leaned back in her chair and let the small team around Casey's conference table absorb her lengthy statement. Childbirth hadn't been as hard as telling the taskforce about her rape, the ugly trial, and what she was going through with Jason now that he'd been paroled. That she'd gotten pregnant as a result of the attack was the one fact she'd held back.

Romeo and Casey's expressions were stoic and unreadable. Compassion reflected in Olivia's warm, brown eyes. J.T.'s hunter green gaze hardened to a fierceness Leigh hadn't seen before. She felt this team supported her more as friends than coworkers.

Casey cleared his throat. "Thank you for telling us, Leigh." He turned to face to group, "Based on the expected court proceedings, I encouraged her to share her situation with the team. I also assured her, everyone in this room would understand how difficult sharing such personal information was for her."

Romeo's hand covered hers. "Tell us what we can do."

"My off-duty time is yours." Olivia leaned forward and rested her hand over Romeo's.

"Jesus Christ." J.T. rolled his eyes. "I'll shoot the person who says, 'All for One and One for All.' So help me." He folded his arms across his chest and scowled, but the corners of his lips couldn't hold the downward curve.

"Damn." Casey laughed. "You stole my line."

Leigh struggled to express her gratitude, her voice breaking when she thanked everyone for their support. Casey ended the meeting and sent the group off with instructions to turn up something on the sniper.

"I've got to stop by the printer," J.T. commented. "I received the report on Preston's trust fund."

Leigh made her way to the restroom, where she turned on the tap and splashed cold water on her face. Hands propped on the counter, she blinked back tears, refusing to give in. Reliving the past in her mind was bad enough, speaking the words out loud had turned her inside out. The pain doubled her over as old memories became new and real again.

Pissed she'd given Jason this much power over her emotions, she ripped a handful of paper towels from the dispenser and dried her face.

The badge hanging from the lanyard around her neck bounced off the marble countertop. She caught the cool shield in her hand, held it to her chest, and drew strength. Life slid into focus. Enough. Work waited outside the door. Leigh held her head high and went back to her desk.

J.T. looked up as she sat in her chair. "I was seconds from coming after you."

"Rescuing me from the clutches of the women's restroom won't be necessary." She joked, and he rewarded her by showing her his dimple. "Although, I remember you have no problem barging in, privacy be damned."

Heat prickled across her skin when his face relaxed completely, and the smile rose to his eyes. "And don't you forget it." He passed her a file, and his demeanor shifted to business. "Doyle Preston's trust fund hasn't had one single inquiry."

Leigh read the statements and found nothing new. "You expected him to try?"

"No, but I hoped. We'll drop this thread for now and move on."

Leigh shared his disappointment. "At least we caught a break. We made it to Thursday without another murder." Leigh's stomach cramped. "I think Jason maybe Doyle's next target."

"It's hard for me to care if he is. Hell, I'd like to kill Jason. Beat him until my fucking knuckles bleed."

"Hey. I kind of like that you're protective but I need you here. Not in jail."

"I'm sorry, but he hurt you and I hate the son of a bitch."

"If you don't stop, I'm going to kiss you right here."

"Don't tempt me." J.T. sat forward in his chair. "Okay. How would Doyle know about Jason? Help me understand."

"Pieces of our conversation keep popping into my memory. The guy asked me about my bruises, and I made some flippant remark about somebody being after me. After he told me his name, he added that he might help me."

"You sure you didn't mention anybody's name?"

"I'm positive."

"It's a long shot, but if the sniper learned your name and researched you." He ran his fingers through his hair. "But he'd have to know your name."

"What are you thinking?"

"We should ask the widows if anyone offered to help them."

Leigh's cell buzzed. Odd. Her dad never called.

"What's wrong?" J.T. asked when she ended the short conversation.

"I have to go. My mother has had a headache since the attack Saturday and didn't tell anyone." She grabbed her purse. "After she'd gotten violently sick to her stomach, she finally told Dad. He's taking her to the Piedmont ER."

****

J.T. caught up with her and ushered Leigh into the elevator. She surprised him by not arguing, which was just as well because he'd have hogtied her before letting her drive across town by herself. He slipped his arm around her waist and felt the full force of her fear when she rested against his body.

"Leigh." Trying to assure her, he lifted her chin and held her gaze. "You'll get through this."

"And then what? This problem with my mother is because of Jason. He'll never leave me alone."

"Did Atlanta PD follow up with your parents after the assault?"

"Hell no. Not even a phone call." She stormed out of the elevator into the parking garage.

J.T. slid behind the wheel and reached across to the glove box. After she buckled up, he handed her a section out of the newspaper. I saw this with my coffee. "Take a look."

Damn, he hated to upset her further. The picture of Jason presenting a check to some charity in the Hamptons proved he wasn't in Atlanta when her mother was attacked.

J.T. kept quiet, allowing her the privacy of her thoughts. The urge to fix things ate at him, driving his temper close to the edge. He had to walk a fine line because she'd flip if he interfered in her personal life.

Leigh crumpled the paper and tossed it to the floor. "I don't care what they say. Jason orchestrated and directed the break-in and the attack at the park." She slapped the dash. Her anger was close to getting the best of her, so J.T. tried to lighten the mood.

"Easy, hotshot. I'm on your side."

When he stopped at the emergency room entrance, Leigh turned toward him. "You're not leaving. Are you?"

"Not if you don't want me to."

"I'd like you to stay."

"I'll park and be right there."

****

Doyle returned to the waiting room with fresh trash bags and started picking up paper coffee cups. His heart dropped to the tops of his work shoes, and he barely stifled the choking noise bubbling up from his throat.

Detective McBride sat with her back to him talking with an older man. Damn, if she hadn't been deep in conversation, she'd have noticed him for sure.

He worked around people all the time. They never looked at his face, but the fact she was a cop worried him. Cops were trained to notice things. He turned away while he stacked a few magazines then emptied another trashcan. She stood, leaned down, and kissed the man's forehead. The guy waved when she glanced over her shoulder at the door.

He pushed his cart around the room and started wiping down the lamp across from the man. He smiled and nodded. "How are you tonight," Doyle asked. He used his friendliest smile while his heart hammered against his rib cage. What if she came back?

"Good. You?" the man said.

"Better now. It's time for my break. May I?" Doyle pointed at the chair across from the guy.

"Please. I'm finishing my shake before I go back upstairs."

A fountain of information sat in front of him, ready to open up and talk. "You have family on one of the floors?"

Chapter Twenty-Three

"Hurry, Ethan." Leigh raised her voice to emphasize the urgency. She'd overslept and was playing catch up. She had to get him across the street to DeeDee's house or he'd miss his ride to school. "Mom's running late this morning."

"Coming." Carrying his tennis shoes, he walked into the living room.

Dressed in jeans and a Falcons jersey, Ethan fastened the Velcro closure on his shoes.

Leigh grabbed her purse and ushered her son out the door. She'd made it down the sidewalk before she realized he was way behind. "Ethan." She turned toward him. "Hurry," she demanded.

He ceased all movement, looking at her as if she were a total stranger. Innocent blue eyes were wide and full of confusion. Bewildered, he threw his hands in the air.

"Can't you see my feet going really fast?" He panted out a dejected sigh.

Guilt slammed into her chest. Heavy guilt. Earned guilt. She'd taken her problem out on him all morning. She rushed back to him and knelt in front of him.

"You were walking really fast, and I'm sorry. I have no excuse for being cross." She opened her arms wide. Head down, he plodded into them. She breathed in his innocence. Love, strong and powerful, gripped her. He was her life. She'd die for him. Protect him at all costs.

"Forgive me?"

"It's okay, Mama. You're worried about Mimi."

His small hands patted her back, offering comfort. Thank God for innocent, unconditional love. Leigh sat back on her heels and looked him in the eyes. "How did you get so smart?"

His smile said it all. He'd forgiven her maternal griping and fussing in the blink of an eye. "I take after my Papa."

"And I know who put you up to giving that answer." Leigh saw more of her father in Ethan every day. "You study hard today."

"Yes, ma'am."

She held his hand and walked at his own pace. "Mimi's going to be fine. They'll probably let her come home today."

Ethan hopped and skipped the last few steps. Happy and full of life, he raced up the walk and rang DeeDee's doorbell. His mood rubbed off on Leigh. After all, she'd been forgiven by the love of her life. She grabbed him by the backpack and hauled him in for a kiss before he dashed inside to join DeeDee's seven-year-old son.

Taking one last look at her boy, Leigh hauled her buzzing phone from her purse and answered without checking the caller ID. "McBride."

"Don't you fucking hang up on me."

Jason's tone, harsh and demanding, smashed into Leigh. Red flashed in front of her eyes in one giant wave. "Leave my family alone."

"Don't you mean our family? That's quite a secret you kept. Believe me, you're going to regret having that bastard."

"Never happening." Pent up frustration bubbled over. "I should've killed you when I had the chance."

"But you didn't."

"Doesn't mean I won't if you don't stay away from us."

"Stay away? Why, Leigh? Don't you think I'd make a good daddy?" His laugh was cold as death.

"Get this straight. You'll never get near my son." Anger became a living entity, wrapping strong hands around her lungs and squeezing.

"Your son?" His voice screeched through the phone. "You mean that bastard who should've never been born?"

The hate in his voice sucked the strength from her bones. Leigh's knees gave way, and she sat down hard on the porch steps. She got back up, fury burning its way through her.

"Stop this, Jason, before I send your ass back to prison." She poured hate and venom into the statement. He needed to hear how serious, how determined, she was to keep them safe.

"For what? It appears you're the one who's lost control, blaming me for your run of bad luck. Maybe you shouldn't have custody of the child."

The bastard disconnected. Damn him and his untraceable burner phone.

She called Karen Parker on the drive to work, relaying the conversation with Jason to voicemail, and requesting a callback. Talking with him had been a mistake. A big one.

****

.

"Goddamn her." Jason threw the cell at the wall in his office. He stormed across the room and gave the phone a swift kick. "Don't call me and don't come near my family," he mimicked Leigh's whiny voice. "I'll send you back to prison."

"What's going on in here?" his father demanded from the doorway.

"Get out," Jason shouted, jabbing a finger toward the hallway. "Get the fuck out of my office."

"Do not use that disrespectful tone of voice on me. I find your language less than acceptable." His father's face reddened, his eyes narrowed to a glowering snarl while he crossed the carpet.

Jason's recent snort of cocaine had filled him with power. He wanted another bump, but, first, he'd explain to the ignorant old fool that his intimidation techniques weren't working. Disgust filled every fiber of his being. He scoffed his loathing before flopping down in his office chair. "Give it up, old man. You don't scare me. Not anymore. Never again."

"Your recent office behavior hasn't escaped my notice, son. You're unprofessional, irrational, and impertinent. I believe you need counseling."

Jason studied the asshole standing in front of his desk. Tall, with gray hair, wearing a two-thousand-dollar suit and a stiff rod up his ass, he pretended to care about his son's welfare.

Poor Daddy had been ashamed of Jason since the day he'd stomped the neighbor's dog to death for barking all night. The old man had taken his son and the dead animal to the woods where they'd buried the carcass with the promise they'd never discuss it again. Daddy didn't keep his word, because he'd thrown it in Jason's face, reminding him of their little secret hundreds of times

Laughter bubbled toward the surface. Wonder what Daddy would think if knew his baby boy had killed Vick? "I'm fine." Jason stood, retrieved the burner phone from the floor where it had landed, and walked out.

"Come back here," his father called out. "I'm not finished with you."

"Sure you are, Dad." Jason flipped the words over his shoulder. "You were through with me years ago."

****

When Leigh's attorney's office contacted her and insisted she come in right away, she hadn't expected a lecture. The harder she tried to justify telling Jason off, the more serious Karen Parker's expression became.

Leigh shifted the gun on her hip in a failed attempt to find a more comfortable position in the plush chair. The acid in her empty stomach multiplied and heated. The professional feel of the office with its mahogany desk and brocade upholstered furnishings didn't calm or soothe her nerves. "How and when did I become the villain?"

"Nobody said you're the villain." Karen rubbed the vein between her eyes. "Imagine my surprise when I received a phone call from Jason's attorney threatening to petition the court for a restraining order against you and your boyfriend."

"What boyfriend? I got mad and threatened him." Leigh understood how Ethan felt this morning when nothing he did was right. "I need to get back to work. My temporary partner's waiting for me."

"Is this the agent who accosted Jason this morning?"

"He's lying. J.T. and I have been in the field most of the day."

"According to Carrington's attorney, your FBI agent threatened Jason. Smacked his head into a brick wall. You're smiling. Who is this agent?"

She should've known J.T. would step in at some point. A mixture of gratitude and concern hit her. He'd risked being reported, maybe sanctioned for his actions for her. She waved off Karen's question.

"Be careful, Leigh." Karen's gaze sobered. "Don't give the Carrington's ammunition for the judge."

"This is bullshit. I'm not the one Ethan needs to be protected from. I'm not the rapist here. I'm not the psychopath. And you're telling me I have to be careful how I act?"

Karen stood, came around her desk, and seated herself next to Leigh. "You should know that a court in Alabama recently ruled the rapist father had paid his debt to society and proven himself worthy of having visitation rights."

Darkness clouded Leigh's vision. "But we're in Georgia." She gripped the arms of the chair and squeezed.

"It's an example of how things don't always go as expected."

"Any idea of when the visitation plea will get in front of a judge?"

"None. The docket is always backed up. I'll call you when I hear."

A warm calm settled over Leigh. She'd have an exit plan in place if the judge ruled against her. She'd never surrender Ethan for weekend visits with Jason.

Karen's voice drew her attention away from strategizing. "You'll remember my instructions?"

"If he contacts me again, tell him to call my lawyer."

"And?"

"Don't give him ammunition to use against me in court."

Karen walked Leigh down the hall to the reception area. J.T. rose, his smile sent her blood moving faster. She doubted there'd ever be a time her heart wouldn't do cartwheels at the sight of him. How cruel of fate to give her someone to love and then force her to leave him behind.

"That's your agent?"

"He is for a while," Leigh answered with a painful ache deep in her soul.

"Tell him to back off," Karen said.

* * * *

J.T. waited by the door, hoping Leigh's meeting with her attorney eased her mind. Leigh gave him a small smile and winked. The underlying darkness in her eyes scared the fuck out of him. The urge to pull her into his arms and say something stupid—like everything will be all right—was overwhelming. "Let me guess. Your attorney heard about my conversation with Carrington this morning."

"She said, 'tell your friend to back off.' "

"I wanted to do a hell of a lot more to the bastard."

She walked ten feet ahead of him back to the car. J.T. shoved an old jazz CD in the player and concentrated on Friday afternoon traffic. No way was he sorry and no way was he apologizing for bouncing that freak off a brick wall. If she didn't get it, too damn bad.

"Sorry. I didn't mean to take your head off."

"No sweat. My head's at your disposal." He tried to lighten the mood as he parked. "How about I take you out to dinner?" A night out with Leigh sounded good. He'd check on his grandmother and touch base with David on Sunday.

"Can't. I've got to pick up Ethan from the babysitter. We'll help

Dad this weekend. Mom's supposed to take it easy."

"Of course. He'll probably need relief."

The stiffness in Leigh's voice added to the fact she'd avoided eye contact with him sent J.T.'s nerves jumping. She'd previously let him into her life. Inside her mind, heart, and body. Why did he feel as if she'd shoved him back out?

Something odd was going on.

Chapter Twenty-Four

David exited the precinct dressed in jeans and a shirt, both of which were wrinkled and looked like he'd slept in them. Ah, yes. Divorced. J.T. decided against commenting.

"I was beginning to think you were being held hostage."

"You could've come inside. We don't arrest feds for trespassing unless they start shit."

"Very funny. I didn't want to start a rumor you'd wised up and decided to become a real law enforcement officer."

"Like I've got time to spend at Quantico."

J.T. clasped David's hand and pulled him in for a half-hug while they pounded each other's back and shared a chest bump. Being around David was good. "Come on, I'll give you a ride in a good car. Might even buy you supper." After he parked at the restaurant, he turned to face David. "I needed one good reason and I'll squeeze Jason's balls until he sings soprano. I hope you've turned up something on him."

David held up his hands in mock surrender. "I'm sorry. The department's not looking at Carrington for anything, but you're still buying my supper." He was out of the car and headed to the front door of the steak house before J.T. could protest.

Talking over old times made for an okay evening. Throughout the meal, J.T. had sensed something wasn't being said. He gave the beers David drank with his meal a chance to relax him and then pressed. "What are you not saying?"

"I've heard rumbles. Hated to mention them." David tossed his napkin on the table and leaned back in the chair. "You ain't gonna like it."

" 'Like' is not a requirement."

"Your girl is getting a bad reputation. People are talking."

"About?" J.T.'s patience wore thin, quickly.

"Over the past couple of weeks, she's insisted Carrington is out to get her. The guys are beginning to think she's got a hard-on for the dude."

The rush of blood hit J.T.'s head. "That's bullshit."

"Don't get pissed at me." David leaned across the table and clamped his hand on J.T.'s shoulder. "She wouldn't be the first woman with a vendetta."

****

Ellen's excitement bubbled out and spilled over. She beamed like a kid at Christmas, and Doyle's belly filled with guilt. She smoothed the tablecloth with her fingers and studied the silverware with curiosity. Her cheeks reddened slightly while she fingered her napkin. "Can we afford this place?"

"Well," he admitted, "we couldn't eat here every night."

"What's special about tonight?" She gazed at him, her face radiant with love and trust."Don. Are you listening?"

"I'm sorry. What did you say?"

"I asked you what we're celebrating."

"I kind of wanted to wait until dessert, but I can't." He slid his hand into his jacket pocket and brought out a small, velvet jewelry box. Ellen's eyes brimmed with tears when he opened the box and placed it in front of her. "Will you marry me?"

"Yes." She held out her hand for him to slip the ring on her finger.

Another dark corner of his heart flooded with light. For Helen, Carrington would be the last execution.

****

J.T. knocked on Leigh's front door. She hadn't come to work this morning. He'd waited until ten before he'd gone to check on her. He stuffed his hands in the pockets of his jeans, undecided whether to be worried or pissed. She'd avoided him over the weekend, turning down his offer yesterday to take her and Ethan to the movies. Movies? Shit, when had he last been inside a theater?

Already short on patience, J.T. walked around back when she didn't answer fast enough to suit him. He slid his hand across the hood of her car. The cool metal indicted the motor hadn't run in a while. He knocked firmly on the kitchen door. He went up the driveway to the front yard and spotted Leigh across the street.

A tall blond male with the biceps of a body-builder held her undivided attention. Ethan sat on the man's hip, and, from what J.T. saw, Leigh didn't appear to be in distress. Her laughter drifted to his ears, sending heat flashes to his brain, which he refused to believe was jealousy. Satisfied she was okay, he haggled with himself about whether to stay or get in the damn 'Vette and go.

"J.T. is here," Ethan shouted, his arms waving.

The kid wriggled out of the guy's arms and shot down the sidewalk at top speed. Shit. He was coming across the street without looking or slowing down. Leigh yelled something J.T. couldn't hear because he was already moving. He sprinted across the road. He reached the small rocket right before he left the curb and snatched him into the air. Ethan's small arms wrapped around J.T.'s neck and squeezed. He closed his eyes against the emotion when his heart clenched as if the boy's hands were inside his chest.

The angry frown on the approaching mother ended the tender moment.

"Little man, you're in a world of trouble," J.T. whispered a warning.

"On the ground, Ethan," she demanded.

Leigh knelt and J.T. slid the wide-eyed kid down his leg. Her steely, blue eyes narrowed to slits making him regret dropping by uninvited.

"What's the rule about crossing the street?" she asked her son.

Head down, he scuffed one toe of his tennis shoe back and forth on the sidewalk. "Not without a grownup." He looked his mother in the eyes with an expression of pure innocence. "And I didn't."

"Don't you try that lame excuse on me. You were going to."

J.T. decided now might be a good time to intervene. "Sorry if I interrupted something. Everyone at the office was worried you were sick. I told them I'd check on you." He knew—she knew—he was lying through his teeth.

"Ethan, go inside with DeeDee. I need to talk to J.T." She kissed him on top of the head and sent him on his way. "Let's go to my house."

Tears filled Ethan's eyes when he looked back over his shoulder. The last thing he wanted was for Ethan to cry because of him.

"Shit, Leigh. I didn't mean to get him in trouble."

"I know."

"Then what has you tied in knots?"

She waited until they were on her porch to start talking. "I'm considering taking Ethan and disappearing. I'm going to the bank today to draw out enough money to keep us going if I have to go underground."

"Excuse me?"

"I'm not letting Jason have access to my son. Not for visits or holidays, ever. It's my job to protect Ethan at all costs, and I will."

"Leigh," J.T. caught her hand and wove his fingers through hers. "You don't know for sure that Jason or his parents will gain visitation rights. Don't let hate and fear make your decisions."

"If I have to go underground, I will."

"And what will you tell Ethan? How will that make sense to him when he knows nothing about his father?" The tension in her body had her shoulders drawn up tight and her back stiff as a board. "Think this

220 |

through before you do something that might give Jason the ammunition he needs."

"I can't discuss this anymore."

"The hell you can't. Do what you have to do, be ready, but don't run because of a maybe." His phone vibrated. As bad as he wanted to ignore it, he couldn't. He read the message and then stood. "The question of whether someone had offered to help them achieved nothing. None of the victim's wives received offers of help from a stranger."

She pulled her hand away. "I didn't imagine the conversation the night of my wreck. Somebody needs to tell Jason."

"And tell him what? You think he'd believe it?"

The soft lines around her mouth deepened. The gentle blue eyes had darkened to a steel gray. Word by word, she was shutting him out. He wanted her to need him. No. He needed her to need him.

"I have to get back to work." Grasping at the remnants of his pride, he inched backward. "I know you'll do the right thing."

Her head moved a fraction. J.T. walked to his car, got in, and drove off.

****

Leigh rolled over and looked at the clock. Nobody called at eleven at night without a reason. She checked the caller ID before she answered. She hadn't heard from him since he left her house this morning. "J.T.?"

"The sniper hit. You want in?"

"Yes." Without thinking, she scrambled out of bed and slid on the jeans she'd tossed across the chair a few hours ago.

"Are you sure?" The chill in his voice sliced through the air space.

"Yes. Text me the address. I'll meet you."

"Not necessary. I'm not far from your house. I'll be outside." He disconnected.

"Shit," she muttered while she called DeeDee. She should call him back. Not ride with him. She shouldn't get that close. Not when she wanted him to hold her so badly she physically hurt.

She dashed to the bathroom and splashed water on her face, dragged a comb through her hair, and slipped on a headband. Her heart lurched when she slid the lanyard holding her badge around her neck. The rumble of his car easing up her driveway drew another expletive while she raced into her bedroom and pushed her hand under the pillow for her Glock.

The sound of a key in the lock followed by the soft chime of the alarm indicated DeeDee was letting herself in and punching in the code. Leigh holstered her weapon and hurried down the hall.

"God, you're a lifesaver."

DeeDee's tousled hair, sleep-heavy eyes, and pink warmups gave her the appearance of a teenager instead of a rock-solid thirty-something friend who came whenever Leigh called.

"Yeah, I know. Be careful."

"I will." Leigh gave her a quick hug before heading outside. "I'll call later this morning." Closing the door quietly, she waited until the deadbolt slammed home and then jogged out to J.T.'s waiting car. Would this be her last call as an officer of the law?

She buckled up and assured herself riding with J.T. wouldn't be a problem. Then the subtle scent of his cologne slammed into her senses, and her heart cracked. Without warning, tears flooded her eyes. Damning herself, she questioned her sanity for getting this close to him. She angled her head, studying his profile. Missing him already.

"What's wrong?" J.T. broke the silence as he maneuvered the car through traffic.

His tone, laced with hurt and anger, sliced open her heart with the precision of a surgeon's scalpel. "Nothing. I'm fine."

"You're on the verge of tears. Arms wrapped around your belly like you're having an appendicitis attack." His voice was low, growling like an injured animal. "Hell yeah . . . nothing's wrong."

The Corvette charged onto the loop at the pace of a hungry panther, and its driver fell mute. He'd given up trying to talk, and Leigh's guilt kept her from trying to make peace.

He'd warned her not to get involved with him. In fact, at one point, he'd been quite adamant. Her disappearing wouldn't be more than a blip on his radar. Was she glad he hadn't fallen in love with her? No, she'd longed to hear him say the words at least once.

The crowd around the crime scene prevented them from parking close. All four major news networks had already arrived and set up lights and cameras. She and J.T. pushed through the crowd. An Atlanta cop saw her badge and motioned them under the tape.

"Straight down the walk, in front of the Georgian Towers Apartment." The cop directed them toward a small cluster of people.

"Thanks." Leigh turned when J.T. caught her arm. She looked into the familiar scowl, with deep furrows between his eyes and hard-set jaw. "What?"

"I know this address." He glanced ahead at the building and back at her. "I have a friend on the force. He sent me information on Carrington—"

She whirled and stormed away. Leigh found her cousin taking pictures of the body. "Charlie," she called out.

Her cousin had seen dozens of gruesome crime scenes, yet, tonight, when he turned and faced her, his grim expression sent shivers coursing across her skin. He skirted the perimeter and came to her.

"You shouldn't be here." Charlie's hands gripped her upper arms.

"Why not?"

"The dead guy is Jason Carrington."

Chapter Twenty-Five

Breaking every rule of training, Doyle hadn't left the execution site. Leigh McBride and the fed were working these cases. Doyle had to be there when she arrived. Albeit from a distance, he had to share this moment with her. He hid among the group of spectators who'd gathered across the street. Overhead lights had been set up, giving him a good view of the small army of officials who moved around the body with the precision of choreographed dancers.

Doyle's hands shook as he contemplated the importance of tonight for both of them. His skin tingled thinking about this, the culmination of his career. No more jeopardizing their relationship, because after tonight there would be no more executions. Not by him.

His commitment and promise to avenge the defenseless was righteous, but, lately, the white-hot, burning need for retribution had faded and vengeance simmered instead of flamed.

Tonight, he'd cleaned his rifle for the last time. He'd left it on the roof of the restaurant where he'd given Ellen her engagement ring. Carrington was his last execution.

The crowd grew in size as more people gathered and craned their necks to get a glimpse of the dead body. His skin became clammy with anticipation. He rubbed his aching left arm. Sweat trickled down his neck while he scanned the group of cops. Doyle shoved his way through the mass of flesh. He had to get closer. His breath caught. Leigh had arrived. The same FBI agent who'd been working with her was at her side.

Doyle barely stopped himself from running across the street when she staggered backward and the fed wrapped his arms around her. She screamed, struggled, and fought against his restraining arms. She broke free and ran toward the remains of Jason Carrington.

Confusion washed over Doyle. Was she upset? He'd executed Carrington for her safety. How dare she pretend an injustice had been done? Her reaction of disbelief and horror exploded in Doyle's chest.

The woman next to him muttered something he didn't understand. His ears roared. Blood rushed to his brain with the velocity of a freight train. Something was crushing his chest. He opened his mouth to speak. The excruciating pain radiated down his arm and across his chest. Fighting for control, he staggered and stumbled, unable to focus. The darkness around him grew thicker, heavier.

Hands roughly shoved him out of their way. With legs melting like butter, and vision dimming, he thought he saw his dead daughter. Had she come for him? Not now. Please. He didn't want to cross that threshold tonight. His new life was beginning.

****

Leigh pushed her way to where the body lay sprawled across the sidewalk. The scene looked much like the other sniper killings. Brain matter and bone had exploded when the bullet hit its target sending blood spatters over the area.

They had to be wrong. This couldn't be Jason. Could it?

Reality slammed into her. Her stomach lurched. A human being had been murdered. She hated Jason and the terrible things he'd done. Weeks of constant fear ending so abruptly sent her thoughts swirling. A myriad of emotions washed over her. Tears rushed from her eyes and down her cheeks while she fought back the loss of control inching toward the surface.

She leaned into J.T.'s strong hands. She turned around, resting her head against his chest. She needed his strength, and, again, he was there for her. "What happens now? Do I have to explain all of this to Ethan? Or can I stick with the story that his dad disappeared? Jason's parents may insist on Ethan knowing the truth."

"You're getting way ahead of yourself. Whatever happens, Ethan will be fine. He'll have your strength." J.T. squeezed her arms. "But if the ID is right and this is Carrington, you should leave the scene. Let the ME and crime scene techs do their job."

"Nonsense." Granted she'd temporarily lost her composure, but she had to see this through. "I'm not going anywhere."

"You're not thinking rationally. The press will have a field day if they tie you to the victim."

She glanced at the horde of reporters behind the barrier. "All they care about is who's dead."

"Detective McBride." Chief Hampton's voice came from behind her.

She whirled, spotting something out of the corner of her eyes as she turned. Her gaze locked on the right hand of the dead man. Her heart dropped straight to the tops of her shoes. She wobbled on her feet.

"Leigh?" J.T. rested his hand on her shoulders. He gently shifted her body, turning her to face him and her boss. "What is it? You're white as a sheet."

"I can confirm the body is Jason Carrington." She blinked hard to clear her vision. "Run his prints. They'll come back as his."

"Walk with me, Detective." Her boss turned and charged across the street.

She caught J.T.'s hand and was grateful when, without hesitation, he fell in step beside her. Together they followed the chief down the block to an ambulance.

"What are we doing?" Confused by her boss's appearance at a crime scene and curious at his brusque tone, Leigh searched his face. His cold stare unnerved her.

"Sit down before you pass out." His tone left no room for

argument.

"There's nothing wrong with me." She grudgingly sat.

An EMT wrapped the blood pressure cuff around her arm. She sat quietly while he took her reading and then listened to her heart. She stated she hadn't taken any blows, while he felt around her head and neck as if checking for a bump. After she followed his finger back and forth then up and down a few times, she'd had enough.

"Well?" She pushed to her feet and stepped away.

The EMT shrugged. "Blood pressure's a little high."

"Why wouldn't it be?"

"Thanks." Her boss waved off the EMT.

"I don't understand why you're here, sir."

"You do understand. I'm expecting a call from the mayor before morning. Perhaps you'd like to explain how you positively identified a body with no head."

"I recognized the ring on his finger, right hand." She answered fast because J.T. looked ready to pop a vein. "Jason wore that thing the night he beat the hell out of me."

"You're positive?"

"Yeah. I am." She shook off the seven-year-old memory of her battered and swollen face, refusing to go there.

"I'll pass the information on."

"That's okay. I'll tell the forensics team."

"No. You won't." His words fell out of his mouth like bricks hitting the pavement. "Go home, Detective."

Leigh's head snapped back as if he'd slapped her. Panic slammed a heavy hand over her lungs and squeezed. "Sir, with all due respect, you have no reason to send me home."

"I don't justify my decisions to you." His nostrils flared. "Your liaison assignment to the FBI is over."

"Why am I being punished? I have a right to know."

"We'll talk in the morning after you've rested and returned to your desk at CID."

The chief whirled and walked away. Stunned, she stared at his back. "Why?" The bitter word burned her tongue when she spoke. She looked up into J.T.'s steady eyes.

"It's procedure and bureaucracy."

"It's bullshit."

"Casey would've done the same."

The weight of a dozen anvils crashed down around her shoulders. "God. Enough. What else can happen?" Her spirit whooshed out of her.

"Be thankful it was the sniper's bullet that killed him."

She recoiled. "What the hell does that mean?"

"Think about it. If he'd been shot in the back, hell, any place other than his head, you could've been considered a viable suspect."

"Please. No more," she whispered. Looking upward, she wished she were at home where she'd crawl in bed, roll into a ball, and hide under the blanket. Instead, she sank to her knees and covered her head with her hands. "No more."

J.T. lifted her in his arms, and she curled into his chest. He carried her farther away from the crowd. Holding her as if she were fine china, he gingerly placed her on the curb, sat behind her, and pulled her between his legs. She leaned back against his chest and cried.

She had no idea of time passing. No real sense of how long the tears flowed, purging the turmoil of the past few weeks. The tsunami of self-pity finally subsided, and Leigh stared up at the vast sky with its twinkling stars and full moon lighting the night. The warm breeze caressed her wet cheeks, a gentle reminder to stop feeling sorry for herself. She'd taken everything life had dished out and had made a good life for herself and Ethan.

"I'm over my bout of poor-poor-pitiful-me."

J.T.'s arms were wrapped snuggly around her waist. "Take your time. I'm in no hurry."

"You held me like this the night Jason broke into my house."

"I remember."

"You do?"

"Yeah. Your hair smelled like grapefruit, and you trembled with a combination of fear and anger. He'd hurt you, and I wanted to kill him myself."

"Thank you." She turned her shoulders, rested her head on his chest, and listened to the strong, steady rhythm of his heart.

"For?"

"For the two long, heartwarming sentences you just said."

He tightened his grip around her waist. "Don't push it."

"I can't believe Jason's dead. Dozens of questions and emotions are running through my mind."

"I can only imagine." His lips brushed the top of her head.

"I hated him. God, how I hated him, and I can't make myself feel remorse."

"There's no reason you should. Maybe now things will calm down."

"I'm sorry about the past few days. I've been a bitch to everybody."

"You do have a talent." His chest vibrated under her with a soft chuckle.

Her spirit lightened. Joking felt good. "I said I was sorry."

"Apology accepted. They don't need me here. How about I take you home?"

"I'd like that."His warm breath shot heat down her neck when he bent his head and softly growled into her ear.

Chapter Twenty-Six

Telling Casey, Romeo, and Olivia good-bye had been much harder than she'd expected. Leigh had welcomed J.T.'s arm around her when he'd escorted her out of the Federal Building to her car. With a promise to take her to supper, he'd thumbed away the brimming tears and sent her back to Atlanta PD.

Since arriving, Leigh had asked for the chief three times, and three times his assistant had given her the runaround. Supposedly, he'd gone downtown to a meeting with the commissioner. Leigh had the nagging feeling he'd made a point of avoiding her.

Her coworkers smiled and nodded at her while giving her a wide berth. She tried to shrug off their behavior, but the air thickened and wrapped around her like a heavy fog. She entered her limited notes from last night and waited for an explanation. Or, at least, a new assignment. Her buzzing cell brought a sigh of relief. Her attorney had returned her call.

"Hang on, let me get somewhere private." Leigh moved to a small interview room and closed the door. "You got my message?"

"Yes. I'm sorry I didn't get back with you sooner. I've cleared my schedule and will be in my office for the rest of the day."

"Thanks, you shouldn't have."

"Leigh, you may need me. You must get into self-protection mode. A multi-millionaire's son, murdered on the streets of Atlanta, will draw nationwide coverage. Be prepared. All of Jason Carrington's dirty laundry will be fodder for the newsmongers."

Leigh blew out a sigh, remembering the parking garage at the Federal Building. "They were waiting for me this morning when I got to the FBI office."

"You didn't talk to them?"

"No comment. That's all they got."

"Good. I've had clients whose statements wound up twisted and distorted. Talk to no one without me present."

"Stop. You're scaring me."

"You don't know much about the Carrington family, especially the mother."

"Never wanted to. Still don't."

"She'll play this like her son was the second coming and his death was tantamount to him being nailed to the cross."

"That's disgusting."

"To you. Not to Carlton or Elizabeth Carrington."

"I'll leave the drama to her. All I want is the visitation hearing dropped."

"My advice is to not push the issue for a while."

"Why? Don't you think Mr. and Mrs. Carrington will drop the case?"

"Think about the implication here. Their only child is dead. Their last tie to him is his son."

"My son," Leigh snapped. "My son." She bit back the urge to shout.

She calmed down and ended the call. Leigh returned to her desk and waited until the chief's assistant came and said, "He's ready for you. Right away."

"Thanks." Leigh marched straight to his office. Pausing at the closed door, she knocked firmly and waited for his booming voice.

"Come."

"You wanted to—" Leigh cut her words off and stopped all forward motion. The chief wasn't alone.

"Hello, Carl." Leigh shook the extended hand of her union rep. "Do I need representation?"

"I'm here to protect your interests." Carl cleared his throat twice and adjusted his uniform shirt over his pudgy stomach.

"Good to know."

The chief shifted his bulk in the chair. "Take a seat, Detective."

A chill raced across her skin, like the cold you feel when you step from your warm living room and face a hard, north wind. Leigh and Carl sat directly across the desk from her boss. She leaned back and held her tongue.

"I spent the morning discussing the current situation and your assignment with the mayor. For the time being, you'll work at a desk."

"A desk?" Her jaw dropped.

"Let me finish. You will assist one of the other detectives."

"You were right to have Carl present because I want an explanation for being yanked out of the field. Tying me to a desk is preposterous." Keeping her voice down and level, she held his gaze without flinching. "If I'm to be disciplined, I want the charges spelled out."

"This isn't discipline. I'm trying to protect you."

Leigh blew out a sigh. "I understand why I'm being taken off the sniper case. My connection to the latest victim precludes my further involvement. Why am I being shackled to a desk instead of being assigned to another case?"

"Okay, Detective. Here's where you are right now." He leaned forward in his chair. "Carlton Carrington bypassed the mayor and went straight to the governor. He had plenty to say, mostly accusations of how you'd conspired to have his son sent back to prison. He's wondering now if you're somehow responsible for his son's death. Be glad you're not on suspension pending further investigation. At least you still have your badge and gun."

Heat prickled her scalp. Sweat dampened her skin. The bun at the base of her neck was too tight. She succumbed to the urge and patted her hair. "Carrington can't accuse me of anything more than fighting to keep his psycho son away from my child."

"Your continued complaints against Jason Carrington haven't helped your cause. Not one shred of evidence has been found to substantiate your claims. If you'd prefer not to work a desk . . ." He paused, opened a file lying on his desk, and studied the page for a minute. "You've accrued vacation days. Perhaps you'd like to use them."

Leigh shifted in her chair and stared at the silent Carl. "Don't you have something to say?"

"The department has the right to give you any assignment as long as they don't violate the union contract," Carl spoke slowly as if he'd memorized the words. "Your job grade doesn't guarantee fieldwork. Take the time. Come back refreshed."

"Et tu, Brute?"

****

Doyle blinked a couple of times against the bright light. Fought against the darkness trying to pull him under. He struggled against the black void tugging at him. A cool hand rested on his forehead. A voice far away called to him.

"Don?" A whisper. A familiar sound. Loving. Pleading.

"His eyelids fluttered," the voice said louder. "I saw them move."

One more time, Doyle tried to breach the black void. The pain stilled him.

"He moaned. Did you hear?"

The woman sniffed and her voice trembled. Ellen was in tears because of him? He forced himself to focus. "Ellen?"

"I'm here." She brushed his cheek with a kiss. "Welcome back."

"Don't cry," he croaked. Without him asking, she slipped a straw between his lips.

"Tiny sips."

Cool and wet, the water refreshed and rejuvenated him. Ellen's beautiful face loomed above him, reassuring him. Something had put him flat on his back in a hospital bed. He shifted and pain wracked his chest. "What happened to me?"

"You had a heart attack."

"I retired. For us." He fought the urge to sleep.

"Sh. Rest." She laughed and patted his arm. "You're not making any sense."

"Am I dying?"

"Not on my watch." A man wearing a white coat stepped into Doyle's line of sight. "You'll be better than new. When I crack a set of ribs and take a heart out, I return it in better condition."

"I appreciate you putting it back."

"Had to. Ellen told me you two are getting married. She'd never have forgiven me otherwise."

"Thank you."

"My pleasure." He put his stethoscope in his ears and listened to Doyle's chest. He pursed his lips and nodded. "We'll miss you around here."

"Pardon?"

"You're retiring?" The doctor patted Doyle on the arm. "I'll check back before I leave for the day."

"Why does he think I retired?" He struggled to keep his eyes open as weariness crept upon him.

"You were talking gibberish when you first woke." She gave him another sip of water. "Sleep. I'll be here when you wake."

His heart monitor sprang to life, the beats per minute raced. "What else did I say?"

Alarm colored Ellen's face. "You were muttering something about retiring."

"Sorry. Can't keep my eyes open." Doyle's body succumbed to exhaustion.

Her soft hand held his, a tether to life.

****

J.T. knocked and stepped back a few paces. He bent his knees and spread his feet wide for stability. Leigh stepped out onto the porch and cocked her head to the side looking at him as if he were nuts. Disappointment Ethan hadn't blasted through the door and jumped into his arms surprised J.T., confusing him.

"You look like a linebacker ready for a blitz." Her blue eyes glittered with humor.

He closed the gap between them, pulling her in for a kiss before peering over her head. "I braced for a rocket launch. Where is he?"

"Peachtree City. Mom's taking him to school in the morning."

J.T. followed her inside, pushed the door closed with his foot, and leered down at her. "We're alone?"

"Totally." She rose on her toes for a kiss.

"He's gone for the entire night?" He looked into her eyes. Buried right below the surface, troubled simmered.

"Yep." Her hands stroked down his back and held him closer. "Until after school tomorrow."

He opened his mouth to ask her what was wrong, but she angled her head and nipped the tip of his earlobe. She nibbled her way to his jaw, sliding her tongue around the outer edge of his lips. A soft hum rolled from her mouth to his when she kissed him. His train of thought vanished, and he dragged her closer.

His growing erection strained against its confinement. The scent of her hair, the taste of her skin made him want to devour her on the spot. He didn't have her alone as much as he'd like, and, tonight, he intended to take his time.

Her tongue stroked up the tendon in his neck. "Hurry." She pushed away, grabbed his hand, and tugged him down the hall.

"Forget that." Somebody had to take charge. With the head of steam she was building, he'd be inside her and spent within minutes.

She glanced over her shoulder. "Excuse me?"

"We're in no rush."

"Speak for yourself."

With one move, her T-shirt came off and landed across his chest. His dick jumped, begging for freedom. A red lacy bra offered a tantalizing view of rosy nipples jutting out, begging him to touch. Zip. Her jeans were loose. She hooked her thumbs in the sides, wiggled her hips, and, with a bounce they were on the floor. A tiny red triangle covered a small patch of blonde hair. He salivated profusely while following her blindly.

"You play dirty." He barely croaked out the words.

"I play to win." Her need-you, blue eyes darkened.

The back of her knees bumped into the mattress. Without taking her gaze off his, she scooted up the bed. J.T. jerked off his socks and shoes and then crawled after her. He sat back on his heels. Sanity slipped out the door when her hips rose in invitation.

"You're right. The hell with going slow." He ran his fingers between her legs. The muscles in her stomach tightened at his touch. Already wet, the scent of her moisture drifted to his nostrils. Sweet nectar. He nudged her knees wider, slid his hands under her hips, and lifted her ass in the air. His fingers slid the thin strip of lace to the side, and he blew warm breath across her sensitive skin. "Mine."

"Please." She wet her lips with her tongue, and her eyes pleaded for relief.

J.T. covered her with his mouth. He couldn't get enough of her. Would never get enough of her.

Chapter Twenty-Seven

J.T. shifted his weight in search of Leigh's warm body but found only empty cool sheets. He bolted upright, instantly awake and alert. Swinging his feet to the floor, his gaze swept the room. She sat on the floor next to the window looking out at her backyard. Moonlight streamed through the open curtains and across the long, curly hair hanging down her back. The sight sent a sharp pain through his heart. This feeling that swelled in his chest when she was near couldn't be anything more than lust. Couldn't be. All he had to do was look at his mother and father for proof love or long-term commitments never lasted. Then Nana's undying love and support flashed across his mind. Shit. He was contradicting himself.

Leigh was grieving for something other than Carrington's death. What troubled her? Tonight had been about forgetting. Twice, she'd used him to forget. Not that he minded being Leigh's sex toy. He slid off the bed and assumed his usual position on the floor, behind her.

His libido sprang to life with her naked body pressed against him. He willed his expanding erection to relax. "What's up?"

"You deserve an explanation." Her voice was soft as a breeze across calm water.

"No. You don't owe me anything."

"The chief gave me a choice today. Work a desk or take vacation time."

"What lame-ass excuse did you get?"

"Carlton Carrington."

"What   about   him?"
Leigh's chest rose while she took a deep breath. On the exhale, she twisted in his arms and faced him. As she turned, moonbeams highlighted tears, brimming, ready to rush down her cheeks. She didn't cry, instead, she laid out the day's events, factual and flat. He felt her undercurrent of anger.

His blood boiled at her boss's treatment of her. She'd been through enough hell during the past few weeks to knock a bull to his knees. Yet she kept getting up and moving forward. He respected her dedication to Ethan and her job. He'd never experienced her kind of devotion from his mother.

"Did you tell him to go f—"

Her finger across his lips cut off his last few words. "I'm on vacation for a few days. When I go back, I'll do what it takes to reclaim his respect."

"I'm sorry. You deserve better." A plan formed in his head. He'd ask Casey to send a letter of commendation on her behalf to the chief of police, and hell, maybe the mayor.

"I'll survive. This is a minor setback." The corners of her mouth lifted. "You'll be fine working the case without me."

"I'm not sure about that." A long curl draped across her breast. He picked up the lock of hair and dragged it back and forth across her nipple. "You haven't heard the latest. The shot that killed Carrington came from the roof of a restaurant across from his apartment building. The crime scene unit found quite a surprise." Leigh shivered and pulled the strand of hair away from him.

"I hate that I'm already out of the loop."

Not to be defeated, he used the tip of his finger to stroke her breast.

"Focus." She chuckled low and sexy. "The surprise?"

"The sniper left a Remington 700, the case, and a partial box of .338 bullets behind."

"You think he got spooked or left them on purpose?" Her hand covered his.

"It wasn't an accident. His rifle was part of him—an extra appendage."

"I agree. He's too methodical to experience fear."

"Exactly. I think Carrington was his last execution."

She leaned back as if trying to get a better look at him in the moonlight. "Am I misreading you, or do I detect admiration in your voice?"

"I'm glad that son of a bitch Carrington is dead but I'm curious. What made him believe he had the right to become judge and jury?"

"When you find him, you can ask."

Even in the dim light, the disappointment on her face stabbed him in the chest. "Catching him now will take a miracle. I'm sorry you won't be there with us."

She lifted her chin defiantly. "You'll get him. Congratulations, you were right about his choice of weapon."

"Was there ever any doubt?" He tried to lighten the mood, anything to make her smile.

"I should feel worse, have some remorse another human being is dead. I'm not glad, but I am relieved."

"I get that. Nobody should live in fear the way you have."

"You have no idea." She stood and offered him her hand. "Come back to bed. Unless you're hungry. We sort of skipped supper."

J.T.'s gaze slid up her long, lean body and came to rest on deep blue eyes. "You, naked in the moonlight, or food? I'll eat tomorrow."

"Good. I'll fix breakfast and send you home in time to change into your 'Men in Black' persona."

He ignored her wisecrack. "I'm proud of you for not letting the chief get under your skin." J.T. backed toward the bed.

Leigh pushed him flat on his back and straddled him. Her breasts, creamy white in the moonlight, swayed with her movement. His mouth watered. He propped up on his elbows and angled his head in for a taste. "That's my girl."

"Am I your girl?"

Her question flipped his brain upside down and turned his voice box switch off. He gripped her thighs and managed to force one word out. "Leigh."

Her muscles tightened, and tendons became ridged under his hands. "Forget it. I didn't mean to scare you."

"Leigh," he repeated, still sounding like a frog.

She rolled off him, turned her back, and fiddled with her alarm. "Seriously. Forget I asked."

Her tone left no room for more conversation. She drew the sheet over them, obviously through talking to him. He slid his arm around her waist. She lay perfectly still, catching his hand in hers.

He should say something. Anything. Instead, he lay in the dark, his thoughts racing at the speed of light. Eventually, her breathing grew soft and steady. He'd missed the perfect opportunity to tell her how much she meant to him.

****

The aroma of food led J.T. to Leigh's kitchen. A hot shower had given his nerves time to calm down and him a chance to think about last night. How damn easy it should've been to answer her with a simple fucking yes. Of course, she was his girl. And more. Much more.

"Something smells good." He stopped in the doorway, hoping the tension between them had eased.

The corners of her mouth lifted. No doubt, she was remembering his earlier slapstick performance when her alarm clock had sent him flying across the room. It had accomplished a couple of things. He'd gotten out of bed. More importantly, she'd folded over laughing.

"Perfect timing." Leigh set a plate of scrambled eggs, bacon, and toast on the table next to a steaming cup of coffee. "Eat. Or you'll be late."

He ignored the aroma assaulting his empty stomach. A need to be near her, to hold her, propelled him across the room. He gathered her in his arms, advancing until she leaned against the counter. "I called work and left word I'd had a heart attack and might not be in today."

He bracketed her with his hands on the tile, leaned down, and kissed her softly. A thank-God-you're-in-my-life kiss. A forgive-me-for-being-a-fool kiss. A don't-make-me-live-without-you kiss. He hoped to convey what he should've said to her last night. What he needed to put into words this morning. He leaned back and studied her face. Again, his tongue locked to the roof of his mouth.

Her eyes communicated nothing. "You think Casey will buy that excuse?"

"It's the truth. That alarm took me straight to cardiac arrest." His stomach protested loudly. He sat and forked in a mouthful of eggs. "You always been hard to wake up?"

"When I'm falling asleep, a creak in the house, wind howling through the trees, or a car idling down the street snaps me wide-awake and has me reaching for my gun. When I finally fall asleep, it's hard and deep."

"Jason's dead. Maybe now, you can lower the volume." He washed down a moan of appreciation for the home cooking with a swallow of strong coffee.

"I hope so." She fixed herself a plate and joined him.

They needed to talk about last night. He was in too deep to lose her. He opened his mouth and brain freeze returned, blocking out the right words. When his cell buzzed, he ignored it. Instead, he ate and drafted sentences in his mind.

"Aren't you answering that?"

"No."

Her jaw dropped. "It may be important."

"This is important."

"This? *This* is breakfast between two friends. Answer your phone."

He hated talking about his feelings, but her frosty use of the word friends was a land mine, and his foot hovered over the blasting cap. One way or another, they had to clear the air. He forced his mouth open and pushed words out.

"We need to talk about last night." There. Now he'd committed himself to clearing the air.

"There's nothing to say. We had great sex." She batted her eyelashes and waved her fork through the air. "Let's do it again sometime."

Jesus Christ. The spear she'd thrown hit him right in the heart. He hated to make bad matters worse. "Can we be serious?"

"If this is a brush off, get it over with." She laid down her fork and leveled her gaze at him. "Otherwise, leave it alone."

"A brush off? That's the dumbest . . ." He had no response to such a stupid statement. Other than his grandmother, he'd never cared enough about a woman to stick around and argue with her. In the past, he'd cut his losses and walked away. No way would he do that with Leigh. Not having her near, in his life, was unimaginable.

Her fingers drummed on the table. "I'm dumb? As in stupid?"

"Bad choice of words. Sore spots, left alone—fester."

"You saw me naked last night. Did you notice any open wounds on me? And you're over thinking what I said."

He stared at her. Did she expect him to believe that crap? He recognized the warning signs. There was a wound all right, one as big as Mt. Vesuvius. His cell buzzed a second time.

"Answer your damn phone." She used her don't-argue-with-me-Ethan expression.

But J.T. wasn't a child. "No." God help him if Casey needed something.

"I'm getting dressed, and we're not having a conversation about last night." She shoved her plate away and narrowed her eyes. "I asked a question I shouldn't have, and you overreacted. Forget it and move on."

For the third time, his cell buzzed. No way to ignore three calls in rapid succession. J.T. snatched the cell from his pocket and flipped it over to read the caller ID. Time stopped. His appetite vanished. He hit the receive button.

"Nana?"

"It's Elva." Her voice cracked and trembled. "I didn't leave a message 'cause I needed to talk to you directly."

"What's wrong?" J.T. interrupted. The hair on his arms stood.

"Your grandmother's on her way to Piedmont."

J.T. shoved his chair back and raced to the bedroom. He could talk and finish dressing at the same time. "Her heart?"

"No. EMT said her hip's probably broken."

"Broken? How?" His mind raced in different directions. He couldn't locate his shoes.

"Don't know. I found her unconscious in the driveway."

"Jesus Christ." The top of his head would detonate if he didn't find his shoes. He knelt and checked under the bed. Where the hell had he thrown them? "Where's my mother?"

The pause lasted too long. Ice crystals locked around his chest wall.

"Elva, where's my mother?"

"I can't rightly say. Wasn't anybody around when I arrived, 'cept your grandmother."

His heart splintered into a million pieces. "I'm on my way."

Of course, his mother was gone. Hadn't she always been missing when something important happened? A nightmarish image of Nana's small, crumpled body lying alone in the dark in need of help flashed through his mind. The chill in his heart melted. Molten lava replaced the cold.

Leigh helped locate his shoes. She placed them on the floor next to where he stood. He slammed his feet into them while she slid her pistol into her purse. "Let's go," she said.

J.T. didn't argue. Later he'd speak his heart. He sprinted to his car with Leigh at his side. The engine sprang to life and soon telephone poles flashed by like tumbling toothpicks.

"I heard you say broken. Did Nana fall?" Leigh reached across and stroked his neck, startling him.

"Huh? Yeah." He retold his conversation with his grandmother's housekeeper. He tried to keep his emotions under control while his mind vacillated between worry, fear, and anger. His fury targeted his missing mother. He slid the Corvette into a no parking zone, slammed on the brakes, and was out of the car in the blink of the eye. A security guard stepped toward them. J.T. jerked his ID from his hip pocket.

"Nobody touches that car," he growled without slowing down.

Leigh held up her hand to silence the guard. "Give me your keys."

"Nobody drives my car." He spit the words over his shoulder. He abruptly turned on his heel and walked back to Leigh. "Except you."

"Go," she whispered. "I'll find you."

He jogged through the entrance unsure if he wanted her to find him. She'd never bought into how dysfunctional his family was, and he feared today might tip the scales.

****

If the doctor didn't bring news soon, Leigh worried J.T.'s nerves would snap. He'd stalked the halls, paced the waiting room, and jumped each time the doors to the examination room opened. He'd pestered nurses and threatened an intern or two. Fear for his grandmother and fury at his mother made the situation highly combustible.

Leigh hadn't returned his car keys. Instead, she held them tightly. The cool metal warmed in her hand while she remembered his expression when he'd handed them over. She'd seen love in his eyes. Maybe he didn't know it, but Leigh not only saw the love buried behind the façade, but she'd also felt it in his touch.

He dropped into the chair next to hers and picked up the paper cup she'd set on the table. "I'll find my mother if I have to turn Atlanta upside down."

"What then?"

His head swiveled in her direction. Eyes narrowed, nostrils flared, he didn't hesitate. "My mother's going to tell me exactly what she did to my grandmother."

Leigh's stomach roiled at the venom in his voice. "You don't believe she'd hurt her mother. You can't."

"She may not have physically hurt Nana, but my mother is responsible. Count on it."

"Mr. Noble?"

J.T. sprang to his feet, and Leigh stood with him. She rested her hand on his back for moral support. She recognized the nurse walking toward them. They'd met a couple of times. Ellen, the woman's name popped into Leigh's mind. After her mother's trip to the emergency room, she'd commented on Ellen's soft kind eyes and gentle hands.

"How's my grandmother?" J.T. towered over the diminutive woman.

"Her vital signs are strong. She's stabilized. The doctor will be along to discuss the particulars."

"Thank you." His bunched shoulders relaxed. "Can I see her?"

"Not yet. I'm sorry."

"I appreciate you telling me."

"You're welcome. My fiancé had a heart attack this past Tuesday. For the first time, I truly understood how it felt not knowing what was going on with someone I care for."

"How is he?" The lines around J.T.'s mouth softened.

"He'll be fine. With my help, he'll start taking better care of himself."

"We've met before." J.T. smiled for the first time. "Haven't we?"

"We have. You asked me questions about a patient who'd been abused. Her husband had been murdered."

"Right." He nodded. "I'm caught up. How much longer before I can see my grandmother?"

"I can't say. The doctor will make that call." She glanced at the clock on the wall. "I'd better go. It's my lunchtime, and I want to check on Don."

She paused in the doorway and spoke to Leigh. "How's your

mother?"

"Doing great. Thanks."

"Hell of a memory." J.T. shook his head. "Better than mine."

"Mine, too. She's a nice lady." Leigh's heart hurt when he brushed his fingers across her cheek. Then he resumed his pacing, scowling deeper with each step.

Chapter Twenty-Eight

Leigh sat in the familiar waiting room with her mom while Ethan played with the racecar he'd brought to the hospital. J.T. was in the intensive care unit checking on his grandmother.

"J.T.," Ethan squealed.

Leigh grabbed for the back of his shirt, her hand closing around empty space. He'd forgotten she'd asked him to use his inside voice while they were in the hospital. The sight of J.T. entering the room had proved too much for her six-year-old bullet train.

"Hey, little man." J.T. dropped to one knee and gathered Ethan close.

J.T.'s gaze lifted and met hers. Dark circles under his eyes and deep lines around his mouth spoke a silent tale. He'd been waiting since eight-thirty that morning. Leigh hoped the visit with his grandmother would give him peace of mind. Judging from the signs of exhaustion on his face, he was still worried. The sadness in his eyes ripped at Leigh's heart.

Her son spoke quiet words Leigh couldn't hear while he rubbed small circles over the scar on J.T.'s cheek. Her heart clenched when he didn't pull away. The expression of tenderness in his eyes made Leigh swallow tears pushing their way to the surface.

He stood as if the child didn't weigh fifty pounds, and then plopped him down sidesaddle.

"Sarah." J.T. turned his attention to her mother. "Thank you for coming. You sure you're up to getting out?"

"Oh, sure. We were in town to pick up Ethan at DeeDee's. You saw your grandmother?"

"Finally."

He put Ethan down next to his toy. He'd lost all interest in playing. Instead, he caught J.T. by two fingers and stared up as if Superman had flown in from Metropolis to save the day.

Leigh's mother alarms went off. Her selfishness had left her son vulnerable for a huge disappointment and heartbreak. If J.T. didn't love her, didn't love Ethan, she'd set him up for a terrible fall. What if she'd been stupid enough to tell J.T. how she felt? The fact remained; she'd fallen in love with him. Hopelessly and forever.

She and Ethan would back out of J.T.'s life quietly. The pain in her chest took her breath away. She forced her attention back to the subject of his grandmother. "Is she awake?"

"In and out. Her hip is broken, and they have her on pain medicine. It's enough to keep her sedated. Surgery is scheduled in the morning."

"In the morning?" she said, not hiding her surprise.

"That's what the doctor said. She's scheduled for six-thirty."

"Rehab next." Leigh's father spoke from behind them.

J.T. turned and shook her dad's hand. "You're exactly right. Doc said they'd get her up and moving as soon as possible to avoid pneumonia and blood clots." His broad shoulders shuddered.

Movement in the hall caught Leigh's attention. A thin woman wearing baggy, gray slacks, and a lacey, white blouse rushed into the room. She stopped. Her hair was brown not black like J.T.'s, but her hunter green eyes matched the man standing in front of Leigh. The woman's gaze swept the room and came to rest on his back. Leigh's breath caught. It was his mother, and she headed straight for him.

"J.T." Leigh grasped him by the arm, interrupting him. She nodded toward the figure walking up behind him.

He whirled, following the direction of her gaze. His body stature changed. His back straightened and he grew taller. The lines on his face turned to cement, his jaw clenched, and the scowl appeared to be permanent.

The woman took a hesitant step toward him. "Where's Mama?"

"Get out." Venom dripped from his words.

Leigh almost felt the blow when he'd fired the two words. He'd struck his target with the accuracy of the sniper he hunted. The woman blinked rapidly, the color drained from her face, and a trembling hand slapped her chest, covering her heart.

"No. I won't leave."

"You're not welcome here." His words were low and menacing.

Roxanne Noble wobbled on her feet, and tears spilled from red-rimmed eyes. The woman teetered on the verge of collapse. Leigh had to intervene.

She grabbed his arm. "You can't mean that."

He cocked his head sideways. Eyes narrowed to slits, his gaze slid from her hand up her arm and stopped when their eyes met. A dark storm brewed. One of epic proportions. Leigh doubted he saw her through the anger boiling up.

"This is none of your business." His lips barely moved. His voice sounded like it came from a stranger.

She understood his mother's previous reaction. Laser-sharp words burned through Leigh's outer layer of flesh and ripped open a hole in her chest.

"You're my business," she whispered. "You and Ethan are my only business."

"Stay out of things you don't understand."

The blow to her heart hit with the force of a runaway train. Who was this man? This wasn't the person she'd fallen in love with. She turned to Ethan, who'd crawled up on a chair, observing with the eyes of a frightened deer. She released J.T. and held her hand out to her son.

"Let's go home." She motioned her parents to follow. Leigh tugged Ethan down the hall. Unwilling to leave, he wanted to know why J.T. was mad. She couldn't explain what she didn't understand herself. She didn't know the stranger who'd passed judgment on his mother without hearing a word she had to say.

"Leigh." J.T.'s voice came from behind them.

Thank God. He'd come to his senses. "Go ahead," she said, passing control of Ethan to her father. "I'll catch up." She stopped and waited.

Hate filled his face, his stride, and his bearing. He extended his hand to her. "My car keys."

Damn him. Blood coursed through her veins, heating to a rolling boil. She wanted to knock a super-sized dose of understanding, compassion, and forgiveness into his stubborn head. She wanted to believe he wasn't this cold and unforgiving stranger standing before her. Instead, she dropped the keys on his open palm, turned, and hurried toward the exit. Gulping air, swallowing hard, and fighting back tears, she prayed he'd snap out of the fog.

****

J.T. had no idea how long he'd stood staring at the empty doorway. He'd wanted to call out, to stop her, to try to explain. She couldn't possibly have understood. The one woman who'd made him believe in home and family was gone, probably forever. Maybe it was better this way.

He shivered when a cool hand rubbed his arm. "Go away, Mother. Haven't you done enough?" Again, she hadn't been there when she was needed. He didn't want to hear her excuses. He didn't want to know where she'd been. He knew where. And he knew why. At a bar. For a drink.

"I'm not going anywhere. I'll never leave again."

"Stop." He spun to face her. There'd been a time he would've believed her, but that naïve young boy had grown up. "Don't lie to me. I've heard those same four words too many times." He scrubbed his hand over his eyes. Four words? She talked in four-word sentences. He looked back at the exit half-expecting Leigh to be standing there smiling.

"Can we—for now—forget how badly I've hurt you and talk about my mother? When I got home this morning, Elva told me what happened. I came straight here." She moved to a group of chairs and sat down.

"What happened last night? Did Nana run after you? Beg you not to leave?" He leaned down, gripped the arms of her chair, and bent close to her face. "She fell after you drove away and lay helpless outside in the driveway while you went barhopping."

"None of that's true."

She tried to rise, but he stood his ground. He wanted her to understand Nana could've died alone in the night. "Didn't Elva tell you where she found her?"

"Yes. Son, please listen. Mama didn't chase me. She knew where I was going. I went to pack my things."

"You packed? To go where?"

"Home. To my mother."

"You're moving in with her permanently?"

"Yes. She didn't expect me back last night. I had to clear things with the apartment manager this morning. Go look. My stuff is still in her car."

He tried to read behind her flashing eyes. She was an expert when it came to lying. And for years, he'd believed her until she'd proven she couldn't tell the truth.

"Mama loaned me her car for God's sake." She returned his glare. Fire flashed in her eyes.

He studied his mother's appearance for the first time since she'd arrived. His resolve slipped. Had he pronounced her guilty too quickly? The redness in her eyes could be from crying, and the old familiar stench of a night out drinking wasn't seeping from her pores. Her slacks and blouse weren't wrinkled or sweaty.

"You had her permission?"

Tears slid down her face. "Yes. I swear I don't know why she was in the driveway."

He squatted down in front of his mother. He searched her face, looking for a shred of truth to believe. He'd been down this road many times in the past, always falling into her trap, trusting her, hoping she'd stay sober. Hell, one more trip wouldn't kill him. "I'm sorry I mistrusted you."

"I haven't earned your trust, but I will." She pushed the hair off his forehead. "When you get angry, you look like Mama."

"No, I look like you." He stepped back and helped her stand. He towered over her, yet she made him feel small. God help him, he wanted to believe. Had she turned the corner? He hoped so. "Did you get all your things from your place?"

"I did." She tucked her hand inside his elbow. "There wasn't much. I'll need help carrying the boxes into the house."

"You got it. First, let's get you in the ICU. You need to see Nana."

"Deal. Tonight, we'll talk. You and me."

He shot a glance at the exit door. Leigh had witnessed him at his all-time worst. He felt like shit for not giving his mother the benefit of the doubt, and now he'd pay for it. He'd known from the beginning the relationship with Leigh wouldn't last. What he hadn't known was how bad losing her and Ethan would hurt.

****

Leigh closed the door to Ethan's room, stood in the hallway, and appreciated the stillness of the night. He'd been quieter than usual all day. At bedtime, he'd opened up and expressed concern over the scene between J.T. and his mother. Far more intuitive than she'd realized, Ethan reasoned no son would get mad at his mama without a good reason. Leave it to a child to notice the pain and suffering of others, especially someone he worshiped. By the time he'd finished talking it out, Leigh's perspective had changed.

She leaned her head back on the wall and closed her eyes. Worshiping a hero was a dangerous thing, and, apparently, she and her son had fallen in love with one. She prayed they hadn't fallen for a false idol. Superman, like Santa Claus, didn't exist.

Where did she go from there? She hadn't grasped the full extent of J.T.'s pain when it came to his mother until today. Leigh showered, slipped on her sleepshirt, and slid between the sheets, determined to sort through the day's turmoil. One thing she knew for sure, he was important to her. No way would she give up on him. Her heart ached, folding her over in pain.

Her love for him and the relationship they shared was worth fighting for, and she intended to put up one hell of a battle. She would prove not everyone he cared about left him. She would always be there.

****

J.T. paced. The doctor had called Nana's surgery a success, but he wouldn't be happy until she opened her eyes and talked to him. Walking into the recovery room, seeing her with all the different bags hanging from the IV stand had about done him in. Hell, his mother had handled the situation better.

She wouldn't hear of his apologizing. He'd assumed the worst yesterday, yet she refused to let him accept the blame for the horrible things he'd said. He and his mother had talked for most of the night, before catching a few hours rest. Again, this morning, he'd tried to say he was sorry. She'd insisted part of her accepting her alcoholism was facing the distrust of the people she'd let down.

He'd about popped his shirt buttons when she announced she'd started attending AA meetings. Roxanne Noble, who'd, in the past, denied and railed against any mention of her illness, had sought out help of her own free will. Still, his skepticism crept back, threatening his newly found belief in her.

His mother smiled up at him. She caught his hand and led him to the couch where she'd been sitting. "They'll let us know when they move Mama to a room. In the meantime, tell me about the woman I didn't get to meet yesterday. Mama talked for days about the picnic you took her to. She thinks you and the lady are in love." His mother sat, pinned him with her gaze, and patted the spot next to her. "Are you?"

Her question didn't surprise him. He tried not to smile when he joined her on the couch. "I can't answer that."

"Sure, you can. It's a yes or no question."

"Yesterday may have been the end for us." No doubt, he'd royally fucked up. Bad enough Leigh had witnessed his meltdown, but Ethan and her parents had been present as well. "She comes from a different world. Different upbringing."

Her hand gripped his knee and squeezed. "I get it. She's too good for our dysfunctional family."

"That's not what I said." A sharp pain stabbed him in the chest. She'd hit the nail on the head. Leigh was too good for him. "But now you've pointed it out, yeah. I've already told her that we Nobles don't do family. I'd wind up hurting her and the boy, which is the last thing I want. We don't make good parents."

She laughed, a bitter cross between anger and amusement. "If you need an excuse for your bad behavior, find something or somebody else to blame. Don't put that burden on me."

"I'm not looking for an excuse." She didn't understand. She hadn't been around to witness him fuck up every relationship he'd ever started.

"I can't force you not to hide behind me. Son, everybody makes choices. Good and bad ones, but make your own mistakes. Don't use mine to define how you'll live."

His mother, sitting right next to him, sober as a judge, was giving him a piece of advice. How many times had he wished for her guidance? How many nights had he lain awake wishing she'd come home? Would Leigh be willing to give him as many chances as he'd given his mother?

His mother shook his knee. "Your mind wandered again."

"It did." Hell, he hadn't led an exemplary life and the cloak of self-righteousness he wore around the woman next to him fit too snugly. He had one hell of a lot of baggage to dump and a couple of bridges to rebuild. No reason not to start right now. "I've used your alcoholism as an excuse not to let anybody get too close. It's a shield, and I've lived behind its protection for years. I'm not sure I can lay it down."

"Anyone in their right mind would understand."

"I got lucky when Leigh came along."

His mother chuckled. "I like her already."

"Me too, Mama. Me too." He hoped and prayed he hadn't driven her away.

"Tell me more."

J.T. spent the next hour talking about Leigh and Ethan. Speaking the words out loud, relaying her history, and everything she'd been through, J.T. realized how proud he was of her. His heart swelled to the point his chest hurt while he described Ethan. "He's a great kid. Something funny happens inside me when he wraps his arms around me and hugs. He has this unconditional love for people. Just blows me away."

"Leigh sounds like a reasonable woman. Tell her what you told me."

****

Standing just outside in the hall, Leigh held her breath. She wished she'd overheard more of the conversation between J.T. and his mother. Maybe, she wouldn't be questioning her sanity for returning. Only one way to find out. She moved farther into the room, unable to keep silent.

"You're right. I am a reasonable woman," Leigh said. "Tell me what?"

J.T. sprang from the couch as if he'd been hit by a hot wire. Leigh made no effort to contain her laughter. The surprise on his face sent her nerve endings dancing across her skin. Yesterday, his mother had worn the look of a wounded animal, with him the predator about to move in for the kill. Today, they were sitting close and discussing her.

"We . . . uh . . . we were shooting the breeze." He shifted his feet like a kid in trouble and looked down at his mother.

"I can see that. Quite different from yesterday." Leigh bit back a smile. The man who fancied himself always in control had stumbled over his words and right back into her heart.

His mother stood and extended her hand to Leigh. "I'm Roxanne Noble. Come sit next to me." She looked up at her son. "Go get an update on your grandmother."

"And leave you two alone? Not a chance."

His mother sighed and then scowled a familiar frown at him. "Son," she said with authority. "I need to tell this young lady about myself. Don't make me do it in front of you."

The expression in his eyes, coupled with the smile he gave his mother, brought tears to Leigh's eyes. "Yes, ma'am, I'll go."

His broad shoulders sagged as he walked away. Leigh shook her head and mumbled to herself. "Again, with the four-word sentences."

"Four words?"

Roxanne's puzzled expression deserved an explanation. "Occasionally he talks in full-blown sentences. Usually, it's rapid-fire bullets of four or five words. It makes him hard to get to know."

"Let me tell you where I think that came from."

J.T.'s mother, her thin shoulders straight, head held high, looked Leigh in the eye and talked. Leigh listened silently. He'd return soon. She didn't want to waste this opportunity to learn more about Roxanne, his past, and his relationship with his mother.

Chapter Twenty-Nine

"She recognized me." J.T. froze for a second at the sight of his mother holding Leigh's hand. "Nana opened her eyes when I called her gorgeous. She smiled at me. A weak one but she's coming around. They're moving her to room 1411. Mother, why don't you ride up with her?"

"I will. Leigh, I'll see you again?"

"Count on it."

His mother pulled Leigh in for a hug. The two women exchanged a knowing look right before the doors to the recovery room swung closed.

"Why do I feel like you two dissected, inspected, and analyzed me? I thought she wanted to talk about herself."

"We did both."

What the hell had his mother said to Leigh? She leaned toward him and, for a second, he thought she might kiss him. At the last minute, she turned away.

"Come on, we'll go upstairs," she said.

He'd never begged for anything, but for a second chance with Leigh, he'd get on his knees. First, he needed to get her alone to plead his case. His luck didn't hold because the friendly nurse from the ER joined them at the elevator.

"Ellen, isn't it?" Leigh's finger hovered above the call buttons. "Up or down?"

"Up, please. Aren't you nice to remember my name?" Ellen shifted a stack of magazines and a book to her hip. "My fiancé had heart surgery recently, but he's healing nicely. When he fell on his face he landed on broken curb. It left a cut on his cheek. He's so afraid I won't love him if it leaves a scar. I always check on him before my shift starts."

"J.T.'s grandmother is on her way to the fourth floor," Leigh said. "Room 1411."

"I'll check in on her from time to time. Until Don's dismissed, I'll be on four a lot."

When the elevator finally arrived and the doors opened, Leigh stepped back. J.T.'s breath caught. She wasn't getting on. "You're not coming?"

"You go ahead. I need to call Mom. If she can pick up Ethan at the sitter's after school, I'll stay with you for a while longer. I'll swing by the cafeteria and bring up some coffee."

What if Leigh left without hearing him out? She reached up and rested the palm of her hand on his right cheek. The scar warmed under her touch.

"Go. I'll be there in ten minutes tops."

J.T. forced a smile and boarded with Ellen. By the time the elevator went up four measly floors, he'd forgotten where he was supposed to go. He wished Ellen a good day and then stopped at the nurse's station to get Nana's room number. Fear Leigh had given him the slip shredded his insides.

Ellen's back was to the door when J.T. strode down the hall. She'd leaned over her fiancé for a hug. The word circulated in J.T.'s head. Fiancé. Fiancé. He liked it.

****

Doyle breathed in the fresh air Ellen always brought with her and tightened his arms around her as best he could. He was determined to continue to regain his strength and moving around had been great.

"How are you feeling?"

"I don't know which makes me happier, the fact you're here or that damn catheter has been removed."

Ellen giggled, hovering over him while she checked him over. She nodded her approval and then moved a chair close to the bed. "Most of your lines have been removed."

"The doctor said I was doing better than expected."

"I heard that. Walking after heart surgery is exhausting."

"Not at all. It wasn't nearly as bad as I expected. I surprise the nurse's everyday with the number of steps I'm taking."

"Good. We shouldn't have stopped jogging. When you come home, we're gonna get healthy. Start walking. Eat right." She adjusted the half on and half off hospital gown. "You're wearing the pajama bottoms I bought you."

"And I appreciate them. I prefer limiting the number of people who see my bare backside." He couldn't wear the shirt because of all the tubes and wires running from his body, but covering his butt made him feel much better.

"The limit is one." Her cheeks reddened.

"Yep, just you. Think you can find out when I'm going home? They won't tell me." Lying in bed gave him too much time to think. He'd replayed the night of his heart attack over and over again. His eyes hadn't deceived him, Leigh McBride hadn't been even a little grateful. He doubted any of the women he'd exacted punishment for were thankful. Did any of them realize the sacrifices he'd made? He'd given up his wife. His life. A nurse walked into his room carrying a tray.

"Time to change that bandage on your head," she said, placing her utensils on his food table. Rolling it next to his head.

Fate had been good to him. His gaze stayed on the blunt tipped scissors while she reached to remove the gauze from his face.

"Don?" Ellen shook his knee. "You spaced out on me. Are you in pain?"

"No. I'm sorry. Tell me about your day."

The longer Ellen talked, the more the beep on his heart monitor increased. He had trouble believing the story she told him. How had she become friends with Leigh and her federal agent? What were the odds of them ever meeting? Ellen was a regular chatterbox. What had she told them about him? Her gaze flicked from his face to the rapid, irritating beep.

"What did you tell them about me?" He tried to keep his voice calm, but the question came out an accusatory demand.

"Not much. What difference does it make?" Ellen stood and took his pulse as if the stupid machine was on the blink.

"Why are you getting so excited?"

"Damn it. Answer me. What did you say?"

Ellen started babbling about how and when she'd met the McBride family. The longer she talked the faster his blood boiled through his veins. Soon, Ellen's mouth moved, but he didn't hear any of her words.

Detective McBride's friend was waiting for her right down the fucking hall in room 1411. What if she looked in the room and saw him? Would she recognize him from the night he'd pulled her from her wrecked car? Why had he told her his name was Doyle? She'd picked up on the name right away. If she saw him, would she question why Ellen referred to him as Don?

He had to get out of the hospital. Now. Before the detective got a look at him. He pushed the nurse away, grabbed the scissors, and opened them. The sharp blade pressed into her flesh. "Remove the IV and the EKG leads attached my chest and back."

Ellen screamed.

"Listen to me, Ellen. I have to leave. Love me enough to help me or stay out of my way." He pushed himself upright. "Shit," he whispered against a surge of pain. He shoved the nurse to the floor, jerked Ellen's hands off him, and spun her around. "Remove the last of these IVs. Now!

"I will not. Are you running a fever?"

"You give me no choice." He jerked her forward by her hair, pushed the open blades against her throat and stared to bear down. "Shut up," he commanded. "Help me or you'll die."

Ellen nodded, gasping for air while tears raced down her cheeks.

Her hands trembled but she did exactly what he demanded. Now what?"

Ellen tried to jerk out of his grasp. Her hands gripped his arms trying to pull the sharp edge away from her skin. For her effort, blood ran down her neck.

"Why won't you listen? If you love me, help me."

"I am trying to help." She was, at this stage, useless. "You're delirious."

He couldn't stop because she was scared. The right side of her white blouse turned crimson but it was too late to stop.

The nurse had recovered and came up behind him. "Release her and get back in bed, Mr. Preston. I need to stop her bleeding," the nurse commanded.

"That's not happening." Fire shot down the middle of his chest. Dots danced before his eyes. "I'll kill her if you don't back away.

"I'm sorry, Ellen."

"I hate you," she cried.

She couldn't turn on him. Not after he'd given up his life's work for her. He jerked her against his body. A white-hot laser shot through him when she slammed into his chest.

Ellen's sobs grew loud.

"Listen closely. I won't repeat myself. Move." He backed through the space the two nurses created. "Shut up. This is life or death for me."

Out in the hall, for one brief moment, Doyle saw freedom. Then the fed pushed his way through the gathering crowd. He issued commands and ordered people out of his way. Damn, Ellen and her wailing.

By this point, his chest had exploded into a raging forest fire, dulling Doyle's thinking. He backed down the hall, in the direction of the bank of elevators he'd seen while on his earlier walk. Dragging Ellen while she tugged at his arm trying to free herself made every step excruciating. He shook his head to clear his thoughts, had to keep an eye on the fed. No doubt, he'd make a play soon.

****

J.T. found the cause of the yelling the second he stepped into the hall. Recognition slammed into him. The forensic artist's drawing. Leigh had recalled the face of the man named Doyle. Her memory was spot on.

Doyle Preston had the same look of terror J.T. had seen many times in battle. Wild-eyed, sweating profusely, the son of a bitch was fighting for his life. No way was this going down easy. Preston's gaze scanned the hall.

Adrenaline pumped into his system as he inched closer to Ellen and the lunatic. Her eyes were wild with fear as blood trickled down her neck. Her gut-wrenching sobs ricocheted off the walls.

J.T. reached behind him, resting his hand on his Glock. No way could he shoot the bastard with this many people around. He had to try to talk Preston down. "FBI. Let the woman go."

"No," Preston yelled. "Stay where you are or she dies. We're getting out of here. Together."

"I can't let that happen." J.T. inched forward. Doyle lurched backward, moving on shaky legs. "And you know it."

J.T.'s heart jumped to the back of his throat when Leigh stepped around the corner. Unseen by Preston, her gaze instantly assessed the situation. She pulled her pistol from her purse and handed the tray of coffee to a nurse. Together, Leigh and the nurse silently backed out of sight.

Slowly, Doyle and Ellen continued moving backward.

J.T. followed them as they reached the corner and turned toward the elevators. Leigh eased up behind Preston. Her pistol pressed against the bastard's flesh.

"Let her go," Leigh spoke in a calm, monotone voice. "Release her and put down your weapon."

J.T. stood in a vacuum as his world shifted off its axis. The hair on the back of his neck stood out. Somewhere in the middle of the bizarre scene, his love for Leigh filled every dark corner in his being. He loved her more than life. Helplessness washed over him. He'd become useless when she needed him the most.

Preston shoved Ellen away and she fell on the tiled floor. He screamed and charged Leigh.

"I killed for you. You and all those ungrateful women." The blade got closer with each step.

"Stop." When he slashed at her, Leigh fired. Screams filled the hall as his body crumpled to the floor. J.T. ran to her, pulling her into his arms.

Ellen scrambled across the floor, blood dripping from her neck to her insane fiancé. "You killed him. You killed him," she cried over and over at Leigh.

J.T. grabbed Leigh's arms. "Talk to me. Are you all right?" He crushed her against him.

"I'm fine," she mumbled into his chest. She surrendered her gun to him and then turned back to the chaos behind her. "I didn't shoot to kill him."

"I know." He never wanted to let her outside the perimeter of his arms.

"Let's get this crowd under control." She stepped back. Her cool, detached tone and serious take-charge cop attitude opened a relief valve, and he laughed, drawing a curious stare from her.

"You got it."

J.T. understood her frame of mind. Right now, every nerve cell in her body ran on high-octane fuel. For a while, she'd feel ten feet tall and invisible. Later, after the adrenaline wore off, reality would kick in and the shakes would take over.

Would she take another chance on him? If she'd allow him, he'd hold her in his arms, tell her how proud he was of her, make love to her, and tell her she was his girl like he should've done when she'd asked. Hopefully, she'd be his girl forever.

Hospital security started sorting through the chaos. Gurneys lined up and Ellen was whisked off down the hall to determine if the blood on her was actually hers.

Two doctors gloved up and knelt over Doyle Preston. "Get this man to an OR," one doctor barked at an orderly. Within seconds, Doyle disappeared on a gurney flanked by two security officers.

Atlanta PD burst onto the scene, bringing with them a completely new set of chaotic activities and questions. J.T. passed off Leigh's weapon to the sergeant in charge.

APD separated him and Leigh when they took their statements. He willingly complied, after he'd checked on his grandmother and mother. Huddled together, both of them refused to admit to being scared. His family in harm's way shook him to the core. Leigh standing so close to danger terrified him. He'd have to learn to deal because she'd never leave the force.

****

Leigh rested her hand on the door to room 1411 but didn't push. She needed a minute to catch her breath. Yeah. A quick deep breath and she'd be ready to join J.T. inside with his mother and grandmother.

APD had taken his statement and cut him loose. Their questioning of Leigh had run much longer. As the shooter, she'd had a lot more explaining to do. At least for now, they'd finished with her. IA would hold a formal investigation, conduct a hearing, and then make a ruling.

The hospital staff and security returned to normal operations. To anyone arriving, everything appeared to be business as usual. Leigh couldn't imagine normal right now. Not while the image of Doyle Preston as they'd rolled him away flashed with every blink of her eyes. Perspiration popped out across her forehead. All the possibilities of what could've happened wormed their way into her mind. They rumbled and thundered until her entire body shook. She'd shot another human. Her stomach roiled, threatening to purge itself.

The door opened, and J.T. stepped out. Off balance, she stumbled forward, slamming into his solid body."I've got you."

She gave way and let her tears soak the front of his shirt. His strong hands gripped the back of her blouse, swaying slightly, he pressed her tightly against him. She slid her arms around his waist and clung to him. Her lifeline.

"You better have me, 'cause I'm never going to turn loose," She cried against his chest.

Her tears soaked through his shirt. He cleared his throat. "Leigh, aside from scaring the shit out of me, you made me face reality. Seeing Preston lunge at you drove home how helpless I was and made me realize I can't lose you.

"You had it together. You stood your ground. Damn, I'm proud of you."

"Thank you. Hearing you say the words helps." She leaned back and looked up at his beautiful face, soaking up the love shining from his eyes. Her world righted itself. He hadn't said the words, but, for now, she was okay with that. "I can't seem to turn off the waterworks."

"Cry all you want." He kissed her forehead. "Shooting somebody is a hell of a lot harder than people think. The aftershock can be a bitch."

"You've killed people, haven't you?" She regretted asking when the spark in his eyes dulled. "Stupid question. Don't answer that. I'm sorry."

"It's okay. I've killed. That's something I've learned to live with. Taking another human's life never gets easier, but I understand the responsibility comes with the job." He leaned down, resting his forehead on hers. "Did I mention how proud I am of you?"

"You did. Say it as often as you like. I love hearing it." Leigh hoped her words reflected her emotions.

The door opened, and Roxanne stuck her head out into the hall.

"Oops. Am I interrupting?"

"And if you are?" J.T. smiled at his mother, and Leigh saw the same mischievous look she'd received from her son. J.T.'s eyebrows rose as if he waited for his mother's comeback.

"I'd say get a room. Mama worried you'd left without saying good-bye." She rested her hand on Leigh's arm. "Come in—when you're done." With a wink, she disappeared back into the room.

J.T. shook his head. "I can't get over the change in her. I hope she sticks around this time."

"Did you learn how your grandmother broke her hip?"

"Yeah. My mother's wallet had fallen out of her handbag. Nana ran outside to catch her, but Mama was already gone. Nana slipped and fell on her way back inside."

"Oh, God." Leigh gasped. "Inadvertently, your mother did cause the fall."

"Yeah. She's hurting."

"She blames herself."

"More like she was afraid I'd blame her."

"I'm glad you talked things out with her."

"Me, too." He glanced toward the hospital room. "We'd better go in for a while. Then I'll drive you home."

She reached for the door but paused. "I drove. My car's in the parking lot."

"We'll get it in the morning."

"Why? You'll have to drop me off at home on your way to work."

"Nana's in the hospital. The sniper's in custody. I'm taking some vacation time."

"Again, with the four-word sentences," she joked. In reality, she didn't care if he talked in short sentences for the rest of his life as long as they were together. She wouldn't say that out loud because he'd frozen up the last time she'd put him on the spot. "Besides, I need to pick up Ethan," she said instead.

"Let me try again. I can do better." He leaned down so close his lips brushed her ear. "We'll pick him up in the morning. Because tonight, I want to take his mother home with me and make love to her all night long." The look on his face was positively delicious. Lighthouse beacon bright, love beamed from his eyes.

"Now that's a sentence I can get into."

"Here's another. Life without you wouldn't be living. I love you, and I should've said it sooner. I'm sorry for being a coward and not telling you the minute I knew."

Before Leigh responded, he tugged her up on her toes and kissed her. Hard. Possessive. Forever. She was breathless and weak-kneed when he released her.

"I love you, too. And have since—"

An instant before his lips crashed down on hers, Leigh heard him mutter.

"Thank God."

Epilogue

Leigh stood at the top of the courthouse steps in the hot Georgia sun. For the first time in months, she breathed in freedom from worry. Breathed in peace. She lowered her gaze to the man waiting at the bottom and soaked in his love.

"I guess this is it for us." Wearing a navy-blue designer suit and matching heels, Karen joined Leigh on the walk down. "I'm glad things worked out for you and Ethan. And, from what I can see, for you and your agent."

"I'm grateful and can't thank you enough." Leigh shook Karen's extended hand.

"My pleasure." The attorney waved at J.T. and headed to her car.

Carlton and Elizabeth Carrington's black limo eased away from the curb. A strong, warm hand slid around Leigh's waist. J.T.'s touch never failed to electrify her skin. He'd had to wait outside the courtroom, but his presence and support had helped her through the hearing, the wait while the judge deliberated, and today when he'd given his decision. Relieved her ordeal was over, she turned into his arms.

"Let's get out of here." Leigh rose on her toes for a kiss.

"Just waiting for you." He smiled a one-sided grin. He'd probably worn a path through the pavement while fretting over her being inside without him to protect her. She'd probably never convince him she didn't need protection. But then she wouldn't try. She loved that part of him. He wore the hero slash defender badge well.

Wearing jeans and a Falcon's jersey, his dark hair gleamed under the bright sun. As usual, he set off a firestorm of hormones in her body. Without questioning her, he tightened his grip and walked her to his new SUV.

Seated, she considered the odd choice he'd made. For him to part with his Corvette and purchase a vehicle the size of Indiana was way beyond weird. Yet, this morning, he'd picked her up with no explanation, just a smile. Leigh leaned back, closed her eyes, and breathed in the new car smell. J.T. slid behind the wheel and the engine hummed to life. The interior improved dramatically with leather and male scent mixed.

"Thank you for being here for me." Cool air caressed the perspiration off her face.

"I love you, remember? There aren't enough Marines in the state to keep me away." J.T.'s hand settled on her knee. She felt stronger, safer, loved, and incredibly sexy whenever they came in contact. She rolled her head to the side and opened her eyes, knowing his probing emerald gaze rested on her face.

"You bet I remember. Knowing that you loved me helped me get through the Internal Affairs investigation, the hearing with Jason's parents, and Doyle Preston's death."

"None of which were your fault. Carrington was murdered, and Preston died on the operating table."

"But I don't say thank you enough." She stroked her fingers down his arm.

"Glad I could be of service."

"I appreciate all the 'services' you provide." Tension in her body eased at the sound of his husky chuckle. "And because the Carringtons finally realized what a monster Jason was, they've backed off and decided not to pursue a relationship with Ethan . . . for now. When I tell him about his father, which I will someday, they asked me to tell Ethan they'd like to meet him. If he's interested and willing."

J.T. caught her hand and then kissed her palm. She leaned toward him, allowing his internal strength to pass into her.

"I'm sorry you had to go through all this crap."

"I'm glad they finally learned the kind of man Jason was."

"Shit." J.T. spit out the word on a cloud of disgust. "They knew. Good riddance to the lot of them."

"You're right. They helped create his personality. Now that IA's wrapped up their investigation, I can go back to work."

"I didn't figure it would be a problem."

The truth was, Leigh hadn't spent much time worrying about Internal Affairs. Her son remained her first priority. "Poor Ethan. How do I explain Jason to him?" She resisted the urge to pat her loose curls into place. "At what age do I try?"

"Will you be okay if he decides he wants to have a relationship with them?"

"I'll have to be. If, and that's a big if, the Carringtons stick to the bargain and let me tell Ethan when he's older."

"We've got lots of time to work through that."

Her heart jammed into the back of her throat. He'd used the word "we" again. Since the shooting, he'd added the word to his vocabulary, lumping the three of them together as if they were one big happy family. She prayed he meant it. Hopelessly in love, she couldn't imagine life without him.

He backed out of the parking spot but stopped in the middle of the lane. In one quick motion, he drove back into the slot where they'd started. He put the gearshift in park, drummed his fingers on the steering wheel, and stared straight out across the hood. The nerve in his jaw twitched. Her heart rate sprang from normal to crisis.

"What is it?" She wrapped her fingers around his flexed bicep. "Talk to me."

"Let's go get Ethan right now."

"Okay. Summer vacation is the time for fun." Confused, she puzzled over his odd behavior.

"Good." He nodded his head once. "Good. I need to talk to him."

"He'd like going to the park."

"That'd work. I'm crazy about him. You know that. Right?"

"I do. And he loves you. You're his hero."

"Oh, yeah?" He shifted so they were facing each other.

"Yeah." She put all her conviction into that one word.

The corners of his mouth curved into his special smile. "What about his mom?"

"Since when do you need reassurance?" She puzzled at his questions. "How else can I show that you'll always by my hero?"

"You—" J.T.'s mouth was suddenly bone dry. He tried to swallow but couldn't. "You—damn it, you can marry me. Become Mrs. Leigh Noble."

Her heart swelled, pounded, ricocheting wildly off the walls of her chest. Love for him brought tears to the surface. She'd prayed to hear the very words he'd just struggled to say.

"There's nothing I want more."

"And I want to be Ethan's father. A real one. By adopting him."

"I'd love you to be his father." Tears slid down her cheeks.

"Then we should go talk to Ethan." Emerald eyes bore down on her face. "What do you think he'll say to you both becoming a Noble?"

Leigh unhooked her seat belt, leaned over, and captured his lips with hers. "He'll be thrilled."

"Thank God. That justifies me buying this Explorer. An SUV is too big of a car unless a guy's got a family."

"You traded your Corvette for us?"

"Yes ma'am, I did."

Her heart filled with love. Expanded. Grew in her chest. Bordered on exploding. This four-word speaking, perpetually scowling loner wanted her and Ethan to be his family. He wanted to build a life with them. Wanted forever. She could live with forever.

Also By Jerrie Alexander

Romantic Suspense
The Green-Eyed Doll
The Last Execution
Hell or High Water
Cold Day in Hell
No Chance in Hell
No Greater Hell
A Helluva Holiday
Till Justice is Served
Till the Dead Speak
Someone To Watch Over Me
Flirting With Fate
Skyway to Hell – coming soon

Contemporary Erotic Romance
Come Hard
Come Hot
Come Together
Come Undone

Meet Jerrie

A career in logistics offered me the opportunity to travel to many beautiful locations in America, and I revisit them in her romantic suspense novels.

I write romantic suspense and contemporary erotic romance with alpha males and kick-ass women who weave their way through life's obstacles to emerge stronger because of, and on occasion in spite of, their love for each other. I like to put my characters in difficult positions, make them suffer, and if they're strong enough, they live happily ever after.

My books are written as standalone with no cliffhangers.